"Unless you have a license to care for protected species, I'm afraid I'll have to shut you down."

As he spoke, Mark pinned his new neighbor with a look.

She crossed her arms over her chest. "I suggest you talk to the Fish and Wildlife Service before you threaten me."

"Lady, I am the Fish and Wildlife Service."

"Forgive me," she said sarcastically, "but you're not exactly dressed

He glanced dow   . "Up there. You   didn't like to a   FWS. A secret a he should have   he shot off his big mouth. "Now let's see the permit."

She sighed. "It would be a lot easier if you simply called the local FWS and checked with them. They gave me these birds to rehabilitate."

She was right. Her story would be easy to check. Since she didn't appear stupid, he figured she had to be telling the truth. "You're legit."

"Afraid so. I'm Cat Randolph. And we seem to have gotten off to a bad start. How about a cup of coffee?"

He'd kill for a cup of coffee. But if he took her up on it, he'd feel obligated to apologize, and just now any thought of apology stuck in his craw. It looked as if getting shot was only the start of his bad luck.

Dear Reader,

The grackle started it all.

One day I was sitting at my computer, working on a book. Actually, I was struggling with a book, so instead of looking at the computer screen, I was looking out the window for divine inspiration. What I found was a dead grackle lying on the ground. A few minutes later, his head came up. Okay, not dead, but injured. Well, crud, I thought. What am I supposed to do now?

I called my friend Sue Gordon who happens to rehabilitate birds. Sue took the grackle home, nursed him and came back over to release him the next day. I watched him fly away and I saw the joy my friend received from being able to help this bird. And I felt good, too, because not only had I helped save a bird—he certainly would have been some cat's meal if we hadn't rescued him—but I had an idea for a new book.

So, if my heroine, Cat Randolph, rehabilitates birds, who would the hero be? Well, a secret agent. No, not that kind of secret agent. Mark Kincaid is a secret agent for the Fish and Wildlife Service, one who busts bird-smuggling rings.

During my research I discovered that the worldwide illegal exotic animal trade is a huge business. Second only to drugs. The methods used to smuggle these animals are unconscionably inhumane, and countless animals die during the process. I'm an animal lover—to say I was horrified is putting it mildly. So it seemed appropriate to me that the hero of my book, and the man my bird-lover heroine falls for, would be a person who works to put a halt to this terrible crime. Of course, it didn't turn out to quite be that easy....

Eve Gaddy

I love to hear from readers. Write me at P.O. Box 131704, Tyler, TX 75713-1704 or e-mail eve@evegaddy.com. Check out my Web site, www.evegaddy.com, or the Superromance authors' Web site, www.superauthors.com.

Trouble
in Texas
Eve Gaddy

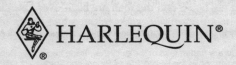

HARLEQUIN®

TORONTO • NEW YORK • LONDON
AMSTERDAM • PARIS • SYDNEY • HAMBURG
STOCKHOLM • ATHENS • TOKYO • MILAN • MADRID
PRAGUE • WARSAW • BUDAPEST • AUCKLAND

ISBN 0-373-71031-3

TROUBLE IN TEXAS

Printed in U.S.A.

This is for my father, David McMahon.
I miss our trips to the bookstore, Dad,
and those Sunday-night steak dinners and
being able to call you up and yell about politics,
or ask you obscure questions you always knew the answers
to. I even miss the football games, because you're not here
watching them and hollering for the Longhorns. I promise,
during UT's first game next season I'll say a great big
"Hook 'em Horns" in your honor. I miss you, Dad.

Acknowledgments:

My thanks go to Sue Gordon,
because I wouldn't have had the original idea for this book
without her, and also for sharing her love of birds
and stories about them with me.

And to Rosalyn Alsobrook,
for talking about the book, critiquing the book, listening to
my tortured ramblings, helping me figure out those pesky
problems (and I still can't write a decent synopsis, so
you're not off the hook in the future). And especially, for all
our talks about your mom and dad. Thanks, Roz, for being
there when I really needed a friend who understood.

CHAPTER ONE

THE SHAPELY BLONDE in Mark Kincaid's arms whispered an erotic suggestion that sent his blood pressure rocketing eight miles high. Smiling, he murmured an appreciative yes. She sighed and snuggled closer. Ran her hand over his chest and began a slow journey south, her talented fingers tracing a warm, steady path to paradise.

Until she screeched in his ear.

Mark shot up in bed with an explosive oath and a wild-eyed glare for the blonde—who was nowhere to be seen. His heart rate slowly steadied. He'd been dreaming. But the obnoxious noise that woke him continued, joined by others, equally loud and grating. No illusion, that. Even in his half-asleep state he recognized the sounds. Of course he recognized them. He spent fifty weeks a year putting up with sounds just like that.

Birds. A lot of birds. Damn, couldn't he ever get away from his job?

Especially since he wasn't even on the job, but still on sick leave. He rolled out of bed, wincing as a bedspring poked him in the rear, and stumbled over to the open window of the second-story room. He scrubbed his hands over his stubbled face, then propped them on the windowsill and grimaced as the screen fell off and crashed to the ground below. Bleary-eyed, he trained his gaze on his next-door neighbor's yard. He blinked. Blinked again. Then shuddered at the sight that met his eyes. Raising his eyes skyward he muttered, "Oh, man, what did I do to deserve this?"

An aviary. A very large aviary, taking up nearly the entire yard.

And a female caretaker, he realized, his gaze narrowing. She was about as far from the luscious blonde of his dreams as it was possible to get. Chinlength dark hair, and a nice, curvy little body. Young, he thought, but somehow he didn't think those curves belonged to a teenager. Too far away to see her face clearly, but man, oh, man, that body was definitely worth looking at. Nice, if you liked your women small, dark and sexy.

Which he did. But sure as hell not at six in the flipping morning after four hours of sleep on a mattress made of gravel.

"What the hell are you doing?" he shouted. She didn't hear him. Not surprising, since the birds made such a racket. He shouted again, and again, until she finally glanced up at him. For a moment she looked startled, then smiled and waved—just as if she hadn't been responsible for blasting him out of the best dream he'd had in a month of Sundays—and turned happily back to her business. Which seemed to be stirring up a dozen species of birds.

Gritting his teeth, he snatched up a pair of cutoffs, yanked them over his hips and fastened them. On his way out of the room he grabbed his gray T-shirt from the chair and pulled it over his head.

An aviary. His frown deepened as his annoyance increased. He'd do something about that. There had to be some ordinance against so many animals at one residence, or if not, surely there was one about excessive noise, even in this godforsaken little town tucked away on the Texas coast. He'd go over there and very politely tell bird lady that if her birds woke him up again at such an early hour, he'd call the cops on her.

He splashed cold water on his face to force himself awake. It made sense now—the Realtor's hesitation when he asked why there hadn't been a whisper of interest in the house. Then the blunt reply that he'd better come down and take a look for himself.

Which he had, finally. After being sidelined with a bullet wound to the thigh, courtesy of the case from hell, otherwise known as the Parrot Blues, Mark had decided to put his downtime to good use and take a look at the house his uncle had left him here in Aransas City.

A small community with fishing as its major industry, Aransas City didn't run to condos and big beachfront developments. Not yet, at any rate. Still, with the town situated only thirty miles from Corpus Christi, Mark had thought the real estate market wouldn't be totally dead.

Now he knew why the house hadn't sold. Sold, hell. Nobody had even asked to see it, according to the Realtor, and it had been on the market four months. And why would they bother to look inside? The moon last night had allowed him a brief glimpse of the exterior, enough to depress him for a week. A perfect haunted house.

Face it, he told himself, the place is a wreck. A falling-down, rat- and insect-infested, two-story, pseudo-Victorian monstrosity. Seeing it now, with its sagging ceilings and garishly dismal decor, didn't make him any more optimistic about its prospects. As for braving the exterior in the daylight, he didn't think he was strong enough to face that. Not before a bucket of coffee, anyway.

So, not only had he inherited a disaster that would take him a good six months he didn't have to make habitable, it happened to be next door to an outdoor aviary, for crying out loud. Who wanted to live next door to a bunch of noisemakers shedding feathers, bird droppings and attracting even more birds to the area?

Nobody in his right mind.

As he limped across the sparse grass to reach Ms. Bird Lover's backyard, he wished he'd thought to put on his shoes. His uncle's yard was as neglected as the house. It consisted mostly of sand, broken shells, stickers and rocks, with an occasional fire-ant mound thrown in to really keep him on his toes.

A few feet away, he stopped and stared at the woman. Hands on his hips and his jaw twitching from irritation, he waited for her to finish feeding the heron before he spoke. She had tethered the bird to a table just outside the aviary and seemed totally unconcerned with the infernal racket coming from the rest of the motley flock.

Unhurried, she held out a fish, and the huge gray-blue bird took it delicately from her. She had a way with birds, obviously. Mark wouldn't have hand-fed a heron. Who knew when it would decide to take a bite out of the hand that fed it? But then, he had more experience with dead birds than live ones, unfortunately.

Finally, she turned, looked him up and down and offered another welcoming smile. "Hi. You must be Gilbert's long-lost nephew."

He didn't bother to respond to the comment. It ticked him off even more that the smile did great things for her face. A pretty face, not gorgeous but intriguing. And, he noticed, big brown bedroom eyes. If he hadn't been so irritated...

"Do you have any idea what time it is?" he snarled.

She glanced at her watch and bestowed another

bright-eyed, cheery smile on him. Didn't the woman ever stop smiling? What could there possibly be to smile about at 6:00-damn-a.m.?

"Six-fifteen," she said, and turned back to the bird. "Come on, Rover. You know I have to check your wing. There's a good boy." She took the wing gently in hand.

Mark ground his teeth together. Another time he might have appreciated the fact that she was dressed in a pale yellow tank top, a skimpy pair of white shorts and battered sneakers. But not now. His bum leg ached and his head hurt, the squawking and chirping of the birds making him feel like Rosie the Riveter was doing a tap dance inside his skull.

Still, he tried to be reasonable. "Could you do this later? Say, three hours or so later?"

She let go of the wing with a murmur of approval. She turned a solemn face to him. Her dark eyes twinkled with, he was sure, ironic amusement. "No. They like to get up early and they want to eat first thing. You get used to it."

"I don't want to get used to it," he snapped. "I want it to stop. I was trying to sleep."

"Well, I'm sorry, but they're birds. They make their own schedule and there's not much I can do about it." She didn't look particularly sorry.

He crossed his arms over his chest and glared at her. "Maybe the cops will change your mind about that."

She laughed, not a bit concerned. Mark couldn't remember the last time someone had laughed at him when he was angry.

"You have a lot of nerve for somebody who only moved into the neighborhood yesterday. Go right ahead and call them," she said in a voice rich with enjoyment. "I'm not breaking any laws." She gestured at her other neighbor's house. "Besides, you really will get used to it."

He stared at her in his best intimidating manner, the one he usually reserved for low-life smugglers and poachers. "Excessive noise. Disturbing the peace."

Didn't anything faze the woman? She openly grinned at him now.

"That's debatable. But it doesn't matter. Inside the city limits, you might have a case. But—" Her smiled widened. "Notice the pavement change? Your place is city. Mine—" she raised her chin and met his glare head-on with a smug smirk "—isn't."

Eyes narrowed, he stared at her, trying to figure out if she was bluffing. Somehow, he didn't think so. He glanced at the street. Damn, she was right. The pavement changed right before it reached her house.

A muscle in his jaw throbbed. "You're outside the city limits?"

"Just." She gave a satisfied nod. "Look it up."

Okay, time to pull out the big guns. He motioned

at the heron. "Are you aware that bird is a protected species?"

In the process of putting the big bird back in its cage, she looked over her shoulder at him. "Of course. Why?"

As she shut the cage door, he pinned her with The Look. The one that made grown men quake and women cry. "Unless you have a license to care for a protected species, I'm afraid I'll have to shut down your little operation here."

"Is that so?" Far from crying, or even looking scared, she crossed her arms over her chest and shook her head indulgently. "I suggest you talk to the Fish and Wildlife Service before you threaten me."

"Lady, I *am* the Fish and Wildlife Service."

Her eyebrows drew together and she frowned, drumming her fingers on a bare arm. A moment later her expression cleared. "Oh, I get it. You must be new."

He shook his head. "Nope. Now, where's the permit?"

"Forgive me," she said sarcastically, "but you're not exactly dressed for the part. Where's your ID?"

He glanced down at his ripped T-shirt and cutoffs before he jerked his head toward his uncle's house. This wasn't going at all according to plan. He needed sleep or a big dose of caffeine, not to be arguing with Ms. Chirpy here. "Up there. You don't want to make me get it." He didn't like to advertise his exact position within the FWS. A secret agent should be secret. Something he should have thought about before he shot off his big mouth.

"Don't I?" She arched an eyebrow. "Why not? What are you going to do? Arrest me?"

"If necessary. Let's see the permit," he repeated.

She huffed out a sigh and shoved her fingers, the ones that hadn't been holding a fish, through her hair. "Look, let's save time here. You can rant and rave all you want, but it would be a lot easier if you simply called the local FWS and checked with them. They gave me these birds—" she waved a hand to encompass the whole passel of squawkers "—among others. Which means, as you ought to know, if you're who you say you are, that I'm fully licensed. I rehabilitate the injured birds and release them back into the wild when possible."

Mark remained silent for a long moment, still glaring at her. "And when it's not possible?"

She looked away, as if she didn't want to address the question. Maybe she didn't. In spite of his fatigue, his professional interest stirred.

Finally she said, "Different things. Sometimes they go to zoos, sometimes private owners. It depends. Now, are you through with the third degree?"

Her voice sounded vexed and she'd finally quit smiling. Mark looked then, at the other birds, several different species ranging from an Amazon parrot to a scarlet macaw, to a seagull, all in varying stages of recovery.

He didn't like what he was hearing, and he wasn't sure he quite bought it. But she was right. Her story would be easy to check. Too easy to check. All he had to do was call the local FWS for corroboration. Since she didn't appear to be stupid, he figured she had to be on the up-and-up.

Which meant he was SOL.

He closed his eyes and leaned his head back. Opened them to see a seagull directly overhead, tail feathers twitching. He swore and jumped aside, hearing something that sounded suspiciously like a giggle. Spinning around, he found her watching him. That smile was back, tugging at her mouth. A mighty attractive mouth.

"You're legit," he stated. It wasn't a question.

"Afraid so." She let that hang a moment. "I'm Cat Randolph. And we seem to have gotten off to a bad start. Truce?" She offered a hand and smiled at him, a remarkably friendly smile considering what had just passed between them. "How about a cup of coffee?"

Coffee. God, he'd kill for a cup of coffee. But if he took her up on it, then he'd feel obligated to apologize, and just then any thought of apology stuck in his craw. He glanced over her shoulder to see another woman bearing down on them. No way did he intend to eat crow, and sure as hell not in front of a witness.

Instead of answering, he gave her his iciest glare, turned his back and left her to her feathered friends.

It looked as though getting shot was only the start of his bad luck.

CHAPTER TWO

"HUBBA HUBBA," Cat's sister, Gail, said, reaching her side and watching her angry neighbor disappear with avid interest.

Cat frowned, dragging her gaze reluctantly from as fine a male backside as she'd ever seen. His front wasn't so bad, either, right down to that intriguing scar peeking from beneath the hem of his cutoffs. "Gail, no one says hubba hubba anymore."

"I do. The man is to die for."

True, Cat thought. He'd obviously just rolled out of bed. But neither the disordered dark hair, nor the stubble shading his strong jaw detracted from those go-to-hell looks—if anything, they accentuated them. Add to that fifty fathoms deep blue eyes and you had a picture women would pay to see.

"Is that the guy we heard was coming to town?" Gail asked, fortunately interrupting Cat before she began truly salivating. You know, Secret *Agent* Man," Gail added, singing the last sentence. She offered Cat a doughnut from the white box in her hand. "Have some sugar shock."

"Yeah, that's him," Cat said. "I don't know about

the secret-agent business, but I can tell you one thing. The man is a grump.'' She waved the temptation away. "You know I'm trying to diet." Cat was forever trying to lose that last five pounds. Not that her sister had any worries. The opposite, in fact. "Why did you bring doughnuts?"

"Sorry. Forgot." She licked chocolate icing off her thumb with wicked slowness. "I'm celebrating."

"Celebrating?" Cat walked into the house with her, pondering her sister's choice of words. Gail had little to celebrate these days. She and her husband, Barry, had been separated for over a year now, ever since he'd left with most of their assets and all the cash. Even so, Cat thought it was the best thing that could have happened to Gail. Well, next to a divorce. Even raising her two girls alone was better than living with that louse.

Both their brothers agreed with Cat. Cameron did, anyway. Gabe thought lynching the bastard was a better idea, especially since he had found Barry putting the moves on Cat—a bare two weeks after marrying Gail. Barry had been lucky to get out of the room alive.

Cat always wondered how he'd explained the handprint on his face, not to mention the bloody nose, to his new bride. But no matter how hard Cat had tried to finagle the information from her, Gail had never told.

"I'm officially divorced," Gail said, jerking Cat back to the present.

Her voice held no emotion, but Cat knew better. "Oh, Gail, I'm sorry."

Gail shrugged away the offered sympathy and pushed baby-fine blond hair back from her face. "Let's not talk about it. I'll have to go into it with Mom later today and I'd just as soon not hash it out over and over again."

Tossing the box down on the kitchen counter, she took a seat at the table and rested slender arms on the wood-grained top. "So spill. Who is Mr. Incredible? Gilbert's nephew? The one he willed the house to?"

Cat bit her lip, wanting to comfort. But she knew Gail wouldn't accept it, at least not right now, so she allowed the change of subject. "I think he must be, not that he'd tell me anything. He stayed there last night, so I can't imagine who else it would be." She hadn't even managed to get his name. She vaguely remembered Gilbert mentioning it. Mitch? Mike? No, Mark. That was it. Mark something or other.

"You have all the luck."

"Luck?" After pouring two mugs of coffee, Cat set one in front of Gail and took the chair across from her. "The man was furious. The birds woke him up. I don't think he likes them."

"Tell him to get in line," Gail said dryly. "Right behind Mom and Mrs. Porter's cross-eyed cat."

"Well, yeah, but considering his line of work, you'd think he'd like birds."

"What line of work? Isn't he an undercover agent? That's what Gilbert always hinted at, anyway."

Cat frowned. "I don't know about that. He says he's with the FWS. That could be a cover, I suppose." She thought about that a moment, but it didn't seem likely, somehow. "Anyway, he doesn't just dislike birds, I don't think he's real happy with me, either."

"Minor detail. He'll get over it." Gail waved a hand. "It's kismet."

"Kismet? Please." Cat looked at her skeptically, wondering where that idea came from. Surely Gail wouldn't try her hand at matchmaking. Cat had enough of that from their mother, who since their father died had taken to meddling even more in her children's lives. She'd been severely disappointed in Cat's broken engagement. Brightening, Cat realized the divorce meant their mother would be bound to focus her ambition on Gail, at least for a time.

"No, really, think about it," Gail continued. "You were saying just the other day that nothing exciting ever happened to you. Well, there it is. Excitement in the flesh."

"What excite—you mean him? Wait a minute, I don't even know the man's name, for Pete's sake. Or if he's married, for that matter. You're pairing me up with a stranger."

"Did he wear a ring?"

She thought about his hands, big, strong, capable looking. And bare. "No, but that doesn't mean anything."

"Find out." She leaned across the table, her blue eyes bright with mischief. "You know you want to. Confess, Cat. You're tempted. Otherwise you wouldn't have noticed he didn't have a ring."

Cat conceded her sister had a point. Really, the guy was to die for, just as Gail had pointed out. She thought about him leaning out of his window just a short while ago. Shirtless. Tanned. Muscled. Closing her eyes, she bit her lip to keep from moaning. Oh, yeah, she was tempted.

"Maybe a little," she admitted, snapping her eyes open and glaring at Gail.

Her sister smirked. "I thought so."

"He's not my type."

Gail arched an eyebrow. "He's tall, dark and gorgeous. What more do you want?"

Cat set her mug down with a clatter. "Are you joining Mom in her quest to find me a husband? Because if you are—"

Before she could erupt into full swing, Gail interrupted. "Don't get so bent out of shape. Of course I'm not. But I think you need to have some fun. With something—or someone—besides those infernal birds."

"I have fun." She sounded defensive, which made her wince.

"Since when? Ever since you and Chad broke up—and that was three years ago—you've been living like a nun."

At the mention of her ex-fiancé, Cat sighed. She had never explained to her mother and sister what had happened between her and Chad Birmingham. Discovering that after they were married, Chad would expect her to work for a big accounting firm and give up rehabilitating birds had been the final straw, the one that finally opened her eyes to his true character. A traditional—some might say narrow-minded—kind of man, he wouldn't have been happy with Cat's more unusual interests. And she wouldn't have been happy to give them up.

But expecting her mother to comprehend her behavior would have been futile, and at the time Gail had been so wrapped up in her own marriage and its problems that Cat hadn't had the heart to go into it.

"You won't even go out with Kyle," Gail continued, "and I know for a fact he's asked you several times."

Cat sighed in frustration. Kyle Peters, the wealthy local vet who lived in nearby Aransas Pass, had all the matchmaking mamas in the area beside themselves. But he didn't do a thing for Cat. "Don't start that again. Besides, I did go out with him." And she'd been incredibly bored. Even though they had common interests, nothing had happened. "There's no spark between Kyle and me. Nothing. Zippo. *Nada*." She shook her head, remembering. Besides that, Kyle was a little too stuck on himself to suit Cat. "No, I'll just continue to keep his books and let the personal relationship remain platonic."

"Okay. It doesn't have to be Kyle. That leads us back to your new neighbor. I bet there could be a forest fire there," Gail said with terrier-like determination. "I know, take him a casserole and a set of earplugs. To apologize for waking him. And welcome him to the neighborhood."

"No!" Horrified, Cat stared at her. "That's so pathetic. I'm not going to pounce on him the instant he gets into town. I'm not that desperate."

"What pouncing? Just a casserole, Cat. You cook all the time anyway. And it's the neighborly thing to do."

"No casserole. And no more talk about my new neighbor."

"But, Cat, I think—"

"Gail, please. Just drop it."

"Okay, okay." Gail threw her hands up in defeat. "You are so stubborn."

"This coming from you?" Cat asked.

She shrugged and laughed. "Guess I'd better go get the girls. Now, where did I put my ke—" She broke off abruptly, pointing an accusing finger at the blue jay sitting on the countertop and plucking industriously at her keys. "That damn pirate! If he takes my keys again, I swear I'll—"

Cat lunged for the key chain, her fingers curling thankfully around it before the capricious bird could make off with it. Bluebell squawked indignantly and flew out the window, deprived of his treasure.

"If you'd shut your windows this wouldn't happen!" Gail snatched the keys from Cat and shook her finger at her. "You just wait until he takes something important. Like a client's tax return."

"I keep the office door closed." Usually. Gail had a point. She ought to be more careful about that.

Cat smiled, thinking of the perky bird. Bluebell was one of her successes. Her niece Roxy had found him, newly hatched and about to be her cat's next meal. Cat had fed him hourly with little expectation that he'd survive. He had not only survived, but thrived. When she'd released him, he'd stayed around, nesting in the huge live oak in the front yard.

And stealing trinkets from her house whenever she left a window or door open.

Cat tried to placate her sister. "I'm sorry, Gail. He doesn't mean any harm, he's just being a bird. Besides, your daughter gave him to me," she reminded her.

"What does that have to do with— Oh, forget it," Gail said. "I'm going to make that bird into soup someday," she threatened with a parting shot.

Hearing Bluebell's mocking squawk, Cat laughed

and waved to her sister, knowing it was an empty threat. Though Gail didn't have any interest in rehabilitation, she did love animals. She would no more injure one purposely than Cat would.

It occurred then to Cat that she should warn her new neighbor about Bluebell's thieving tendencies. His air conditioner obviously didn't work well, if the open windows were any indication. And his screens, what few of them still hung on precariously, were mostly useless. To Bluebell an open window was an engraved invitation to enter. Yes, she decided, telling him would definitely be the right thing to do. Not pathetic, not as if she wanted to move in on him, just…neighborly.

It had nothing to do with the fact that she couldn't get his voice, deep, husky and sexy as sin, out of her mind.

MARK WORKED straight through the day, stripping filthy wallpaper from the kitchen walls. He didn't mind renovation and construction work. He'd worked construction in the past—supported himself and his younger brothers that way. Usually he enjoyed working with his hands, but today his heart wasn't in the job. Still, the sooner he whipped the place into shape the sooner he could unload it.

Two to three months, he estimated, less if he contracted out some of the heavier work. His budget was almost nonexistent, though, which meant he'd be doing the majority himself. The house desperately needed a new roof, but he couldn't see putting that much money into it—unless that was the only way the place would sell.

Time was no problem, even if he didn't like the idea of not working actively with the FWS for several months. He'd already been away for six weeks, recuperating before he came down to Aransas City. And he admitted, he didn't enjoy knowing his last case—the Parrot Blues—proceeded without him. Even though they hadn't busted the exotic-bird-smuggling ring yet, Mark had a feeling it wouldn't take too much longer. After all the work he'd put in, not to be part of the final sting irritated the hell out of him.

No sense obsessing over things he couldn't change. He had plenty to do right here.

He climbed to the top of the ladder, armed with a steamer to help him pry loose a stubborn scrap of ancient paper. Seven layers of old wallpaper, and he'd only worked on the kitchen. Who knew what problems the rest of the house harbored? Why hadn't anyone ever stripped the walls instead of simply slapping another layer of paper on top of the last one?

Come to think of it, why had his uncle, who he'd only seen a few times in his life, left him this albatross of a house? He knew the answer to that, though. According to the lawyer, Mark and his siblings were his only living relatives, so he'd left the house to the eldest. Him.

The doorbell groaned. Mark winced at the grating sound. His uncle, he decided, must have had a peculiar sense of humor, since instead of ringing, the doorbell bellowed like something out of *The Addams Family.*

"Yeah, yeah, I'm coming," he muttered, then swore when his leg stiffened up and he slid the rest of the way down the ladder to land in a heap at its base.

The doorbell sounded again while Mark continued to swear, clutching his leg and waiting for the spasm to ease. Damn it, he'd thought his leg was better but he'd obviously pushed too far too fast.

Eventually he made it to the door, jerked it open and found his neighbor on the step. Smiling. Again. What was it about this woman that she managed to irritate him at every turn?

"What?" he said sharply.

The happy expression on her face collapsed. Mark felt as if he'd kicked a puppy. Until she spoke.

"I had this silly idea I should be neighborly. I brought over some food for you." Her eyes narrowed, sweeping him with disdain. "But on second thought, forget it. I'll take it home and eat it myself."

He had to say, she wasn't easily intimidated. And by that time he'd had a whiff of a dangerously appetizing aroma and remembered he hadn't eaten all day. His stomach rumbled, clinching the matter. He dredged up his most engaging smile, which, when he wanted, could be pretty damn charming, and offered it to her. "Sorry, my bum leg's getting to me. Come on in."

Tilting her head to one side, she considered him. "I don't know your name," she remarked pointedly.

His lips twitched. "Mark Kincaid. Gilbert's nephew. I'd offer a hand but yours seem to be full."

She nodded, and glanced down at his leg. "What did you do to your leg?"

"Had a run-in with somebody meaner than me," he said, remembering the smuggler who'd shot him before getting away. Stepping aside to let her in, he added, "It's not fully operational yet."

Still standing in the doorway, she gazed at him thoughtfully. "Line of duty?"

Mark shrugged, and gave the standard answer, even though it wasn't true. "Poacher." He didn't like to outright lie, but the less said about the true nature of his job, the better. Let her think he was a game warden or a park ranger. Anything but what he really was. "Come in," he repeated.

"I didn't intend to stay," Cat said. "I just thought—"

"Look, do you want me to grovel? That smells like my favorite dish, and I'm starved. Why don't we call a truce?"

Her mouth curved in a wry smile. "We tried that. It didn't work."

"We could try it again," he said hopefully, damn near salivating over the aroma drifting toward him.

Her cheeks dimpled and she walked in. "Okay. And here I thought you were just terminally grumpy."

"I am," he said, his grin widening. "But I can control it if I'm fed well. Is that what I think it is?"

"Lasagna." She set the dish on the wobbly green Formica-and-chrome table and made his day—hell, his week. Sure beat the few canned goods that had been left in the house or the no doubt cardboard-like pizza he had thought about having delivered.

"Have a seat and I'll see if I can scrounge up some plates and silverware." A bright spot, finally. Maybe his luck was turning. About damn time.

"I already ate," she said. "But thanks. You go ahead."

Finding a plate wasn't too hard, but his uncle had apparently had odd ideas about where to keep the silverware. Rifling through the cabinets and drawers, he wondered if the old man had ever thrown anything out. He ought to just back his truck up to the door and start shoveling. Finally, he unearthed the silverware and grabbed a fork and a serving spoon, not caring to look at them too closely.

His cell phone rang. "Perfect timing," he muttered, the scent of Italian spices tantalizing him as he grabbed the phone and put it between his shoulder and ear.

"Yeah. Kincaid."

"Mark, long time no hear."

"Simpson?" Surprised, he asked, "How's it going, man?" His partner on the Parrot Blues case, Simpson wouldn't call just to chat. He must have something new to tell him, Mark thought, his interest piqued.

"Better and better. I've got news you won't believe. That's why I'm calling."

"Yeah?" Mark glanced over at his company, who instead of taking a seat, wandered around the kitchen. Nosy, he thought as she busily rearranged a pile of circulars. His eyes narrowed as he watched her. At least his credentials were locked up tight. Not that he had any reason to be secretive in Aransas City, but in Mark's experience it paid to keep a low profile, even when off duty.

Keeping an eye on her he said, "Look, I'm kind of involved right now. Let me get back with you."

"Okay, but make it tonight. We've got a new lead on the Blues case and you'll never believe where we've placed one of the major players."

Damn, no way could he pass on that teaser. Mark didn't believe in coincidence, but the skin on the back of his neck tingled. *Nah, it couldn't be,* he thought. Still tracking his curious guest, who'd now poked her head into one of his partially unpacked boxes, he bit. "Talk to me."

"Truth is stranger than fiction."

He snorted. "Aransas City."

Cat's head came up, but she quickly looked down. To the contents of yet another box. And her ears were obviously tuning in to every word.

"You got it, buddy," Simpson said. "And aren't we lucky we just happen to have a special agent already in place? Call me back ASAP."

Mark hung up, unable to stop his grin from spreading. It looked like he'd be in on the final sting after all.

And Curious Cat was going through the mail like she owned it.

CHAPTER THREE

"WHAT ARE YOU DOING?" Mark asked, setting his phone on the table.

Startled, Cat looked at him, then down at her hands. The very hands rearranging the man's mail. Mortified, she dropped the papers. "Oh, I—I'm so sorry, I forgot."

"Forgot what?"

His eyes sharp and hard, he studied her. Cat squirmed, uncomfortably aware of her besetting sin. "Forgot I wasn't at my house. Or my sister's or brothers'. When I see papers scattered like that, I have to—I mean, I need to..."

Her voice trailed off, but she began again, determined to make a clean breast of it. It wasn't easy though, with him looking at her as if she belonged on a lab slide. Lifting her chin, she sucked in a breath and said, "I can't help it. If I see something messy, I straighten it." Pictures, knickknacks, junk, papers. You name it, she straightened it.

She could imagine what he thought. *Boy, you are one weird lady.*

He continued to stare at her. "You straighten other people's mail."

Cat bit her lip and nodded. "I said I was sorry. It's a nervous habit." Compulsive, Gail always said.

He shook his head, muttering something she couldn't quite make out, and took a seat. She pulled out the chair across from him and plopped down in it. Crossed her leg over her knee and bounced it a time or two. He already knew her most annoying character flaw, might as well be totally herself. Leaning forward, she said brightly, "Gilbert said you were a secret agent."

He glanced up, those blue eyes zeroing in on her. Then his mouth tilted into a half smile, devastatingly attractive. *Lord, what would it be like when he really put some effort into it?* she wondered.

"If Gilbert went around telling people that, then it's not much of a secret."

Now there's a nonanswer. "You said you worked with the FWS. From the way Gilbert always talked, I thought he meant you were CIA or FBI or something."

"Nope." He took another bite, half closed his eyes and sighed appreciatively.

Nope, what? "Are you a FWS special agent?" Special agents went undercover, which might explain Gilbert's remarks. They spent their time trying to break up wildlife smuggling rings and enforcing wildlife laws. A very worthy job, Cat had always thought.

He seemed to hesitate a moment, then shook his head. "Game warden. Grapevine Lake."

"Where's that?" Tilting her head, she considered him. Couldn't the man speak in complete sentences?

"Near Dallas," he said. "You're a hell of a cook. This lasagna's incredible. Thanks."

Apparently, he could, though not about what she wanted to know. Cat waved the thanks away. "After all, my birds did wake you up. And I'm afraid they're going to continue to do it." She worried her lip, deciding not to press further. He obviously didn't want to talk about his job.

She tried again, hoping to find a subject he might actually open up about. She wanted to know more about him. What made him so grumpy? Was it simply his injury, or something else as well? What would he be like if he relaxed? But even more than that, she wondered what he was doing in a tiny place like this when he had big city written all over him.

"I take it you're not here because of the job."

He shook his head. "I'm here to get this—" he gestured at the walls with his fork "—junk pile in order so I can sell it."

One mystery solved. "You don't like the house?" She'd always thought the house had character. Maybe a little too much character for some people, she admitted.

He shot her a sideways glance. "Lady, nobody in their right mind would like this house."

"I think it's kind of—" she glanced around, searching for the right word "—charming. In an odd sort of way."

He snorted. "Odd is right. Also ugly, falling down, piece of—"

Cat laughed. "I'm sure someone will think it's just the place for them. You have to admit, it's different."

"Right."

She watched him eat for a minute, thinking that he made a plain navy T-shirt look better than any man had a right to. Maybe it was the firm muscles of his arms, or the way the soft cotton stretched snugly across his shoulders. The face above the shirt, with those unbelievably blue eyes, didn't hurt, either. She bit back a sigh. He's just passing through, she reminded herself, then broached the subject she'd come to discuss. He deserved a warning, after all. "I should tell you about Bluebell."

"You brought ice cream, too?" His mouth lifted at one corner. "What a woman."

"No, not the ice cream. The bird. Bluebell is a blue jay."

"Too bad. I have a real weakness for ice cream." He rose and took his dish to the sink.

She noticed he took a moment to rinse off the plate and fork and put them in the dishwasher. Most of the men she knew, her brothers included, would have left the dishes to molder.

"You're awfully neat," she observed. "You're not married, are you?"

Turning around, he leaned back against the counter and crossed tanned arms over a chest broad enough for a linebacker. "No." He gazed at her a minute, then added, "What does being neat have to do with being married?"

"Nothing, I suppose." She flashed him a brilliant smile. "I was just curious."

He blinked, looking baffled. "Do you always ask whatever pops into your mind?"

"Usually. Don't you?"

"No, I can't say that I do."

"Maybe you're repressed."

The wicked smile that curved his lips didn't look at all repressed. And it was every bit as tempting as she'd imagined it would be.

"Not when it counts," he said.

Stifling the impulse to fan herself, she decided it might be safer to return to her original purpose. To give her hands something to do, she put the foil back over the lasagna. "About Bluebell. He lives around here and he tends to, uh, well, he's a thief."

She glanced up to find him watching her with an amused expression. "If you leave your windows open he'll come in and take things. You know, oddball thing. Shiny objects, glittery things. Hair from the hairbrush, keys. Once he took my niece's—''

He broke in. ''The bird isn't afraid to fly into houses?''

''Well, no. You see, he's kind of domesticated.''

There went that dynamite half smile again. ''Let me guess. You domesticated him.''

''I nursed him and raised him,'' she corrected. ''And returned him to the wild as soon as I could. But since he spent his formative weeks with me, thinking of me as his mother, he has no fear of humans. So—'' she spread her hands ''—there you go.''

''Sounds like he's a pet.'' He dropped his arms, resting his hands on the edge of the counter. ''No wonder you brought me dinner.''

''What do you mean?''

''It's illegal to keep wild birds. Which, I'm sure, you know.''

Frustrated, she stood. ''I told you I released him. He's built a nest in my tree. I'm not keeping him anywhere, he's free to go whenever he wants. I simply wanted to warn you, not receive a lecture on bird laws.'' She quelled an urge to pick up the remainder of the lasagna and dump it over his hard head.

Then he smiled at her. An achingly gorgeous smile. A zing of pure lust shot through her veins, reminding her exactly how long it had been since she'd been involved with a man.

"Sorry. Just my lame attempt at humor." His voice washed over her like a midnight tide. "I really appreciate the meal. And the warning." He picked up the stoneware dish.

When he handed it to her their fingers touched. She could have sworn she felt a spark, but dismissed the idea. Static electricity, she told herself, aware there was no carpet to have caused it. "No, no," she managed to spit out, shoving the dish toward him. "Keep it until you're finished."

"Thanks. I'll bring the dish back to you soon."

Cat left, wondering what in the world had happened in there. Her arm wasn't tingling. Of course it wasn't. No one's arm tingled simply from touching a man's hand.

Right, she'd just keep telling herself that.

Mark Kincaid was trouble. She knew what people said about inviting trouble in.

But Cat had always found trouble tempting.

THE FOLLOWING MORNING was too pretty to stay cooped up inside a mausoleum, Mark decided. Instead, he opted to work on the roof, hoping he could repair rather than replace it. A ten-minute inspection sent that hope up in smoke, so he spent the rest of the morning buying building supplies and groceries in Corpus Christi.

On the roof after lunch, he considered his second conversation with Simpson the night before. After

Cat left, he'd called his partner back for more details. As Simpson had mentioned in his previous phone call, the Dallas Special Agents team had intercepted a message indicating someone in the Aransas City area was a key distributor of the exotic birds smuggled into the country by the very ring they'd been attempting to break. Since Mark was already in place and had a great cover, that put him back on active duty.

He pried off a particularly stubborn shingle and swore when it popped up, hitting him in the face. Normally, infiltrating a local ring took several months. This time, they wanted to move more quickly. The quicker Mark could infiltrate the birding community, the better.

Which made his neighbor—the local bird rehabber—someone he needed to get to know. No hardship there, he thought, remembering those dark, sultry eyes.

He'd succeeded in stripping a small portion of the ruined shingles when the sound of a motorcycle pulling into his yard caught his attention. Squinting against the glare, he tried to figure out who it was. He didn't know anyone who rode a Harley around here. In fact, he didn't know anyone period, aside from his neighbor and the realtor. But when the rider slid off the bike and straightened, Mark knew that lean, rangy body instantly.

What was Jay doing here? Last he'd heard, his younger brother was in medical school in California.

He set aside the scraper. ''Why the hell aren't you in school?'' he called down by way of greeting.

Leisurely taking off his helmet and stretching, Jay flashed the grin that had earned him the nickname *heartbreaker*. It didn't work on his brother, naturally.

''I'm taking a break.''

''How long a break?'' Mark asked.

Jay tilted his head back and looked up at him. ''A couple of weeks. Don't worry, I haven't dropped out. Yet.'' He climbed the ladder, appearing beside Mark on the roof a few seconds later. ''Though it's a tempting thought. Aren't you glad to see me, bro?''

Mark eyed him suspiciously. He doubted Jay had come simply for a visit. He had something on his mind. Mark assumed he'd find out what soon enough. Damn, but it was good to see the kid. It had been too long. He grinned and punched him in the arm. ''Not especially.''

Jay laughed outright. ''Liar.''

''Not me, surfer boy.'' That particular nickname dated back to Jay's teenage years, because of his blond good looks and success with girls. It fit even better nowadays, Mark thought, considering Jay lived in California and counted surfing as his favorite activity—after women, of course. Long blond hair, a dark tan and a small turquoise stud glinting in one ear enhanced the image still further.

"So, what gives?" Jay glanced around at the tools and supplies. "I thought you gave up construction for a living five years ago?"

Mark shoved a hand through his hair and grimaced. "Yeah, well, I thought so too. Welcome to my inheritance." He waved a hand to encompass the house. "I could use a break. Then you can tell me why you're here, since I'm sure you have a reason besides missing my pretty face."

"As a matter of fact, I do. But you won't like it," Jay said, following him down the ladder.

The kitchen, Mark noticed, looked worse this morning than it had yesterday. Chunks of plaster showed through the partially stripped wallpaper. Mark hadn't cleaned yet, preferring to start with the major problems, consequently, a grayish layer of grime coated the appliances and countertops. Not that they'd been any too attractive to begin with. He pulled out a couple of soft drinks from the refrigerator and set one in front of Jay, taking the seat across from him.

"There isn't a habitable room in the house." He popped the top and drank. "This is as good as it gets. I hope you have a sleeping bag, because there's only one bed and it's mine. Or you can use the couch, but it's lumpy as hell."

"No problem. I can give you a hand with the repairs while I'm here."

His eyebrow lifted. When his laziest brother offered to work, he knew something was up. "Okay, Jay, talk. Why are you really here?"

Jay didn't speak for a moment, twirling the can between his hands. Expression wary, he looked at Mark before he finally spoke. "It's, uh, it's about Mom."

"Mom?" Mark gazed at him blankly. "You actually heard from her? When?" He hadn't seen or talked to his mother in years, not since she'd walked out of their lives, leaving him with custody of his younger brothers.

Barely twenty-one, Mark had been scared to death he couldn't support all of them, much less raise the boys decently on his own. He was all they had, though, since their father had left long before their mother. Both boys had turned out great, but Mark didn't kid himself that it was due to his parenting skills. He attributed it to luck and the fact that they were good kids.

Jay shifted uncomfortably in his seat. "She contacted us—Brian and me—about a year and a half ago. We've kept in touch since then."

"First I've heard of it," he said, unable to stop the sense of betrayal tightening around his heart. Not only Jay, but Brian as well. Mark had talked to his youngest brother shortly before he came here, and Brian hadn't mentioned a word of this.

Lillian Kincaid hadn't been there for her sons, not once over the years. She'd spent little time with them even before she'd abandoned them. Mark had been both parents to his two brothers from the time they were twelve and thirteen. Yet the instant their long-lost mother called, his brothers had seen her, apparently without a moment's hesitation.

"Why didn't you say anything? And why tell me now? Obviously, neither you nor Brian had a problem keeping me in the dark."

Jay winced and shot him another uneasy glance. "Brian and I knew how you felt about her. And she was afraid you'd convince us not to see her."

He gazed at Jay grimly. "She was right. I'd have tried." But not because of how Mark felt. Because he remembered, even if Jay and Brian didn't, how much their mother's desertion had hurt them.

"She's remarried."

"Yeah?" He took a sip of his drink, pretending to be at ease, but inside, his emotions were boiling. "How'd she fit that in among her many causes?"

"She's changed, Mark. Not so caught up in things the way she was when we were kids."

Mark slapped his can down on the table, rocking it. "People like her never change."

"I really think she has. She wants to see you. The only reason she hasn't tried is that she's afraid you'll slam the door in her face."

Mark didn't answer. He didn't know what he'd do if he saw his mother. And he had no intention of finding out.

"There are things you don't know," Jay continued. "She knows she screwed up, but she wants to patch things up, Mark. With all of us, but especially you."

Something twisted inside him. Once, he'd have given anything for his mother to make such a gesture. But it was too late now. Years too late.

"Look, Jay, you're an adult. If you want to see her, it's your decision. But I'm having a hard time buying this contrite act of hers. Why wait so long to contact any of us, if she was so interested in making things right?"

Jay's gaze met his. "She had reasons. Good reasons she wants to explain to you herself."

Mark spared him a sardonic glance. "Yeah, right. I'm sure some species of snail needed saving and that took up all her attention for the past twelve or thirteen years."

"Hey, I know she wasn't the best mother—"

"She was a lousy mother," Mark said flatly. "When she was there at all. Or have you forgotten?"

"No, I haven't forgotten a thing. But she's still our mother, no matter what she did. Or didn't do. Can't you give her a break?"

"Why should I?" He got up, stalked over to the sink. Taking a deep breath, he reminded himself none of this was Jay's fault. He had a soft heart and had obviously been taken in by their mother's sob story.

"Why should I give her a break?" he repeated.

"She sure as hell didn't give Miranda one." He gripped the edge of the sink, memories he'd buried for more than a decade pouring back.

His sister, his only sister, had left home at fifteen and no one had heard from her since. It still hurt him to think of her, a kid so young, completely on her own. He didn't even know if she was alive or dead, and figured he never would. Once he'd taken custody of his brothers and made enough money to afford it, he'd hired a private investigator to find her. The man hadn't come up with a clue to her whereabouts, and considering the amount of time that had passed, he hadn't given Mark much to hope for.

Jay walked over to him and laid a hand on his shoulder. "Mark, you can't blame Miranda's taking off totally on Mom."

"Why not? It was as much her fault as our father's."

Jay threw up his hands n defeat. "You're being illogical. Maybe we should talk about this later."

"Maybe we shouldn't. You see her if you want, but I'm not interested." He would never put himself in such a vulnerable position again. Better to avoid seeing her entirely.

He shook Jay off, went to the back door and pulled it open. "I've got work to do," he said, and left.

By the time Jay joined him on the roof half an hour later, Mark had managed to shove most of their conversation out of his mind. They worked companionably, Jay entertaining him with a story about his latest failed love affair. Since the kid dated an incredible variety of women, and generally parted as friends, Mark wasn't too concerned. Someday Jay would settle down, but in the meantime he was having way too much fun.

"Something wrong?" Mark asked, aware that Jay had abruptly stopped working.

"I think I'm in love."

He pried up a stubborn shingle with a grunt. "Yeah, I heard. You'll get over it."

"No, really. Who's the babe? Is she hot or what?" Jay asked in reverent tones, craning his neck.

He was staring at the house next door, damn near drooling. Mark glanced down to see Cat in her driveway washing a ten-year-old red pickup truck. A nice picture, he admitted, noticing the smooth length of leg exposed by her shorts. Very nice.

"My next-door neighbor. Cat Randolph. She runs a bird sanctuary."

"Man, she can shelter me anytime."

Surprisingly, Mark felt a stab of annoyance. "You're too young for her, Heartbreaker."

Jay grinned. "I like older women. Oh, man, do I ever." His gaze returned to her. "She can't be much more than twenty-eight or thirty, and I'm twenty-five. What's a few years?"

"Come back when you're grown up, sonny," Mark advised.

Cocking his head, Jay winked. ''Planning on seeing a little action there yourself, Mark?''

Damn straight, he was. The smuggling case gave him the perfect excuse for getting to know Cat Randolph. And if his plan led to other things, so much the better. He smiled, considering what those other things might be. Besides, someone needed to protect her from Don Jay. ''I just might be,'' he murmured.

CHAPTER FOUR

THOUGH CAT MADE a valiant effort, she couldn't put Mark Kincaid out of her thoughts. No matter what she was doing, he seemed to work his way into her dreams, both day and night. Sighing, she set down her coffee cup. If she had any sense, she'd forget about him.

But in all honesty, she was tired of being sensible. Why not be impractical for a change? Her lips curved into a thoughtful smile. Have a little fun? Nothing permanent, just...fun.

Then again, he hadn't exactly been beating down her door. In fact, she hadn't seen him at all since she took him the lasagna. Minor detail, she told herself. Sometimes all you needed was a little initiative.

Settling down with her quarterly reports, within moments she lost herself in the world of numbers. She didn't hear the doorbell, but the sound of Buddy, her African gray parrot, mimicking it and screeching "the door" in raucous tones, brought her out of her absorption. She glanced at the clock—8:00 p.m. already—wondering who it could be.

Propping her reading glasses on her head, she answered the door. "Oh, hi, Kyle," she said upon seeing the local veterinarian. She stepped back to let him in, hoping she hadn't forgotten some promised work. At the sight of the visitor, Buddy shrieked anew from his perch in the living room, hurling a tirade of obscenities at the intruder. Fortunately, most of what he said was unintelligible. "Sorry, let me take care of him."

She put the foulmouthed bird in his cage and covered it, hoping that would quiet him down. Turning back to Kyle she remarked, "I can't figure out why he has such an aversion to you. You've never even seen him professionally."

"No accounting for taste," Kyle said, shrugging. "As long as you don't dislike me, I'll survive. I know it's late but I thought I'd bring these daily reports by." He dropped a manila file on her coffee table among a pile of other papers.

Cat bit back a sigh of irritation. While she did the books for his business and he often stopped by, sometimes daily, he didn't usually come after hours. Couldn't he have waited?

Kyle stepped closer, reaching out to twirl a stray strand of her hair around his finger. "And I'll confess I had an ulterior motive." His smile deepened. "What do you say we go out? Take in a movie, or—" He leaned closer still and she wondered if he was about to kiss her. "Or there's a place I know over in Corpus. Quiet, elegant."

Cat sidestepped him quickly. Periodically, Kyle tried his luck with her. She liked him, but she didn't want to go out again. Once had been enough. For no reason she could put her finger on, either.

Maybe it was because her mother considered him the perfect man for her. But even if she didn't want to date Kyle, she still needed his business. Besides, he was a good vet, an avian vet, as well, so she couldn't just blow him off. But every few weeks he'd start again, obviously believing that if he were only persistent enough she'd give in. Stumped for a way out of the tangle, she studied him.

Divine inspiration hit. "I really can't. I'm sorry, Kyle. I've been seeing someone."

His skeptical expression said he didn't believe her. "This is sudden, isn't it? Anyone I know?"

Too late, she saw her error. Of course, Kyle knew all the single men around here and he'd know good and well she wasn't dating any of them. She opened her mouth to claim her new man was from Corpus Christi, when the perfect answer struck like lightning. "He's new to town."

Kyle strolled over to her and stood looking down at her, amused. Sliding an arm around her, he said, his voice low, and she had to admit, pleasantly sexy, "If I didn't know better, I'd think I make you nervous."

So much for subtlety. She could take a frying pan to his head and he probably wouldn't notice. "You're not making me nervous. I just told you, I'm dating someone else.''

"I heard you," he said, giving her another indulgent smile. "It can't be very serious, not in this short time. Besides, I haven't heard of any newcomers." He bent his head, apparently intent on kissing her, despite her claims.

The doorbell rang again. *Salvation,* she thought, squirming out of his grasp. "There he is now,''she said, praying it wasn't her mother or Gail, but knowing it probably was.

She swung the door open. Her neighbor and another man stood on the doorstep. The man with Mark was several years younger, with a killer smile, blond hair and moss-green eyes. A relative maybe? The younger man held her clean casserole dish in his hands. Perfect.

She grabbed Mark's wrist and pulled him inside, leaving the other man to follow. "Mark! I thought you told me you'd be here at seven-thirty?'' His eyes widened in surprise, but she didn't care. "Don't worry. I forgive you." Bent on convincing Kyle of the truth of her claim, she threw her arms around Mark's neck and kissed him passionately.

He only hesitated a moment before his arms came around her. The instant their lips met, Cat totally forgot why she'd kissed him, but boy, howdy, was she glad she had. He returned the kiss, slowly and very thoroughly. As her heart rate kicked up, she relaxed in a puddle against him. *Oh, man, is he good.*

Eventually something penetrated the haze of her mind. The sound of a man clearing his throat caused Mark to release her. Dazed, she stared at him. Or rather, at his mouth.

What a mouth. It ought to be licensed as a lethal weapon.

"I guess this means I'm forgiven," he said with a grin.

Fascinated by the beautiful dimples that appeared, she remained silent. "Forgiven?" she echoed finally, surprised she'd been able to speak at all.

He raised an eyebrow. "For being late." He stepped farther inside and motioned to the man beside him. "Cat Randolph, meet my brother, Jay."

"I don't suppose you reserve that greeting for all Mark's relatives?" he asked, a playful smile lifting one side of his mouth. When she laughed, he held out a hand and smiled engagingly. "Jay Kincaid. Mark's younger and more charming brother," he added with a mischievous grin. "And having tasted your lasagna, I now worship at your feet."

Mark shot his brother an amused glance but didn't speak.

What had she done? Mark was bound to think she was some kind of nut. Or worse, a man-hungry vampire. Oh, well, it couldn't be helped. She stole a glance at Kyle, pleased to see him frowning.

Cat grasped Mark's arm and squeezed it in warning. It felt like rock. Though tempted, she resisted stroking it. "Nice to meet you, Jay." Dragging Mark with her across the room, she introduced everyone. "Kyle Peters, Mark Kincaid." She waved a hand at Jay. "And this is his brother, Jay."

The men all shook hands. Kyle looked a bit disappointed at meeting her imaginary boyfriend in the flesh. Cat inched closer to Mark and smiled up at him dazzlingly before speaking again. "Kyle is a vet. He lives in Aransas Pass, but he takes care of our animals here as well."

Kyle's superior smile beamed. "So, Mark, is it? When did you and your brother move in? Very recently?"

"Oh, I'm just visiting," Jay said. "I live in California right now."

Focused on Mark, Kyle didn't seem to hear Jay's comment. "What brings you to the area? Job?"

Mark shook his head. "Personal business. I'm renovating the house next door. To put it on the market."

"Ah. So you don't plan to be here long." He grinned at Cat, as if to say, *I can wait.*

Again, her fingers tightened on Mark's arm in warning.

His lips twitched. "That depends." He glanced at Cat and smiled. "On several factors."

She let her eyes convey her gratitude, before turning to Kyle. "Don't let us keep you. I'm sure you have a thousand things to do. I'll call you about that work."

"No hurry. Well, I'll leave you to your date, Cat."

She walked him to the door. His voice pitched low but still loud enough for the others to hear, he said, "Give me a call when he leaves town. Or if you get tired of him before that."

Cat waited until she heard Kyle's car start before she turned around. Mark studied her, his mouth lifted in a half smile. His brother had set the casserole dish down on the coffee table beside her papers, and watched both of them with cheerful interest.

"You must think I'm a lunatic," she said after a long pause.

Mark's smile widened. "No, but I'll admit I'm curious. Not that I mind kissing a pretty woman, but what was that about?"

"It was unforgivably presumptuous, but I was stuck. I've been trying to disinterest him without hurting his feelings." She crossed the room. "Although I'm beginning to think his ego doesn't leave room for feelings, hurt or otherwise. Thanks for bringing the dish back. Great timing."

"Yeah, I noticed. Are you going to kiss me like that every time I come over?"

She frowned. "That was an emergency." Just because the kiss had been one of the best she'd ever had didn't mean she intended to do it again. Unfortunately.

"An emergency kiss," Mark said. "I can live with that. Any particular time of day you have these emergencies?"

His brother choked, then laughed. "I'll volunteer for emergency duty. I'm a med student, I'm used to handling trauma."

"Scram, sonny," Mark muttered.

"Not on your life. I haven't had this much fun since Amy dumped me."

"The least I can do is offer you some cookies," Cat said, chuckling at the byplay between the brothers and glad to be back on familiar ground. Brothers she could deal with, she had two older brothers of her own. "Thanks for the offer, Jay, but I think Mark did the trick. Emergency over."

She hoped she appeared more blasé than she felt. Whatever she'd expected when she'd kissed Mark, she hadn't thought she'd be reduced to a babbling fool. Okay, maybe not that bad, but she did feel a little out of control. Not her normal state at all.

The men followed her into the kitchen. "Have a seat," she said, grabbing the cookie jar, filled with fresh peanut-butter cookies, and setting it on the table. "I should explain about earlier. Kyle wants to date me. I keep turning him down, but he doesn't get the picture. So tonight, I changed my strategy and claimed to be seeing someone." She poured two glasses of milk and put them on the table as well. "Unfortunately, Kyle knows all the single men around here, and he knew I wasn't dating any of them."

She picked up a cookie, remembered those five pounds and put it down. "So, since you showed up on my doorstep at the exact moment I needed someone, and you're new in town to boot, it seemed like fate." Kismet, as Gail put it. Maybe she had something there. Cat glanced at Mark and sighed. She should be so lucky.

"Glad to oblige," Mark said. "These cookies are great." He finished one and continued. "Why don't you just tell the guy to take a hike? Why the charade?"

She shrugged and took a seat. "He's a client of mine. Besides, he's the only vet anywhere close, and avian medicine is his specialty. For obvious reasons, I need to be on good terms with him."

"Mark said you rehabilitated birds. Does the vet supply you with them?" Jay had managed to put away more than his share of cookies, Cat noticed. Nothing shy about his appetite, either.

"Not usually. I get a lot of them from the FWS. Or sometimes someone local will find an injured bird and bring it to me. Kyle's a client for my other job." She took a sip of milk. "You can't make a living rehabilitating birds. Or at least, I haven't found a way yet. In my other life, I'm a CPA. I work out of my home, so that way I can keep the birds and make a living, too.''

''A CPA?'' Mark repeated. He looked more surprised now than he had when she kissed him.

Accustomed to that response, she laughed and put on her glasses. ''There, is that better? Now do I look more like an accountant?''

Mark smiled. ''Nope. Not even close.'' Angling a sharp glance at his brother, he said, ''Didn't you tell me you had a call to make, Jay?''

Jay grinned. ''Never let it be said that I can't take a hint. See you later, Cat. Thanks for the cookies. And remember—''

''Beat it,'' Mark interrupted. He waited until Jay left, then took another cookie. ''Don't believe everything Jay says,'' he told her.

''Such as?''

''He's not more charming than I am.'' A corner of his mouth lifted. ''He just thinks he is.''

She laughed. ''I wouldn't have believed that the first time we met. Your charm wasn't exactly apparent.''

''Temporary insanity,'' he said. ''Brought on by lack of sleep.''

They laughed companionably. Mark took another cookie, then leaned back in his chair. ''So tell me, how did you get started rehabbing birds?''

''I've been rescuing them since I was a little girl. I don't know why, but they seemed to find their way to me. By the time I was a teenager, everyone in the area knew to bring me any injured birds.''

''Is the rest of your family interested in birds?''

Remembering her mother's exasperation, Cat shook her head. ''No, I'm the only one. For which my mother is eternally grateful. She didn't really approve of my interest in birds, but my father convinced her she might as well give in gracefully. He helped me set up a small hospital when I was a teenager. I was in heaven after that.''

She sighed, remembering the unconditional support her father had given all his children. Too bad her mother didn't seem to have that ability. She loved her children, but after her husband's death, she'd become increasingly manipulative. Cat thought remarrying would be good for her mother—it would give her someone else to focus on, other than her kids.

''Sad memories?'' Mark asked sympathetically.

Cat nodded. ''A little. My dad died when I was in college. I miss him.''

''Do you have a big family?''

''Two brothers and a sister. I'm the youngest. What about you?''

''Two younger brothers. When did you make your bird rehabbing official?''

Apparently, he didn't want to talk about his family. He was an odd combination, she thought. Interested in drawing her out, but not in sharing much himself.

"In college. At the same time I worked for an accounting degree."

"Practical and beautiful. What a combination."

Her eyes narrowed. "I have to tell you, flattery makes me suspicious. What is it you're after?"

His teeth flashed white in his tanned face. "A date. Go to dinner with me tomorrow night."

A mercy date. Just what she didn't need. "You don't have to do that. I know I put you in an uncomfortable position, and you're being incredibly nice—"

"Do I seem like the type to ask a woman out to be nice?"

She thought about what he'd said and done when she first met him. He had a point. "Maybe not. You sure weren't this friendly the other day."

His smile widened. "You hadn't kissed me the other day. Yes or no, Cat."

Go for it, she thought. What harm can it do? "Yes."

"Great, I'll pick you up around six-thirty."

She watched him leave with mixed emotions. Despite what he said, she couldn't be positive he hadn't asked her out of pity. Well, she'd find out soon enough.

"When are you going back to work?" Jay asked Mark late the next afternoon.

They were back up on the roof, pulling off shingles. The roof needed the most work and Mark figured he should take advantage of Jay's help while he had it.

"Don't you want to get those suckers who put you in the hospital?" Jay continued when he didn't answer.

Mark shot him a contemplative look. Jay knew about his work and knew he had to keep it quiet, but it wouldn't hurt to remind him. "I *am* back at work. It landed in my lap when I came down here."

"You're on that case again? The one that sent you to the hospital?" Jay pried up a shingle, sent it sailing downward, then paused to look at his brother. "How did that happen?"

"Yeah, and I'd appreciate it if you kept that to yourself. As far as everyone down here knows, I'm just renovating my uncle's home to sell it." Remembering Cat's comment about Gilbert's big mouth and secret agents, he frowned. "At least, I hope that's what they think. Gilbert talked some apparently, and I'm not sure exactly what he said." Mark was hoping his cover story had taken care of any doubts his uncle's big mouth might have caused.

Ignoring his remarks about their uncle, Jay focused on his previous comments. "Who could be involved in illegal bird smuggling in this burgh? Hell, it's too small to— Wait a minute." He glanced at the aviary next door, then back to Mark. "You think Cat's involved?"

Mark shrugged. "Possibly. According to my partner, someone in town's involved—in a big way. The FWS thinks Aransas City has been a way station for smuggled birds for some time now. The local office has intercepted a few messages that are very suspicious. Somebody here is making a profit—and we're not talking peanuts. If my team's information is correct, then another shipment is due soon. We just don't have the exact date."

"But Cat? Why suspect her?"

"I don't necessarily. But she is involved with exotic birds. No one questions her much from what I can tell. The local FWS seems to trust her." Gazing at the aviary, he added, "She has contacts in the birding community. Even if she isn't smuggling, she may know something. May not even be aware she knows it."

"Is that why you're dating her?" Jay shook his head and whistled. "Man, what a waste of a beautiful woman."

Mark frowned and laid his hammer aside. "I don't want to think she could be involved, but I haven't totally ruled out the possibility. And I'll do whatever it takes to figure out who the key man is in this smuggling ring." His job, his obligation. But that didn't mean it sat well with him.

"She doesn't seem like the type." Jay pulled off his cap and used the end of the hammer to scratch his head beneath thick blond hair.

"Yeah, neither did Miller," Mark said, naming the man he'd busted several months before, considered a world authority on exotic parrots. "And he had a multimillion-dollar operation going."

"I don't know, Mark, I just don't get that feel from her."

"You met her for ten minutes. What do you know?"

Jay rubbed a hand over his jaw and stared at his brother. "So is that the only reason you're dating her?"

Evading a direct answer, he said, "She's not my type. If it turns out she isn't smuggling birds, then she's a cause junkie. You know how I feel about cause junkies." People like their mother, who had all the time in the world for her causes, and none for her family.

"Which is why you're with the FWS busting exotic-animal smugglers. That's not a cause, now, is it?"

"It's a job, Jay." He gritted his teeth, aware they'd had this conversation before. Numerous times.

"Right. You know, I could point out that rationale doesn't make a lot of sense."

"Look, it's a puzzle. I like putting the pieces together."

"Whatever you say." Jay spread his hands and resumed working. After a moment he added, "So if

Cat's just a means to an end, you wouldn't mind if I try my luck with her.''

His eyes narrowed as he gazed at his brother. ''Back off, Jay. You're leaving in a few days anyway.'' Even as he said it, Mark knew that his job wasn't the only thing behind his interest in Cat Randolph.

He liked her, damn it. Too much for his peace of mind.

CHAPTER FIVE

MARK HAD JUST EMERGED from the shower when Jay appeared in the bedroom doorway. Lounging against the doorjamb, his younger brother gave him a pitying smile. "Looks like you're out of luck tonight. Cat called while you were showering. You've been dumped."

Mark snorted and tossed his towel in the direction of his bed before stepping into his jeans and jerking them up over his hips. "Nice try, but it won't work."

"Would I lie to you?"

"In a heartbeat." He grabbed a sky-blue knit shirt and pulled it over his head. "Especially if you thought it would get you a date with a pretty woman."

Jay grinned. "True, but I'm not lying. She said she had to baby-sit her nieces."

Baby-sitting? He felt a jolt of disappointment. Business, he told himself. Nothing personal.

Like hell it wasn't.

Jay added, "For what it's worth, she said she'd be at home if you wanted to call. And I heard the theme song from *The Little Mermaid* and kids screaming in the background.''

Distracted for the moment, Mark tucked his shirt into his jeans. "How would you know the theme song to *The Little Mermaid?*"

His brother's eyes lit with humor. "I've dated a few single mothers."

"Good, you had me worried for a minute there."

Jay chuckled, then straightened. "I'm going to track down some dinner. And if I'm lucky, the company of some nice, friendly women. Heard about a place in Corpus that's supposed to be good. Want to come?"

Mark shook his head. "Thanks, but no." Maybe he could still salvage the evening. "I'll take a rain check."

"Suit yourself."

An hour later Mark showed up on Cat's doorstep, with an extra-large pizza and a six-pack of beer in hand. "I brought dinner," he told her when she opened the door. She wore short beige shorts and a T-shirt, which had once been white but now had some sort of grape stain on it. Looking closely, he decided the green stuff in her hair was paint. "Tough night?"

A smile spread like dawning sunshine over her face. "What are you doing here? Never mind, you've saved my life." She grabbed his arm and tugged him inside. "Tell me that's pepperoni."

"Half cheese, half pepperoni. Did I guess right?"

"Bless you. Come in and meet the minions of hell." She turned around and snagged a toddler who had climbed up on the back of the sofa and was preparing to launch herself. "Watch it there, Sky Princess." Settling the girl on her hip, she spoke to Mark. "This is Mel. The child knows no fear."

She led the way to the kitchen, waiting only long enough for him to set down his offerings before handing the toddler to him. "I'll be back with the other one in a flash. I hope," she added with a shudder. "Roxy and Buddy, my parrot, disappeared into my bedroom a little while ago. I don't even want to guess what they're doing."

Nieces, Mark thought, not particularly disconcerted to be presented with a squirming bundle of sticky young female.

"I'm Mark," he said, taking her to the sink. "How about we wash up before dinner?"

"Uh-uh." A pint-size angel with blond ringlets and a stubborn chin sparkled at him. "I'm free," she said, holding up three remarkably grubby fingers.

"That a fact? I thought you were much older. Four at least." She rewarded him with a beaming smile. "What if I wash my hands first and then you wash yours? Or we could have a race. Bet I can beat you."

She giggled. "Me first! Me first!"

Mel won the race, managing to dump a load of water down his shirtfront in the process. Better water than pizza, but there was still a chance for that, he knew.

A few moments later, Cat entered with another angelic-faced blonde of maybe five or six. "This is Roxy. Roxy, this is Mr. Kincaid."

"Mark. Nice to meet you, Roxy."

Roxy was a slightly larger version of her little sister, with blond hair, blue eyes and cherry-red lips, and a mouth that never stopped running. At the moment she chattered about a spinning lamp shade and blue feathers.

"Want me to get them something to drink?" he asked Cat when the little girl paused for breath.

"I'll do it, but thanks." She finished anchoring a high-chair seat to the table. "You must have kids. Or does Jay? You know what you're doing," she said as he slid the baby into the seat.

"No kids," he said. "And none for Jay, either. Or my other brother, Brian." But Mark had plenty of experience in taking care of kids. "I was the oldest, and a lot of the child care fell to me." Even then, his mother had been willing to let Mark shoulder many of her responsibilities. And of course, his old man hadn't lifted a finger to do what he called *woman's work.* "I raised my younger brothers alone for several years. I guess it shows."

"That must have been hard on you, raising your brothers. You can't have been very old."

"Old enough." He shrugged. "But it wasn't

easy,'' he agreed, wishing he hadn't brought the subject up. He didn't usually share that with others. Something about Cat loosened his tongue.

Though he couldn't say he talked one-on-one with Cat much during dinner, the evening did provide insight into her character. She was very patient with her nieces, taking it in stride when they flung pepperoni at each other, effectively subduing them with the threat of no dessert.

After dinner—and a brief argument he won—they cleaned up the kids, the kitchen and the light fixture above the table, then went to the living room.

''I promised the girls we'd play Candyland,'' Cat said. ''I really appreciate your bringing dinner and helping me clean up, but you don't have to stay.''

''I don't mind. I play a mean game, myself.''

She blinked at him. ''You play Candyland?''

''Well, it's been a while, but I bet I can still figure it out.''

''But…Candyland?''

He smiled at her shocked expression. ''I had a sister,'' he said slowly, remembering Miranda when she was about Roxy's age. ''This was her favorite game when she was little.''

''Had?'' she asked softly. ''I'm sorry.''

Why had he brought up Miranda? ''We…lost her a long time ago.'' But he'd never lost the pain. He slid in a deep breath.

''That must be tough. I can't imagine being without my brothers and sister.'' She paused a moment, then asked, ''What about your other brother? Where is he?''

''Studying for his master's degree. In Dallas. He's the computer fiend of the family. Jay's like you, he wants to fix things. Only he fixes people, not animals.''

''Is Jay going to be here long?''

Mark shook his head. ''No, he's heading back to medical school soon.''

''Oh, I thought he might be staying a while.''

''He's just here for his break.'' And to force Mark to talk about things he had no interest in discussing. Such as their mother. Changing the subject, he said, ''So, how did you get drafted for duty?''

''My sister's divorced. She's trying to earn a real estate license. It's not easy working full-time, going to school and trying to raise two kids totally on your own.''

''Sounds like she's not on her own. She has you.''

''Our family is pretty supportive. But Gail doesn't want to impose on everyone. She'd never have called me if she hadn't been desperate.''

He hid a smile at her quick defense of her sister. The obvious love she had for her family was nice to see.

The game went well, even with the parrot's help. Both Cat and Mark made sure the little girls stayed ahead. Roxy won, which suited everyone, since Mel didn't really grasp the concept of losing. In an aside to Cat at the end, Mark said, "That bird cheats."

She laughed. "I know, I know. I've tried to cure him but it's no use. Since he cheats in the girls' favor, I figure it's okay."

"Yeah, but you'd better not take him to a poker game," Mark said.

Cat returned Buddy to his cage, settling him down for the night. A short time later, Cat's sister arrived to pick up the kids. Mark recognized her as the woman he'd seen the first time he met Cat. Her daughters looked a lot like her, fair and slight, but the mother had smudges of weariness beneath her eyes.

After greeting him and thanking her sister, Gail said, "Cat, why didn't you tell me you were having company?"

"Because I knew you wouldn't have asked me if you'd had any other option." When Gail protested, Cat simply ignored her. "So how was the exam? Do you think you passed? Are you going to get your real estate license?"

Her eyes lit up, and she nodded. "I know I'm cursing myself to say this, but—" She hesitated, then said, "I aced it."

"Wonderful!" Cat threw her arms around Gail and hugged her. "I never doubted you would."

Gail blew her hair out of her eyes and grinned. Suddenly Mark saw the resemblance between the two. "It's not official, but I'm sure I passed. Once the confirmation comes in the mail, I can job hunt."

"First we're celebrating," Cat stated. "Tomorrow night. Tell Mom she's baby-sitting."

"But Cat—"

"No arguments. This is on me."

Apparently tired of adult conversation, Roxy tugged on Mark's hand. "I like you," she announced. "If you marry Aunt Cat, then I can see you all the time."

Cat choked and Gail laughed. "My little matchmaker," Gail said, and ruffled her hair. "Just like Grandma. Come on, we need to go home and put you two in bed."

AFTER CAT CLOSED the door behind Gail and the girls, she became aware of a taut silence. She turned and found Mark watching her with an expression she couldn't read. Then he smiled, and she had no problem at all reading the invitation in that. "I should change my shirt," she said, and cleared her throat nervously. She wouldn't have chosen to have a date with a man like Mark sporting grape juice on her shirt and pizza in her hair.

"Purple looks good on you."

"Right. Sticky purple stains look good on everyone. I'm going to change. Be right back."

"Need any help?"

On her way out of the room, she looked over her

shoulder and laughed. "I think I can manage. But I could use a hand with icing a cake. Why don't you wait for me in the kitchen?"

When she returned minus grape stains and with her hair brushed for the first time that night, she felt almost human. Mark waited with a hip propped against the counter. Reaching for the mixing bowl at the back of the counter, she knocked some papers off the drain board. Mark picked them up as they fluttered to the floor.

"Thanks. Just put them over there," she said, pointing at the opposite end of the counter. "Don't want to get icing on them." Her brother Gabe's financial records looked bad enough without smearing chocolate on them. She frowned, knowing they needed to talk about his failing business, but so far Gabe had managed to avoid that conversation. Which took some doing, considering she was his accountant.

"Problem?" Mark asked, having come back to her side.

Shaking off her concerns, she smiled at him. "Nothing I can do anything about." She rifled her cupboards, gathering the ingredients for chocolate icing. A short time later, she had everything assembled, ready to begin. A whiff of Mark's aftershave drifted to her nostrils, a pleasantly sexy, masculine scent.

"Why aren't you a caterer or some kind of cook?" he asked. "Every time I see you you've either just made something to eat or you're about to."

"It wouldn't be fun if it were a job." Dumping the ingredients into the bowl, she started the blender, swearing under her breath when batter splattered in her face. "I keep forgetting to buy a new one," she muttered, wiping a hand over her forehead. She was doomed to wear food around this man. She grabbed a towel and wiped her face, hoping she hadn't smeared icing everywhere.

The blender hindered conversation, but she felt Mark's gaze on her as she worked. Soon she had a bowl full of fluffy icing. "Catering requires a larger community than this one. I'd spend all my time on the road to Corpus and the surrounding areas. Then I wouldn't enjoy it anymore. Besides, I need something home based so I can take care of the birds."

"Are there any other bird rehabilitators around here? I'd think this area of the coast would have a large birding community."

"No, I'm the only one. Or at least, the only licensed one. Most of the people just want to own exotic birds, not rehabilitate injured ones. There's an African gray club, and I'm a member of that. Buddy, my African gray parrot, came from the FWS, when they seized him in a raid. He couldn't be returned to his native country, so I took him."

"Smuggled?"

She gave a sharp nod. Her lips tightened into a grim line, thinking of what her bird must have endured. "Yes. Don't get me started on what I think about animal smugglers."

He leaned against the counter, crossing his arms. "I take it you're not too fond of them."

"I've seen their methods," she said. "Working with the FWS has made me aware of how inhumane they are, and the destruction they cause." She glanced at him. "You'd know about that, since you're FWS."

He shrugged. "Some. My work's been mostly in other areas."

"I guess you don't see a lot of smuggled animals running through Lake Grapevine," she said.

He laughed. "Not too many, no. We have some poachers, and a lot of people trying to exceed their fishing and hunting limits." He moved a little closer to her.

"I noticed your flock is shrinking. What's happening to them?"

"A couple of them went to zoos. Another to a private owner. I released the heron this morning." She started icing the cake, making artful swirls with the pastry knife. "Took him to the preserve over near Port Aransas. The birds come in sporadically, anyway. Depends a lot on what the FWS has cooking." They fell silent a moment, then she added, "Tell me, do you like being a game warden? Is that the only job you've had with the FWS, or have you done other things, too?"

"I've held several positions," he said after a moment. He rubbed his thumb over the corner of her mouth. "You missed a spot," he murmured. His gaze holding hers, he brought his thumb to his mouth and the dab of icing disappeared. "Tasty."

Cat sucked in a deep breath. His eyes said he wasn't just talking about the frosting.

"Would you like another taste?" She held out the spatula, covered in thick, dark swirls of creamy frosting.

"Oh, yeah," he said, but he didn't take the utensil from her. Instead, he leaned in very slowly, his eyes never leaving hers. His head lowered and his lips touched the corner of her mouth as the tip of his tongue gently darted against her. She stood frozen, spatula in hand as his lips cruised slowly over to the other side of her mouth. "Sweet." When his lips covered hers fully, she dropped the spatula on the counter with a clatter.

"Easy," he murmured against her mouth, his breath warm, moist, inviting. This time there was no audience to pretend for. Better yet, this time, he'd kissed her. He teased, taunted, his tongue seeking hers and drawing her out, his hands cupping her face. Cat's arms crept up around his neck. Easy is right, she thought. Too easy. But she didn't move away. Instead, she edged closer.

Her head started to spin. She felt as if she was melting into a gooey puddle of sheer lust. *Oh, honey, you'd better watch it,* she thought. She pulled back and looked at him, his hands still against her cheeks. To hell with it. She tugged his head down to hers. His hands fell to her waist and she settled against him, her breasts flush against his chest.

The guy kissed like a fantasy come to life. Who would have thought such a hard mouth, gorgeous as it was, could be so gentle? She couldn't remember the last time a man had knocked her senseless with a kiss. Wrapping her arms around his neck, she poured herself into another kiss and her brain shut down entirely.

The sound of someone pounding on the back door eventually penetrated the haze of lust. Cat pulled back and sucked in a deep breath. ''I'd better get that.''

Mark shook his head ruefully and released her. ''Bad timing.''

Or maybe not, Cat thought, attempting to calm her racing heart. Given many more kisses like that, she'd have been horizontal in no time. She opened the door, irritated to see her brother Gabe standing on the step.

''Hey, what's up, sis?''

She glanced pointedly at her watch. ''It's nine-thirty at night.'' She'd wanted to talk to him, but his timing sucked.

He walked past her, into the kitchen. ''Yeah. Your point?'' He halted when he saw Mark, then glanced at her, a considering lift to his eyebrow. "Am I interrupting?"

"No," Mark said.

"Yes," Cat said at the same moment.

"Sorry." Gabe's lips twitched. "I'm Gabe Randolph, Cat's brother," he said to Mark, offering a hand.

"Mark Kincaid," he said, shaking hands.

Gabe picked up the frosting-covered spatula and licked it, grinning at her over the utensil.

"Don't lick that," Cat said automatically, unsurprised when he ignored her. She loved her brother, she really did, but just at that moment she wanted to kick him.

"You must be new to town," Gabe said. "I haven't seen you around."

"I moved into the house next door just a few days ago," Mark said.

"Gilbert's house? You're his nephew?"

Mark nodded. "I'm renovating it so I can sell it."

Gabe shook his head. "I hope you have some talent in construction. That place is a mess."

"You got that right. I used to work construction. But this is a challenge."

"I've been wanting to talk to you, Gabe. But I didn't expect you to show up tonight. What do you need?" Cat asked him, hoping to forestall a question-and-answer session.

"Oh, I just brought over some receipts. Cat keeps

my books,'' he told Mark. ''I run a charter fishing service.''

''Bay or deep-sea?'' Mark asked.

''A little of both. Whatever the client wants. Do you fish?''

''Freshwater. I like deep-sea fishing, when I get the chance,'' Mark said. ''It's been a while.''

Cat waited patiently while they discussed fishing, the weather, and whether recent reports of tarpon moving back into the area were true or not. Since she saw her brother nearly daily, she didn't pay much attention to the actual discussion, but instead spent the time looking at Mark and wondering what would happen if—

Hastily, she channeled her thoughts away from sex. Just because he'd kissed her like there was no tomorrow didn't mean anything. But still, she thought, perking up, why had he bothered to bring pizza and stay with her while she baby-sat? No man did such a thing unless he was at least a little interested.

She realized both men had fallen silent and were looking at her expectantly. ''Sorry. My mind was wandering. Did you say something?''

Mark smiled, that killer smile that effortlessly revved up her heartbeat. ''Just that I've got to go. I'll call you.''

''Thanks for the pizza. And the company.''

She watched him walk toward the door, that pur-

poseful, sexy stride tempting her to drag him to the
closest flat surface and have her way with him. If
only Gabe hadn't showed up, she might have. As
soon as the door shut behind him, she turned to her
brother, frustration bubbling. "Why does everyone
think I have nothing better to do with my life than
run numbers every night?"

Gabe shrugged, eyes sparkling with more mirth
than usual. "Maybe because you don't."

Unfortunately, Gabe was right. Nonetheless, she
glared at him. "I have an office, Gabriel. I work during the day. Not, as everyone seems to think, at ten
o'clock at night."

"Gabriel? Uh-oh, I'm in big trouble now. You're
just sore because I interrupted your—" He broke off,
cocked his head and raised an inquiring eyebrow.
"What was going on between you two? Pretty heavy
tension when I came in."

"I'm not discussing my personal life with you. It's
absolutely none of your business."

"Fine by me. I don't want to hear it. But you just
met this guy, right? And it's pretty clear there was a
lot of heat going on in here, and not from your oven.
How do you know this guy's not…" He waved his
hand, spattering chocolate on the cabinets. "A
weirdo or something." He scooped up an errant dab
of chocolate and stuck his finger in his mouth.

She parked her hands on her hips. "You talked to
him. Did he seem like a weirdo?"

"No, but then neither do you when you're not around forty thousand birds. So there you go." Regarding her over the spatula, he licked more icing. "This isn't as good as usual," he added. "But I guess you were distracted." He gave her a challenging smile.

Her gaze narrowed, but she didn't take that bait, either. "Trust me, he's not a weirdo. And why are you so worried? You're acting as if I'm sixteen instead of twenty-eight."

"You were engaged to Chad. That doesn't say a lot for your choice in men."

"Like your taste in women is any better?" she asked indignantly, snatching the spatula from him before he did any more damage. "I could point out that the women you date generally have IQs in the double digits."

He grinned, completely unabashed. "You know I'm not into complicated relationships. And we were talking about you." He rested his hands on her shoulders. "Look, Cat, I'm just saying be careful."

"I intend to be. Now, are you through with the obligatory older-brother lecture?" He nodded. "Okay, let me have the receipts."

Reaching into his back pocket, he pulled them out and handed them over. "You're one in a million, sis," he said, and kissed her cheek.

"Don't I know it. And don't think you can sweet-talk me now, either." She thumbed through the receipts and glanced at him. "Business is up from last week. That's good, but we still need to talk, Gabe." She picked up his records from on top of the counter and handed the sheet to him. "About this. It's the financial statement for *El Jugador*." His boat, his pride and joy. And right now, his failing business.

"It doesn't take a genius to see I'm in the red, Cat. What's to talk about? Fishing's a cyclical business. I'll come around."

"I know you will, but—"

"Gotta go, Cat. Thanks."

He left so fast she barely got a goodbye in. Staring at the back door, she tapped her fingers on the counter and frowned. Gabe was going to have to do something, and soon. She didn't believe declaring bankruptcy was high on his list of what he wanted to do, though.

Pray God he didn't decide to gamble again. While Gabe hadn't been an addict, he'd made some major errors in judgment. Cat could only hope that the disaster he'd faced last time would be enough to deter him from trying that again.

CHAPTER SIX

"NOT THAT I MIND cold beer and fresh boiled shrimp, but tell me again why we're going to this place?" Jay asked Mark as they drove down the shell-paved road to the waterfront.

After asking around, Mark had discovered that the Scarlet Parrot, a waterfront bar and grill owned by none other than Cat Randolph's brother, Cameron, was a favorite hangout of the locals.

"I need information, and this should be a good place to start. And remember to keep your mouth shut about my job. As far as people around here are concerned, I'm a game warden on Grapevine Lake." He hoped that story would counteract whatever wild rumors Gilbert's big mouth had been responsible for circulating.

"No problem." Jay peered out the window and shook his head. "I still can't believe this place is the headquarters for the scam you've been working on for two years."

"It's not the headquarters, it's a major distribution center. We think." The animals passed through the designated cities by the thousands, on their way across the country to private bird fanciers. Ones who didn't mind a touch of illegality as long as they got the rare birds they wanted.

"Yeah, but—" Jay gestured at the small, placid marina "—I mean, look at it. Thriving it isn't. There can't be more than ten or twelve boats docked here. Wouldn't it be kind of obvious if one of them was smuggling birds?"

"Not if the boat had a legitimate reason to be here," Mark said, spotting a sign for Gabe Randolph's charter fishing service. "A business reason," he added. An explanation that allowed a man to cruise the coastline whenever he wished, or meet someone out at sea.

Seeing Randolph's financial statement at Cat's house the night before had been pure luck. The quick glance Mark had gotten at the paper had been enough to tell him the man's fishing business was in deep trouble. Not suspicious in itself, but intriguing enough that Mark called his team to have them run a thorough background check on the man. Randolph had no criminal history, but results of the complete check would take some time.

In the meantime, Mark intended to see if he could ferret out any local gossip.

After parking, Mark and Jay entered a small, whitewashed, wooden building, nondescript except for the huge sign of a painted scarlet parrot hanging over the doorway. Once inside, they crossed the plank floor to the central bar, and pulled up a couple of captain's-chair stools, more comfortable than most. A big-screen TV hung suspended at one end of the bar, and the obligatory jukebox against one wall stood silent in deference to either the ball game or the early hour. Mark had been told the place would be jumping later in the evening, when local bands played various types of music.

He pegged the bartender as the owner right off, partly because of his air of command, but mostly because the cute little redheaded waitress called him boss.

Fair-haired and big, Cameron Randolph had a deep voice and piercing gray eyes. He resembled Gail more than either of his other siblings. Then he grinned at a comment from a customer, and Mark saw the likeness to Cat. His motions swift and sure, Cameron slid a couple of cardboard coasters imprinted with a picture of a scarlet parrot in front of Mark and Jay. "What can I get you?"

"Rumor has it your place has the best boiled shrimp around," Mark said. The place didn't reek of shrimp, probably because the big ceiling fans situated throughout took care of circulation. It carried a definite smell of the waterfront, though.

The bartender grinned and told the waitress, "Two pounds, boiled, Sally." Glanced at Jay and added, "Or should that be three?"

"Two will do it," Jay said. "At least for now. And

two drafts. He's paying,'' he said, jerking his thumb at Mark.

''Just passing through?'' Randolph asked a few moments later, setting two frosty mugs of amber liquid in front of them.

''My brother Jay is, but I'll be around a while. Mark Kincaid,'' he said, offering a hand. ''I have a feeling you'll be seeing a lot of me. I'm not much of a cook.''

''Cameron Randolph. Glad to have you.''

''Randolph?'' Mark rubbed his chin. ''Any kin to my next-door neighbor, Cat Randolph?''

He pulled a towel out of his back pocket and wiped down the bar. ''Her brother. So, you moved into Gilbert's place? You're a braver man than I am.''

''I didn't have much choice. He willed it to me,'' Mark said. Randolph gave a bark of laughter, then left to attend to other customers.

A short time later he returned with their meals and seemed inclined to linger. He and Jay got into a discussion about the merits of a couple of the baseball players on the tube. Mark listened and tried to decide how to introduce a more useful topic of conversation. He couldn't exactly say, ''So, hear anything about smuggled birds lately?''

A man's voice called out irritably, ''How about a little service, Randolph?''

Mark glanced over to see Kyle Peters standing impatiently at the bar. The man's gaze passed over him as if he were invisible. Randolph still hadn't turned around, but continued to talk to Jay. Peters spoke again, louder this time.

"Let me go take care of this guy," Randolph said, casting an exasperated glance over his shoulder. "He's a pain in the ass, persistent, too."

Mark considered following him over. The vet had ties to the birding community, but that didn't set him up as the contact, necessarily. Too bad, because he'd rather bust Peters than Cat or Gabe Randolph. He seemed a more likely suspect, but Mark couldn't be sure his prejudice didn't stem from attempts to put the moves on Cat.

"Who's the foxy blonde in the doorway?" Jay asked Mark.

"My other sister." Randolph set another round in front of them. "Gail Summers." His face darkened while watching Peters approach her and guide her to a table. "Great, now he's sniffing around Gail. Does he have to go after both my sisters?"

"Damn," Jay said. "She's married?"

"Divorced." He raised his eyebrows at Jay. "Want me to introduce you?"

"Absolutely."

"She has two kids. Still want an intro?"

"I don't have any problem with kids. Not when their mother looks like she does."

Randolph's gaze narrowed. "Remember this is my sister we're talking about."

Jay smiled disarmingly. "I'm harmless. Just ask Mark."

"Basically true. Besides, he's not in town for long," Mark said, amused. "I don't know about Gail, but Cat doesn't seem to have a lot of use for Peters."

"Really? How would you know that?"

Mark smiled, remembering the kiss. "Long story. But she's not interested. Why don't you like him?"

His jaw tightened. "Got more money than he knows what to do with. Drives a Jag. Thinks he's God's gift to women and the world. What's to like?"

So the vet had money. Mark wondered where it came from. In his experience, vets in dinky little towns in Texas didn't make a fortune. As one of the main contacts in a nationwide smuggling distribution ring, however, he'd have loads of cash. "So what's he doing here if he's got so much money?"

"Beats the hell out of me, but I wish he'd leave. Preferably before my mother manages to marry off one of my sisters to him. And speaking of sisters, there's Cat." He lifted a hand to wave.

Mark followed his gaze. Tempted to whistle, he sucked in a breath instead. It was the first time he'd seen her wear anything besides shorts and a T-shirt. Her short denim skirt ended several inches above her knees. A bright pink sleeveless knit top clung to her curves, showcasing generous breasts. Tidy. Very tidy.

Her face clouded the minute she saw her sister with Mr. Romeo. She stopped at their table, one of a dozen dark wooden tables that had seen better days. After a brief discussion, Cat left them and headed for the bar.

"Cameron," she began, dragging her gaze from her sister. Then she saw Mark. "Hi," she said, a little breathlessly.

"Hi." He smiled, watching her nervously moisten her lips. He had an idea she was remembering the night before, and how the evening might have ended if her brother hadn't come over. He sure as hell was thinking about it.

"Back in a minute," Cameron said, leaving to wait on another customer.

Jay cleared his throat. "Hi, Cat. Can I ask you a favor?"

Blinking, she tore her gaze from Mark's and turned to Jay. "Hello, Jay. What favor?"

"Introduce me to your sister."

She glanced back over her shoulder. "Gail?" She tilted her head, considering him as a smile grew. "You know, I think that's a great idea." She smiled at Mark, as well. "Would you two like to join my sister and me?"

"Funny you should ask," Jay said before Mark could speak. "Since that's exactly what I had in mind," he added, picking up his beer mug. "Come on, Mark. Get moving." To Cat he said, "Consider me your slave for life."

"I thought you were already my slave," Cat said. "The lasagna, remember?"

Mark decided it was a good thing his charming little brother didn't intend to stay in town long. Cat liked him a little too much for Mark's taste. A few moments later they all crowded around a small table. Jay immediately zeroed in on Gail, which left Mark free to talk to Cat. Peters wasn't too thrilled with the arrangement, but seemed civil enough.

"What line of business are you in?" Peters asked Mark. "Construction? Didn't you say something about renovating a house?"

"Oh, Mark's not in construction," Cat piped up. "He's with the Fish and Wildlife Service."

Peters stared at him a moment. "Really. In what capacity?"

"Game warden at Grapevine Lake," Mark said, giving him his prefabricated story. "I'm on a leave of absence, though. I inherited a house I need to unload. Can't afford the taxes forever." Was it his imagination or had Peters relaxed at his answer? "As for construction, I've worked it in the past. Just not for several years now."

He tried to draw Peters into more conversation, slipping in a couple of pertinent questions about his ties to the community, particularly the birding community, but the vet wasn't interested. The most Mark got out of him was that he'd been in the area a couple of years and had a small-animal practice, including avian medicine. All of which Mark already knew.

The band arrived and after tuning up, they started into a zydeco rhythm. Further conversation became tough as the musicians played their instruments with great energy, but unfortunately, not a great deal of skill. Jay and Gail left for the dance floor. "Your brother works fast," Cat commented, leaning close so he could hear over the swish of the washboard. Mark caught a whiff of her perfume, a faint fruity scent that reminded him of strawberries. Lush, tasty strawberries.

So much for pumping Peters. He didn't think the man would give up much, anyway. "He has to. He's not here for long." Mark smiled at her. "But enough about my brother and your sister. I would really like to dance with you."

"I would really like to dance with you, too," she said, her gaze on him. "So why aren't we?"

"I'm not much of a dancer, even without the bum leg."

"Oh, I didn't even think of that. You move so well, I—" She broke off, a faint pink tone washing her face. "I mean, you don't limp much or anything."

"We don't have to move a lot," Mark said. "We could just stand there and sway." And he could hold her in his arms. That sounded good to him.

Peters spoke before she could answer. "How about a dance, Cat?"

"Sorry, Kyle." She tossed him a brilliant smile. "Mark just asked me."

They got up and squeezed onto the tiny dance floor. She went into his arms as if she belonged there, which should have given him pause, but didn't. They danced in silence for a short time, until Mark broke it. "Tell me, are the bands here ever any good?"

She laughed. "Some of them are great. But Cameron has a soft heart, and anyone who wants to can have a turn. They play for a free dinner and tips, so it actually works to Cam's advantage. And if they make it, they come back for old time's sake."

"Nobody seems to mind," Mark observed, watching the dancers gyrate with enthusiasm equal to the band's.

Her lips curved upward. "Story is that Janis Joplin sang here in the sixties. Cam doesn't believe it, but he loves to circulate the rumor, for obvious reasons."

The music grew on him, or maybe it was holding Cat in his arms. "You're going to have to tell Peters to get lost. He doesn't seem to be taking the hint."

She gnawed her lip. He wanted to do that himself. "I suppose you're right. Maybe I should try the direct approach. If I lose his business I'll just have to find someone else to replace him." She sounded a little doubtful.

"Or you could sic your brother on him." He nodded toward the bar. "He doesn't much care for your would-be boyfriend."

"Cameron never has liked him. I'm not sure why, but I think it has something to do with a woman."

"That happens," Mark said, and pulled her closer. "Why don't you like him?" He breathed the question in her ear, smiling when he felt her slight intake of breath.

"Hmm?" She looked as if she'd forgotten the question.

"What do you have against the vet?"

She blinked and wet her lips with a smooth flick of her tongue. "I don't know, exactly. Kyle's nice, most of the time, but...he reminds me too much of my ex-fiancé. Maybe it's the superior attitude. Inherited wealth seems to do that to some people."

So he'd inherited the money. Interesting. Maybe a background check on the vet was in order. "So you don't like his attitude."

She shrugged. "He's good-looking, wealthy and can be very charming if he wants. He can't figure out why every woman in town isn't dying to date him."

"You think he's after you just because you turned him down?"

"Sure, don't you?"

Mark gazed down at her and smiled. "No. I think he's after you because he wants you. And I don't blame him."

She stared at him a moment. "Why are we talking about Kyle?"

"I have no idea. Why are we?"

She laughed and shook her head. "Let's change the subject, then."

"Okay. Tell me about the ex-fiancé. What's the story there?"

Her head came to rest against his shoulder, and she sighed. He leaned down to hear her better. "The short version is that we had different ideas about my career. We had a hell of a fight, and when he realized I wouldn't change my mind, he called off the wedding."

"And the long version?"

Her smile was quick and sweet. "Is long and most likely boring. Tell me about you. I know you said you aren't married, but have you ever been? Or engaged?"

"Nope. Not even close. Remember I told you I had guardianship of my younger brothers? The youngest is just now getting out of college. Not too many women were interested in taking on those two hellions."

"When did your parents die?"

"Oh, they're not dead. The old man might be, but our mother's alive."

"I'm sorry, I just assumed... If you'd rather not talk about it, I understand."

"It's a long story, and probably boring," he said,

taking her own words and adding a smile. "Let me take you home and we can find something more—" he paused and studied her mouth "—interesting to do."

Going suddenly still, she stared at him. Slowly, she licked her lips again and cleared her throat. In another woman, he'd have labeled it a come-on. In Cat he wasn't sure. But he was sure of what he wanted to do. He lowered his head, but as his lips came within a fraction of hers, she blurted, "I forgot! I can't believe I forgot! I met Gail here to celebrate her passing her real estate exam, and I've completely ignored her."

"Your sister's doing just fine with my brother. They've obviously hit it off." He turned her to face them and nodded to the pair, who had returned to the table and were deep in conversation. Peters, apparently fed up with trying to talk to two people who were totally oblivious to him, stalked off a few moments later.

Just then Gail threw back her head and laughed. "I have to admit, I haven't seen her have this much fun in months. Still, isn't he kind of young for her?"

Mark shrugged. "Maybe if he meant anything serious. But Jay's heading back to California in a few days. He's in his last year of medical residency. Serious is the last thing on his mind. Which I imagine he's told her."

Her eyebrows drew together in a frown of concern.

"I worry about Gail. She's just been through a bad divorce and I don't want her hurt again."

"None of this is really up to us, is it?" Besides, for all his faults, Jay had always been up front with the women in his life. And it hadn't appeared to ruin his chances with them, Mark mused. Maybe they liked the challenge of trying to change him.

Still watching them, Cat sighed. "True. Okay, let me ask her if she minds. But before we go, I should tell you something."

"What's that?"

Her eyes gleamed, a deep chocolate brown that hinted at sultry nights. "I'm not going to sleep with you tonight."

He bit back a grin at her frank comment. "Damn. And here I was all set to show you my etchings."

Cat laughed. "Do you have any etchings?"

"Nope." He pulled her a little closer and murmured in her ear, "But once I got you to the bedroom you wouldn't have missed them."

Her lips twitched and she laid a hand on his chest. "Tell me something. Are you always this sure of yourself?"

He smiled down at her. "I prefer to think of it as optimistic."

CHAPTER SEVEN

MARK AND CAT stepped out of the noisy bar onto the somewhat quieter deck overlooking the ocean. They threaded their way through the crowd of diners, to the stairs leading down to the parking lot and the beach.

I must be a masochist, Mark thought. Why else would he have suggested they be alone, when he knew he needed to keep his hands to himself?

Or did he? As long as Cat wasn't a suspect, there wasn't a problem with the two of them getting closer. Though Mark hadn't been able to totally rule her out, he didn't buy her as a suspect. Everything about her, from her passionate feelings for the birds she tended, to the background check his team had already run— and the fact it had come back clear so rapidly—convinced him Cat Randolph was exactly who she said she was. She was no more guilty of smuggling exotic birds than he was. She loved birds. To her, illegal trafficking in animals would be the most heinous of crimes.

So, she wasn't a suspect, but her brother might be. Then again, half of Aransas Pass *might* be a suspect.

Until Mark had more proof, he didn't see his suspicions concerning Gabe Randolph's involvement as a stumbling block to his and Cat's relationship. And he wasn't thinking about marrying her, for crying out loud. Taking her to bed, now, that was another matter.

Still, Cat had told him up front she wouldn't go to bed with him tonight, and he suspected she meant it. But there would be other nights.

"Let's take a walk on the beach," he said, watching as Cat breathed in the salt-tinged air.

"Sounds good, but I'm dumping my shoes," she said, and he followed suit. "There's something I've been wondering ever since you moved in," she said, then laughed. "Actually, I think everyone in town has wondered at one time or another. Local legend holds that Gilbert had a lot of money. I guess the rumor started because he was such a miser. Some people believe he buried millions in cash in his backyard." She smiled and added, "I wouldn't go that far, but Gilbert was a pretty strange old bird."

Mark stared at her a moment before grinning. Trust Cat to say exactly what popped into her mind. "Afraid not. As far as I know, the only thing of value he had left was the house. And you know what kind of shape it's in."

She nodded decisively. "Too good to be true, just like I thought."

He'd never known a woman to be as frank as she

was. As unguarded. "Cat?" She glanced at him and he smiled. "I'm not loaded, if that's what you were asking."

"Oops." She placed a hand over her mouth and her eyes danced above it. "Sorry, I didn't mean to pry. I'm just curious." She laughed at the contemplative look he gave her. "Don't worry, you'd be safe from me even if you did have money. I'm not looking to get married. I don't think it agrees with me."

"That fiancé you talked about?"

"Ex-fiancé."

He took her hand as they walked. "Tell me that long story." The beach was quiet, almost deserted. Cat's hand felt soft in his. He wasn't supposed to like her so much. But he did.

He liked her concern for her sister. He liked seeing her with her nieces. Still, staying with the two girls occasionally wasn't the same as having kids of her own. It didn't mean she'd devote herself to family if it meant interfering with her career.

"I love rehabbing birds," she said, her voice dreamy. "It makes me feel as if I'm doing something not a lot of people can, or will, do. I'm making a difference, and I really enjoy that feeling."

"Yeah, I can see that. So what's the problem?"

"Eventually I want to be able to do it full-time. Chad, that was my ex-fiancé, hated the birds. Absolutely detested them. He didn't approve of me working from my home, either. Said my clients were a bunch of losers and I'd make more money if I went with a big company.''

''He had a point. If money's your object.''

''It isn't. Well, money's important, of course, but it's not my only goal in life. I need to make enough to cover my expenses, so I can care for the birds. But Chad knew from the beginning where my real interests lay. I never made a secret of my career goals.''

He believed her. She came across as the least secretive person he knew. Another reason he didn't think her part of the smuggling ring. ''You didn't know how he felt when you agreed to marry him?''

She threw her free hand in the air for emphasis. ''That's just it! I knew he didn't care much for the birds, but I thought he'd adjust to them, that he would come to realize what they mean to me. Instead, he assumed when we married I'd go the corporate route and get rid of the birds. Me, wearing a suit and heels in an office all day.'' She shuddered. ''I'd have lost it after the first week.''

She pulled free of him to prop her hands on her hips. He saw her eyes flash in the full moonlight. ''Do you know, he even wanted me to get rid of Buddy? Can you imagine?'' She let out a disgusted huff. ''I told Chad I'd had Buddy longer than I'd known him and there was no way I was giving up my bird. Or the other birds, either. I said if I had to choose, I'd take the birds over him any day.''

"Ouch, that must have done a number on his ego."

"It didn't." Her nose lifted in the air. "Chad had the sensitivity of a snail."

His lips twitched and he asked, "What happened then?"

She began walking again, taking his hand once more. "He broke the engagement."

"His loss."

"Oh, I'm sure he thanked his lucky stars for his close escape. Besides, I should have known it wouldn't work when Buddy started calling him Bad Chad and Chad the Cad."

Mark laughed. "And since then, have you been tempted?"

"Not to get married." She grinned at his skeptical expression. "Don't look so surprised. Why should men be the only ones who aren't interested in marriage?"

He halted and pulled her into his arms. Smiling down at her, he said, "You're the only woman I know who says exactly what she thinks."

Her face tilted up to his, she frowned. "Speaking my mind has gotten me into trouble so many times I can't count. You talk about it as if it's a good thing."

He cupped her cheek, stroked a hand down her throat. Her skin was soft, inviting. Tempting. "It is.

I like it,'' he murmured and lowered his head to kiss her.

Her lips opened beneath his, warm and mobile. Her sweet-hot taste went to his head and spread through his bloodstream like a straight shot of tequila. He slid his tongue over the edge of her teeth, gently thrust it inside until hers answered. Her arms tightened around his neck and he released her lips long enough to press his mouth to the pulse fluttering madly at her throat. His hand sought her breast, cupped it. When she didn't protest, he slipped it beneath her sweater and caressed the soft silky fabric of her bra, so sheer he felt her nipple bead.

She thrust her fingers in his hair and groaned. ''Maybe—'' she panted slightly as his lips cruised her jawline ''—I might have been too hasty.''

''Hasty how?'' he asked against her skin. Had he lost track of the conversation? It wouldn't be a wonder, with her scent driving him mad and her taste making him crave more.

''When I said I wouldn't sleep with you tonight.''

He stopped sampling her skin and looked at her. ''Do you mean that?'' Her soft curves pressing against him was already playing havoc with his self-control.

She nodded and put her hands on his face. ''Kiss me,'' she whispered.

THE SIGHT OF HER BROTHER Gabe's black pickup parked in front of her house shot to hell any romantic fantasies Cat had harbored about the remainder of the evening. What was it with Gabe? she thought irritably. He was becoming a major crimp in her style.

Mark pulled up behind her and got out of his Blazer. "Company?" he asked, motioning at the truck.

"Gabe," she told him. "I can try to get rid of him, but it depends on what he wants as to how long that's likely to take. I'm sorry."

He took her hand, squeezed it and smiled. "Me, too," he said simply.

"Where the hell have you been?" Gabe said as they reached the porch. "Cam said you left the Scarlet Parrot nearly an hour ago."

She started to answer him, then decided against it. Gabe had no right to question her movements. "I'm here now. What do you want?"

He gestured at the large cardboard box beside the front door. "I found that on my doorstep a while ago. Brought them right over to you, but you weren't here," he said accusingly.

"What's in the box?" she asked, with a sinking feeling she knew.

"Birds. And they weren't doing too well when I found them. They're probably—" He broke off, rubbing a hand across his forehead. "If you'd been here— Oh, forget it."

"Let's go to my quarantine room and I'll examine

them." But if they'd looked bad to Gabe, then there probably wasn't any hope of saving them. For protection, most birds didn't actually *look* ill until they were too far gone to save.

"I'll get them," Mark said when Gabe didn't respond. "Where's this room?"

"We can go in through the garage. I don't want to expose Buddy to anything."

They walked around back with Mark carrying the box. Cat opened the door, and he took them inside, Gabe following silently behind.

"What kind of birds are they, Gabe?" Cat asked.

"How the hell should I know? I'm not the resident bird expert. Some kind of parrot, I think."

Her heart sank further. If they were parrots, that meant they were most likely contraband. How in the world had Gabe ended up with illegal exotics on his doorstep? The question bothered her enough to ask him. "Why would anyone bring the birds to you? Why not just bring them directly to me?"

He gave a bad-tempered shrug. "Maybe they knew you were my sister. Look, Cat, all I know is I came home to find the box on my porch. They looked bad and I didn't know what else to do with them, so I brought them over here."

Mark set the box on a steel table. Other than a couple of large cages, there wasn't much else in the room.

"Want me to open it?" he asked.

He's trying to spare me, she thought, seeing his grim expression. He didn't believe they were alive, either. She shook her head. "No, I'll do it." Briefly, she closed her eyes and sucked in a deep breath, steeling herself for what she feared she'd find.

She pulled open the flaps and looked inside. Two yellow-naped Amazon parrots lay side by side in the bottom of the box, utterly still. Cat blinked back tears as she reached inside to pick up one of the brilliantly colored birds. Cradling it in her hands, she stroked a finger over the yellow band running across the back of its neck. These birds belonged in the wilds of Mexico or Costa Rica, not smuggled into America to become some rich person's plaything.

They were dead. Both of them. Almost undoubtedly caused by the inhumane methods used to smuggle them across the Texas border. She bit her lip and laid the bird gently inside the box. She didn't speak, but knew her silence spoke for her. Mark's arm came around her, reassuringly strong. Uncaring of the tears now pouring down her cheeks, she took the comfort he offered, turned her face into the curve of his shoulder, and let the pain wash over her.

She hated to think of the misery the birds had endured, hated that she hadn't been home when Gabe had first arrived. Most of all, she hated she hadn't been able to help.

"Damn it!" Gabe said, and slammed his fist down on the table. "What a waste!"

Cat pulled away from Mark, wiped her cheeks and tried to pull herself together. "We have to report this to the FWS."

Gabe turned and glared at her. "The FWS? Why bring them into it? These birds are dead. There's nothing they can do now."

"Odds are they're illegal, Gabe. Somebody smuggled them in. Why else would they have been left on your doorstep like that, rather than taken to a vet? Don't you think so, Mark?"

His sharp gaze rested on Gabe. He nodded. "Seems logical. I'd take them down there first thing in the morning."

Gabe stared at both of them in exasperation. "What the hell do you know about it, Kincaid? I thought you were a game warden? How many smuggled birds have you seen in the wilds of Grapevine Lake?"

"I know what everyone who works for the FWS knows. Suspected contraband has to be reported."

"If it's so damn important to you, then you and Cat take them down there. I have a fishing trip set up for tomorrow morning. If you think I'm missing a paying job to take a couple of dead birds to the FWS, think again."

"Gabe—" Cat began.

"We'll take them," Mark said. "But FWS officials will still want to talk to you."

If possible, Gabe's expression grew even more

frustrated. He jammed his fingers through his hair, muttering a curse. "Fine, I'll stop by after my trip. I can probably be there late tomorrow afternoon. But this is a pain in the butt I don't need."

Gabe went home a short time later, leaving the birds for Cat to take care of. Unable to bear looking at the animals any longer, Cat closed the box and turned away from it.

"Is he always that much of a jerk?" Mark asked. "It was obvious to anyone who's known you for more than ten minutes that you'd be upset about those dead birds. Yet he dumped them on you like it was nothing."

Compelled to defend Gabe, out of family loyalty if for no other reason, she said, "I'm sure he didn't mean to be…insensitive. He's having a rough time lately. His business hasn't been—" She hesitated, not wanting to say too much about a client's finances. "The fishing business hasn't been doing so well. He probably just didn't think."

Mark looked skeptical. He grasped her upper arms gently. "He was way out of line. You couldn't have done anything for those birds, even if you had been here. They were too far gone or they wouldn't have died so quickly."

"I know. I told you, he didn't mean to hurt me."

"Not being able to help those birds is what's hurting you," Mark said shrewdly. "Are you going to be okay?"

"I'm fine."

"Right." His hands slid to her shoulders and squeezed gently. "I mean it, Cat. You can't blame yourself for any of this."

"I won't." He looked doubtful and she smiled. "I promise. I know I can't save them all. I hate it, but I do understand it."

"What time do you want to go to the FWS in the morning?"

"You don't need to go with me. I appreciate it, but—"

"Cat," he interrupted. "I'm going with you. I'll pick you up at eight, all right?"

Too tired to fight about it, especially since she wanted his support, she nodded.

"Not the best way to end the evening, is it?" he asked, cradling her cheek in his palm.

"No. I'm sorry, Mark."

"There'll be other nights."

"Will there?" she couldn't help asking.

He smiled, slow and sure. "Definitely." He kissed her then, a long, drugging kiss that accelerated her heart rate and sent a zing of desire coursing through her. He drew back, rubbed a thumb over her still-tingling lips. "Do me a favor and don't beat yourself up about those birds."

MARK GRABBED his cell phone and called his partner as soon as he stepped through the door. "Had a little incident here tonight. My neighbor's brother brought her a couple of yellow-naped Amazons.''

Simpson gave a low whistle. ''Interesting. Did he say how he came by them?''

''Story was, somebody left them on his doorstep. He claimed they were alive when he brought them over, but by the time we got here, they were gone.''

''High-dollar birds,'' Simpson commented. ''Smuggled, I assume.''

''Seems likely. And very dead.'' He remembered again how upset Cat had been. He wanted to slug Gabe Randolph for dumping them on her the way he had.

''Any clues where they came from?'' Simpson asked. ''Do you think your neighbor had something to do with it?''

''No and no.'' He reached into the refrigerator and liberated a beer from the six-pack. Twisting the cap off, he said, ''Cat's in the clear. No way is she the link. Trust me on that. But the brother's another matter. I don't suppose you've completed that background check I asked you to run on him?''

''Sorry. Not much progress there, but we'll keep trying.''

''I've got someone else for you to run, too. Kyle Peters. He's a vet from Aransas Pass. An avian vet, which gives him ties to the birding community. Story is, he inherited money, and lots of it.''

''Hey, you inherited a house.''

"Yeah, but you haven't seen this piece of junk." He looked around at the faded wallpaper and broken-down couch, nearly all the furniture left in the living room. "It's no blessing, believe me. Just check out Peters, okay?"

"Will do. Hey, Mark, I have to ask, why are you so sure the girl isn't involved?"

He thought about Cat's reaction to the birds earlier that night. "Aside from the fact that she doesn't have much money, is nuts about rehabbing birds and fell apart when she saw the parrots were goners? No reason. Just a hunch."

"Maybe she's a good actress."

"No," Mark said positively. "She's a rotten actress. With Cat, what you see is what you get."

Simpson was silent a moment. "You've fallen for her, haven't you?"

Mark laughed. He liked Cat. Wanted to take her to bed. But he hadn't fallen for her. "Nope. So if you're worried I'm going to let her interfere with the job, think again."

"Women are nothing but trouble at times like this," Simpson cautioned. "You know it, I know it. Be careful, buddy."

"Don't worry about me. Let me know as soon as you find out anything about Randolph or Peters. And if you hear anything else from your end, either."

Mark hung up, took another sip of beer and frowned. He hadn't fallen for Cat...yet. But he had a feeling it would be easy to do.

CHAPTER EIGHT

CAT'S VISIT to the FWS office lasted just long enough to infuriate her. As promised, Mark had taken her. He'd remained silent most of the time, letting Cat tell the story and only adding a comment when directly appealed to.

She let herself into her kitchen and said to Mark, "Thanks for going with me. I'll see you later."

He foiled her attempt to shut the door in his face by placing a palm against it. "You know, I'm pretty good at reading people. I get the feeling you're mad at me."

Rather than continue to struggle to shut the door, a fight she obviously wouldn't win, she let him follow her inside. "I'm not mad at you. What gives you that idea?"

Leaning back against the counter, he crossed his arms. Distracted for a moment, she noticed that his stance threw his chest and arm muscles into relief. The man had one seriously beautiful set of pecs and arms. Must be the construction work that did it. But she didn't intend to let his body, however wonderful it was, distract her from her irritation with him.

His lips twitched. "You didn't say a word on the way home. I've never known you to be that quiet."

She shrugged. "You haven't known me all that long, have you? Maybe I just didn't feel like talking."

He raised an eyebrow and gave her a disbelieving look. "Come on, Cat. Come clean. Why are you mad?"

One hand on her hip, she drummed her fingers on the counter and shot him a dark glance. "You heard Hargrove. He acted like Gabe was trying to cover up something." Bill Hargrove, the FWS officer who'd questioned them, had very plainly disbelieved Gabe's story. Cat had known the man for years, and until today, had always thought him a pleasant and fair man. "All those questions about how Gabe came by the birds." She snorted in disgust. "Hargrove thinks my brother is smuggling exotic birds."

"He didn't say that," Mark corrected her. "He simply asked you some routine questions. The same questions he'll ask Gabe when he sees him."

"It was the *way* he asked them," she muttered, flashing him another annoyed glance. "And you just sat there like a lump, not saying anything. I had to drag every word out of you, and you didn't sound any too sure of Gabe yourself."

He frowned. "You have to admit, Gabe having those birds is a little suspicious. I don't know him. How do I know what he would or wouldn't do?"

"Bill Hargrove knows him. And he certainly knows me. Why would he think I'd turn a blind eye to someone—brother or not—who was doing something illegal? Especially something as horrible as smuggling wildlife?"

"He didn't say that, either. He said he didn't think you'd believe anything bad about your brother, no matter how suspicious the circumstances."

"What are you, a tape recorder?" she snapped. "I can tell you right now, Gabe wouldn't smuggle birds," she said hotly, stung by Mark's patient, logical tone. "If he were doing that, do you think he'd stay here in Aransas City, for Pete's sake, eking out a living by running a charter fishing service?"

Mark didn't answer.

"Well, he wouldn't," she said, warming to her theme. "He'd be off in the Caribbean or somewhere like it, drinking tropical fruit drinks and eating mangoes with beautiful women waiting on him hand and foot."

Mark grinned at that. "Nice picture."

"The point is, my brother isn't a bird smuggler. It's ridiculous to even think it."

"So you're mad at me because I didn't leap to your brother's defense, the way you have."

Put that way, it sounded silly. She gave him another dirty look. "It just seems to me you're jumping to conclusions about Gabe. You and Hargrove both. And your opinion matters to Hargrove. Even though you aren't an agent who pursues smugglers, you're with the FWS, so naturally he'd listen to what you say." Still angry, she tapped her fingers on the drain board again. "Why doesn't anyone suspect me? I'm just as likely to have done it as Gabe."

"No," Mark said emphatically. "Why would you have dumped them on your brother? That doesn't make sense. Besides, I saw your reaction last night. You're no smuggler."

"Neither is Gabe." At least Mark believed in her. He was right, he didn't even know Gabe. Maybe it was unreasonable to expect him to take Gabe on faith, simply because she did.

He sighed and walked over to her. "Cat, I don't want to fight with you. If your brother didn't do anything wrong, then nothing will come of this. Hargrove just wants to question him. Relax, it's not as if Gabe's being carted off to jail."

"Relax? I can't relax."

"Sure you can. Start by thinking about something besides your brother and the FWS."

"Such as?"

"Try you and me."

"You and me?" The atmosphere in the room

changed, becoming tense, anticipatory. She stared at Mark, taut and tan in a classic short-sleeved white T-shirt and faded jeans. His dark hair fell over his forehead and his eyes blazed blue and wicked as sin.

''You want me to think about you and me?'' she repeated, this time her voice a little huskier. ''Right now?''

''Yeah. You and me—'' he traced her cheek with gentle fingers ''—and what didn't happen between us last night.'' Then he smiled, a slow smile that promised any number of things. His arm slid around her and he eased her close. ''I know a lot of ways to relax a woman.''

Her eyes widened. It might have been a long time for her, but she knew what an aroused male felt like, and Mark was definitely in that category. Suddenly her run-in with the FWS didn't seem quite so...urgent. And sure as heck not as intriguing as the man holding her in his arms.

''Are you—'' Her breath caught as his lips skimmed lightly down her hairline. ''Are you suggesting—'' Now he was nibbling at her neck. He pressed a sizzling kiss to her galloping pulse. Her legs began to feel wobbly.

''I'm not suggesting,'' he murmured, his breath warm against her skin. He smiled and then his lips covered hers in a deep, hot kiss, his tongue sweeping her mouth with leisurely, masterful strokes. "I'm seducing."

"You're doing a good job of it," she managed to say before she kissed him back, searching, nibbling, finding his taste exotic, exciting. His hands slid up her rib cage to rest just beneath her breasts. She strained, aching for him to caress her, seduce her.

His hands didn't move, but that skillful mouth did, sliding over hers with clear intent, igniting explosions of sensation in her blood. She wanted to touch him. So she did, putting her hands on his chest and spreading her fingers, wondering what all that smooth, bare skin was going to feel like.

"We're going too fast," she said, but didn't pull away.

"Are we?" His gaze locked with hers. His hands had yet to move, but they burned through the fabric of her shirt.

She nodded, wondering if she would come to her senses. "I can't seem to care." *Apparently not.*

He slid his hands under her T-shirt and nudged it upward, inch by tortuous inch, until he drew it over her head. Cat gave momentary, desperate thanks that she'd chosen today to wear her new lingerie. Soft peach and barely there.

Stroking a finger over the lacy edges of her bra, he smiled. "Pretty." He popped the front catch and slowly peeled the cups back to reveal taut nipples just begging for attention. His eyes darkened and he closed his hands over her bare breasts. "Beautiful," he murmured.

"Mark, maybe before this goes any farther—" She moaned and her head fell back as his warm, wet mouth covered her nipple. His tongue circled it, flicked it, then he sucked it deeper into his mouth. Her head swam, her breasts ached, pleading for more, and he gave it to her, applying the same delicious treatment to her other breast. She couldn't think, could barely breathe. But every nerve in her body stood at attention.

"The bedroom," she choked out on a gasp. "I need to—" Words fled as his rough palms replaced his mouth at her breasts, rubbing, gently tugging, and all the while, his gaze stayed locked on hers.

"We'll never make it," he said, and released her long enough to jerk his shirt over his head. "Besides—" he flung her bra out of the way, gathered her close again, bare chest to bare breasts "—I've had this fantasy about your kitchen table. Ever since that night we iced the cake."

Fantasy? She was living one right now. "Tell me," she demanded.

"It involves you and me. Together. Naked." Cupping his hands on her rear, he pressed her against him. Whispered an erotic suggestion in her ear. "And seeing just exactly how hot I can make you."

Boiling, she thought. "Take me, I'm yours," she said, surprising a laugh out of him.

The newspaper littering the table hit the floor. Mark boosted her up onto the table and stepped between her legs. His thighs were hard, muscled, the soft denim of his jeans warm against her skin. He kissed her, his tongue teasing, hands taunting her breasts. Gulping in air, she wrapped her legs around his waist and pulled him closer.

"I'm not going to last long if you keep doing that," he said.

She rolled her hips and rubbed against him, relishing the hard ridge of his arousal. "That's all right, because I won't, either."

He unbuttoned and unzipped her shorts, slipped them down her legs and dropped them to the floor. His eyes glowed brighter as he gazed at the tiny scrap of pale fabric covering her. His smile broadened. "My kind of woman," he murmured huskily, pulling the panties off with a quick move.

He kept his eyes on her as he stepped back and rid himself of his own jeans and briefs, first taking a moment to pull a condom from his pocket. The sight of all that gleaming, naked, masculine flesh made it hard to speak, impossible to concentrate. But she forced herself to ask.

"Do you—" She lost her train of thought as she watched him cover himself.

He moved closer, putting his hands on her knees. "What's wrong? Change your mind?"

She shook her head, but forced out the question. "Do you always keep one of those in your pocket?"

"No." He smiled, slow and wicked. "Just since you kissed me."

"Good answer," she said, and opened her arms to him. "Kiss me again."

His tongue made leisurely thrusts that deepened the longer he kissed her. He didn't hurry, but caressed her until she said his name breathlessly and lifted her hips. And wanted.

He traced her center with a finger, eased it inside her, withdrew and did it again. And again. They both groaned, panted. Her muscles tightened around him and she thought she'd die if she couldn't have him soon. "Now," she gasped.

He opened her, slid inside her. Then he braced his hands on either side and began a gentle rhythm that grew faster and harder. Her back arched, her hips thrust upward. She wrapped her arms and legs around him and rode with him until her mind turned blank and her body became a mass of sensations, all centered on that driving, primitive beat.

Her orgasm hit hard and fast. Dimly, she heard his guttural cry as he lost himself, too, plunging into her with a final deep thrust before he stilled.

"Oh, my," she said, long moments later. "Who screamed? You?"

"I think it was you." His lips moved against her neck. He drew back to look at her, his mouth lifting at the corners in a satisfied smile. "I like a screamer."

Her eyelids felt heavy, her mouth tingled from his kisses. Her heart rate had yet to steady. "Good, but I still think it was you."

He laughed and cuddled her closer. "You have crumbs in your hair. It's kind of sexy."

"Breakfast. I didn't clean off the table before I left. You have crumbs in your hair, too." She reached up and touched it, enjoying the lovely silky strands as she sifted her fingers through it. "You're right. It's kind of sexy."

"I should go home and paint. But this beats painting all to hell."

She allowed herself a small pout. "I suppose you have to go to your house and get to work."

"I should." He pushed against her and her eyes widened as she felt him hardening inside her again. "Or we could both blow off work and make our way to your bedroom."

Her lips curved upward. "Second choice. Definitely."

SOME TIME LATER, they were on Cat's bed, replete for the moment. Mark stroked her bare hip, while she lay on his chest with her hand tracing circles over his heart. She made a heart shape and then kissed it. Instead of freaking him out, the gesture made him smile.

The sex had been great. Not just great, spectacular. That didn't surprise him so much as the fact that he didn't have the urge to leave immediately afterward, the way he did with most women. With Cat, he wanted to stay with her, to talk with her, even if they weren't having sex.

Oh, man, maybe he *was* falling for her. Just like Simpson had said. He could be in deep trouble, here. Still, just because he might be falling for Cat didn't mean there had to be anything serious between them. She was passionately dedicated to her career. His eyes narrowed as he thought about that. A career that more than likely would take all her time and attention. Mark couldn't consider what they had to be anything more than an interlude. But one that was great while it lasted.

Cat stretched and made a sound like a purr. "I need to check on Buddy. Usually when he's out of his cage, he's with me. I'm afraid to see what he's done to the living room."

"I thought you said he liked TV."

"He does, but he likes humans better. Parrots need a lot of one-on-one with their owners. You might have noticed, he's a teensy bit spoiled.'' She fell silent a moment, then said, ''What are you doing?''

Mark toyed with her breast and smiled. Her breasts were beautiful. Lush and full, and judging from her reactions to his earlier lovemaking, incredibly sensitive. ''You're a smart woman. What do you think?''

''I think you're trying to distract me again, and you couldn't possibly—''

He rolled her over onto her back and slid between her legs. ''I couldn't?''

A breathless sound, between a laugh and a moan, emerged from her throat. ''Okay, maybe you can, but—''

He kissed her, and she kissed him back, and soon, neither one talked.

CHAPTER NINE

THE FIRST THING Mark saw when he finally forced himself to leave Cat the following morning was Jay's packed duffel bag sitting beside the back door. His good mood downshifted. He'd known his brother would leave, of course, but he'd enjoyed having him around.

Jay sat at the wobbly table, drinking coffee and reading the local paper. He glanced up when Mark came in, raised an eyebrow and grinned. "Get lucky yesterday?"

"Yeah, but if you're expecting details, forget it."

"I'm your brother, remember? You can tell me."

"Nope." Mark poured a cup of coffee. Like most brothers, Mark and Jay had talked about women they'd dated in the past, but Mark didn't want to share what had happened between him and Cat. He didn't analyze his reluctance, but he recognized it.

"Sounds serious," Jay said.

Mark frowned at the comment. "Just because I don't want to talk about her doesn't mean it's serious." He changed the subject before Jay could probe further. "Did anybody call? I didn't have my cell with me."

Jay nodded, taking a sip of coffee. "Simpson. He said to call him back ASAP. Something about some information you've been waiting for."

"Why didn't you tell me that when I came in?" Mark asked, picking up the phone and punching in numbers.

"Forgot," he said, returning to his paper.

"What have you got for me?" Mark asked when Simpson answered.

"Took your sweet time, didn't you?" his partner asked. "We finally ran down something in that background check on Gabe Randolph. Seems our friend had—possibly still has—a gambling problem."

Damn, not the news he wanted to hear. "Go on. What else did you find out?"

"He was doing all right, businesswise, until he got into gambling about three years ago. Apparently used up his savings and then the fishing industry took a nosedive. Randolph ended up having to mortgage his boat. All this fits with the numbers you saw. The man's in financial trouble. How deep, we don't know yet."

Mark glanced at Jay, who appeared absorbed in his newspaper, but Mark knew better. Jay had ears like a hawk. "You said he might still have the problem. Have you looked into that?"

"Not yet. We'll start today, checking out the boats in Louisiana and the racetrack. Since he's a fisherman, could be he's betting on tournaments. It's not legal, but people do it all the time. If nothing turns up, we can take it to Vegas."

"Good work," Mark said, though the information Simpson had given him was the last thing he'd wanted to hear. "Any news on the other one?"

"Peters? Not much. So far, no sign of a wealthy relative, but that doesn't mean much."

"Let's find out where he was before he moved here. Might be some tie-in there." Especially if the place the vet had moved away from had been connected to the smuggling ring. Someplace like Dallas, say. It would sure be nice to have someone besides Gabe Randolph to suspect.

"I'll be in touch," Simpson promised.

The news Simpson had just delivered, on top of what they already knew, pushed Gabe Randolph from a possible to a likely suspect. The man's gambling and financial problems didn't have to be connected to any criminal activity, but they sure as hell could be. Mark hadn't liked Randolph's actions the night before, but some of that could be because he hadn't liked the way Gabe had treated Cat. *What a waste,* Randolph had said. Had he meant a waste of life…or of money?

"Problems?" Jay asked.

"Yeah." The scenario bothered him. He took a seat at the table, debating how much to tell his brother. Jay knew some of the situation already, and was about as safe a sounding board as Mark had—in Aransas City, at any rate. "Remember I told you about those birds Gabe Randolph discovered?"

Nodding, Jay laid down the newspaper. "What happened with that?"

"The local FWS thinks he might be smuggling. Cat's hot about it."

"They told her they suspected her brother?"

"It was obvious from the tone of Hargrove's questions. And it will be even clearer after they question Randolph himself."

"Do *you* think Randolph's smuggling? Do you think he's the link you're after?"

"I think someone wants to plant that idea with the FWS. It's a little too convenient, though." Mark relayed what Simpson had told him. Ticking items off on his fingers, he said, "So we know Randolph needs money, he has connections in the birding community, through his sister, he has a boat capable of carrying large cargoes of birds and he has legitimate business reasons to travel to and from other coastal cities in that boat. Then he finds dying illegal exotics on his doorstep and what does he do?"

"Gives them to his sister," Jay said, and took a sip of coffee. "Who immediately talks to the FWS."

"Right." Mark clasped his hands together and frowned. "What's wrong with that scenario?"

"Nearly everything. He'd have to be pretty stupid to take the birds to Cat and expect her not to tell the FWS. I mean, I hardly know her and I know she's a straight arrow. And her saving the birds doesn't accomplish anything, either. She'd have called the FWS in that case, too. He had nothing to gain, and a lot to lose by taking those birds to Cat."

"So if he's guilty, why would he do it? He wouldn't," Mark said, answering his own question. "And that's what bothers me. But I don't really have any leads on anyone else."

"You're having Simpson check out someone besides Gabe Randolph."

Mark nodded. "The vet. But so far, we have nothing on him. Still—" He thought back to the night before last, and his conversation with Peters at the Scarlet Parrot. "I find it interesting that those birds showed up on Randolph's doorstep the same night Kyle Peters found out I was with the FWS."

"Kind of coincidental," Jay agreed. "But he thinks you're a game warden, doesn't he?"

Mark shrugged. "Maybe. Or maybe he heard Gilbert's ramblings and is suspicious of me because of them. Added to that, the ringleaders must realize we're getting close. They may not know we've traced them to Aransas City, but they know we popped their colleague in Dallas. They can't be sure how much information the man spilled. Their man here could be getting nervous. Best way to draw attention away from himself is to put somebody else in the hot seat.''

"Like Gabe Randolph," Jay said.

"Yeah." He sighed heavily. His lover's brother. Great, just great.

"What are you going to do about Cat?" Jay asked, mirroring his thoughts.

"You mean now that her brother's my prime suspect, even though I think he's probably being framed?"

Jay smiled ruefully. "Yeah. What now?"

"The short answer is, I break it off with her." Now, before they became any more involved.

"Is that what you want?"

"No, but it's the right thing to do. Whatever happens with her brother, she's bound to think I used her."

Mark went to pour himself another cup of coffee. "Enough about my problems. I thought you didn't have to be back at school for a while yet." He gestured at Jay's bag. "Why are you taking off?"

Jay leaned back in his chair, his gaze meeting Mark's, an odd expression in his eyes. "I'm going to Dallas for a few days before I head back to California."

"Why Dallas? Visiting Brian? Or friends?"

"Not exactly."

Dallas. Where their mother lived with her new husband. "I'd like to think you're going there to see a woman, but that's not what you're doing, is it?"

He shook his head. "Not the kind of woman you're thinking of. Mom asked Brian and me to come stay with her and her husband for a few days."

Mark closed his eyes, surprised at the stab of pain his brother's words caused. It was normal for his brothers to be curious about their mother. But she could still hurt them. Mark wondered if either of his brothers remembered how devastated they'd been when she left. Every night the boys had cried because she was gone, and the only person they'd had to depend on was Mark.

He shook off the past, tried to get rid of the feeling of betrayal along with it, but that was harder to do. "Your choice," he said. "Be careful. I don't trust her, but then, you know that."

Jay picked up his mug and sipped, contemplating his brother over the rim. After a long pause, he said, "You used to tell Brian and me that people deserve a second chance. Was that just bullshit or did you mean it?"

Mark winced. That sounded like the kind of stupid-ass comment he might have made to the boys at one time or another. But he hadn't been talking about their mother when he'd said it.

He turned his back on Jay, to stare unseeing out the window. "She's had plenty of chances. What makes you think this time is different?" He remembered, even if Jay didn't, how many times their mother had promised to see the boys, then never showed. Finally she'd quit calling altogether. And who'd been there to deal with the heartache? The guilt that somehow they'd been at fault. Him, that's who.

"That all happened a long time ago, though," Jay said. "There's a lot you don't know about her. She kept quiet because she thought it was better that way."

Better for her, maybe. He turned around, his hands behind him, gripping the edge of the counter. "Why the sudden change of heart? Why contact you two now, after all these years?" She hadn't even atempted to see Mark. He didn't know whether to be grateful or hurt.

"Her husband talked her into it. I think she was afraid. Hell, I know she was. She was scared to death of what you'd told us about her, scared we all hated her."

Mark didn't hate her, but it was impossible not to resent a woman who had walked away from her family without a backward glance. Yet he'd tried not to let his feelings about their mother color the boys' memories. Tried not to speak badly of her, figuring they already hurt enough without adding that burden. Obviously, he'd succeeded. Brian and Jay didn't seem to see the problems Mark did in letting her back into their lives.

Jay got up and walked over to him. "She wants to see you, Mark. To try to explain, maybe start over. Will you give her a chance?"

"I'm on a case here, Jay. There's no way I can leave." Even if he wanted, which he didn't.

"When it's over?"

He shrugged and met his brother's gaze. "I don't think any good will come of it. I'm not like you, Jay. I can't just blow off her leaving as if it never mattered."

"She doesn't expect you to."

"I'll think about it," Mark said, as much to close the subject as any other reason. "But I'm not making any guarantees."

Jay nodded. "It's a start. I'd better take off now. My flight leaves Corpus in a couple of hours."

"You're not driving?"

"Are you kidding? Eight hours on a motorcycle and my butt would be numb for days. Besides, it's a rental."

Mark laughed and they hugged and pounded on each other's backs. "Be careful. And tell Brian to call me sometime and let me know he's alive."

Emotions mixed, he watched Jay get on his motorcycle and leave. Then he saw Cat crossing the yard. Great, another conversation he didn't want to have. He sucked in a deep breath. Better to get it over with, though. Nothing to be gained from putting off painful reality.

"Bad news?" Cat asked as she reached him.

"Why do you ask that?"

"Well, you've got a grim look on your face and Jay's driving off with his bag behind him. I take it he's leaving? Did you receive bad news?"

"Not...exactly. Come on in, we need to talk." He stood aside, holding open the door.

She cast him a puzzled look, and walked past him. "I'm not sure I like the sound of that. I came over to invite you to dinner. I'm making bouillabaisse."

Bouillabaisse. He bet she made a dynamite one. Oh, man, sometimes life really did suck. "Thanks, but I'd better not."

"Mark, what's wrong? You look so serious."

He held out a chair for her to sit. "I think we need to cool it."

Confused, she blinked at him. "Cool what?"

"You and me. This thing between us. I think we should take it easy."

Her confusion cleared. "You're dumping me?"

"I'm not dumping you. I just think we should...back off. For a while." *Way to go, Mark,* he told himself.

"You are dumping me. You didn't feel this way yesterday. Or did you?"

He jammed a hand through his hair and wished he were better with words. "Yesterday was great. You're great. But I'm not looking for anything serious. I think it's better to cool it now, before we regret getting too involved. I don't even know how long I'll be in town."

Big brown eyes flashed with anger. "If you'll recall, we decided that neither of us is looking for serious. That excuse won't fly." She got up, put her hands on her hips and glared at him. "I really didn't have you pegged as a man who'd dump a woman once he'd scored. I guess I'm more naive than I thought."

"Cat, it's not like that." He reached for her, but she held up a hand to ward him off.

"I'd prefer you didn't touch me right now. Or ever again, for that matter." Her gaze narrowed and she looked at him as if he were something nasty stuck to the bottom of her shoe. "I can't believe I fell for your routine." She left, slamming the door behind her.

Smooth move, Kincaid. Now she hates your guts.

IT RAINED the next day, which gave Mark a break from roofing. On his first day through the house, when assessing what needed to be done, he'd found that someone had carpeted over the hardwood in the dining room and living room. He decided he might as well get started ripping out the carpet and seeing how bad the floor underneath was. With any luck, he could refinish it and make it into a real selling point.

He peeled back a strip of carpet and winced when he found paint stains. "Criminal," he muttered. He ripped up more, brightening as he realized that the paint only covered a small area. Maybe there was hope after all.

Midmorning, his phone rang. "Kincaid," he said, grabbing the cordless beside him.

"Mr. Kincaid, this is Roberta Flemming. I know you're going to be pleased. I had an offer on your house this morning."

He sat back on his heels and let go of the piece of carpet he was holding up. "No one's been through it. They're offering sight unseen?"

"The buyer says he's seen it in the past. He's buying it for a company that plans to turn it into a bed-and-breakfast."

He wiped his face with his shirtsleeve. "Without seeing it again?"

"Apparently. It's for the asking price, too. They must want it pretty badly."

She sounded baffled and he didn't blame her. To go from no traffic at all to an offer for the asking price seemed weird to him. He realized he was screwed if it was a bona fide offer. Without the house as an excuse, he'd have no legitimate reason to stay in town.

"Do they know the shape it's in? Don't they want me to do some repairs first?"

"They know, and they don't care. They say it's perfect for their plans."

Sure, a peaceful bed-and-breakfast next to an aviary with birds squawking at dawn daily. If this offer was for real, he was Tom Cruise. He went to the kitchen to find paper and pen. "Who's the company? And the contact?"

The Realtor told him and he scribbled the information down. Something to check. "I'll get back to you. I've been considering taking the house off the market."

There was a stunned silence before she finally spoke. "You're going to stay in it? Live there?"

"Possibly. I'll get back to you later."

He hung up and called his partner. "I just got an offer on the house," he said without preamble. "Asking price, no haggling. And not a soul's been through it. Think I'm making someone nervous?"

"Interesting," Simpson said. "Want us to check it out?"

"Yeah." He relayed the information the Realtor had just given him. "Any more about Randolph?"

"He was a regular customer on the gambling boats

in Shreveport, Louisiana. But he's either quit going to his old haunts or he's doing it under another identity."

"You might send someone down there with a picture. But I've had some thoughts about Gabe Randolph." He shared his suspicions that Gabe Randolph was being framed.

"I agree, it sounds a little convenient. Still no word on Peters, though. We can't seem to find where he came from. Maybe you can ask around. Is he the only other suspect you have?"

"Yeah, if you can call him that." His distrust of Peters was more hunch than anything else, but Mark had learned to trust his gut reaction.

"We intercepted another message late last night," his partner put in. "It sounds like something's going down soon. No firm date yet, though."

"That's good. It fits with the offer, then." He shifted the phone to his other ear and tossed the note with the buyer's information on the counter. "Okay, I'll tell the Realtor I've decided to take the house off the market."

"Sorry, Mark. I know you were anxious to get rid of it. Once this is over—"

"After we bust the ring I'll put it back on the market. It will have a better chance of selling once I finish some of the renovations, anyway." *Wishful thinking,* he told himself, and hung up.

CHAPTER TEN

THREE DAYS LATER, Cat had gone from angry, to hurt, to angry all over again.

"Whatcha doin'?"

She stopped digging through her files and turned to look at Buddy, perched on her computer monitor.

"Working," she told him. "What are you doing?"

"Brrrr—ing," he chirped, imitating the telephone. "Hello, how ya doin'? Brrrr-ing." He spread his wings and preened, clearly proud of himself. The bird's voice bore an uncanny resemblance to the phone, and Cat often picked it up when it hadn't rung.

"No phone calls today." Not from her clients and most especially, not from Mark. The jerk. She hadn't seen or heard from him since the day after they'd made wild love in her kitchen, in her bedroom and on several other available surfaces. *Don't think about it,* she told herself.

They hadn't exchanged a word since the day he'd told her he wanted to "cool it." And pretended that it was for her own good, yet. She still couldn't believe she'd fallen for him, hook, line and sinker. What kind of fool did that make her, that she hadn't seen what kind of man he really was?

"Well, what did I expect?" she asked aloud. "Undying love? Ha!"

"Fat chance," Buddy said.

His comment forced a grin from her. "You got that right. Still, I didn't expect to get dumped immediately, either."

"Life's a bitch," the bird observed, nodding sagely.

"Ain't it the truth." She couldn't believe Mark's behavior, not after what they'd shared. Even if their lovemaking hadn't meant as much to him as it had to her, she knew he'd thought the sex was spectacular. What kind of man walked away from fantastic sex after one shot at it?

"Pretty girl." Buddy tilted his head, gray feathers ruffling, his bright yellow eyes expressing sympathy. "Poor baby."

A lot of people would think her crazy, but sometimes she thought Buddy read her emotions better than most of the people she knew. Even her brothers and sister. Infinitely better than her mother ever could.

"Men are pigs, Buddy. Be glad you're a bird. Come on, I need a glass of tea." Wary of leaving him alone in the office, she shooed him into the living room and shut the door behind her. "I'll be right back," she told him.

She entered the kitchen just in time to see Bluebell making off with Roxy's favorite barrette. "Damn it, Bluebell, you come back here!" She could imagine Roxy's face crumpling at the news that her barrette—the butterfly one she'd paid her own money for—was gone for good. Roxy would forgive her, but Cat couldn't forgive herself. Pure carelessness on her part, for not making sure the item was safe.

She rushed out the door and saw the bird disappear into the branches of the live oak in her front yard. No telling what treasures he'd feathered that nest with.

Halting underneath the tree, she stared upward in despair. She couldn't even reach the lowest branch without a ladder. Which she didn't have. Turning her head, she gazed at her neighbor's house. She heard hammer sounds, and knew he was on the roof again. Luckily for her, he'd begun work today on the back side, but the ladder stood out front, just waiting to be borrowed. If he weren't such a jerk, she'd ask him.

But he was. So she didn't.

A few minutes later, she appropriated the ladder, leaving Mark pounding away. For a wistful moment she thought about leaving him stranded, but decided she couldn't be that childish. Besides, he'd probably just shimmy down the drainpipe and come get it, and undoubtedly think she'd used it as a ploy to get to him. No, she would use the ladder and return it without him ever missing it.

Unhappy about her raid, Bluebell made his displeasure known by dive-bombing her, stopping just short of pecking her. Lucky for her, he still thought of her as his mother. But his outraged shrieks gave her a headache and she suspected if she stayed too long he'd forget his qualms and resort to more physical means of driving her away.

Fifteen minutes later, flushed with victory, she backed down the ladder. Several long-missed items were stuffed in her pockets, including the coveted barrette. Why hadn't she thought of this before? A couple of rungs before she touched ground, strong hands snatched her around the waist. Startled, she shrieked and lost her grip.

"What the hell did you think you were doing?" Mark yelled after he set her down.

She winced at both the volume and the tone, but he wasn't through.

"Do you have a death wish or something?" Eyes blazing, he gripped her arms and shook her. "Are you crazy?"

"No, I—"

His mouth came down on hers, rough, hot, and simmering with anger.

A traitorous warmth stole over her. Her mouth

opened, and she answered him back with tongue and lips. Then she remembered he'd dumped her flat, the day after they'd made love. Her first impulse, to shove him away, she quelled. Instead, she stopped responding, but it wasn't easy. To help, she repeated tax codes in her mind until he let her go.

"Feel better now?" she asked. "I have to tell you, your style could use some work. Some women might like the Neanderthal approach. I'm not one of them."

He didn't look repentant. If anything, he still looked blazingly angry. "Any fool could see that ladder is unstable. You could have broken your neck."

She laughed, pleased to see it made him even angrier. "But I didn't. Don't you think you're overreacting?"

His eyes narrowed. "Why didn't you ask me for help?"

"I didn't need help. Other than your ladder, that is." She looked him up and down indulgently, as if he were one of her nieces. Only he didn't look like her nieces.

Stubble shaded his jaw. His navy T-shirt stretched tight across that beautifully muscled chest. A chest she remembered every inch of, naked and ranged above her. She raised her chin and met his furious gaze with a bland one of her own. "Was that all you wanted? I'm a little busy," she couldn't resist adding.

"We need to talk. About what I said the other day."

"Oh, that." She shrugged. "I really don't think a postmortem is necessary, do you?"

His expression grew more thunderous, his jaw becoming granite. "Let's take this inside. Unless you want all your neighbors to get an earful."

With a sigh of exasperation, she glanced at her watch. "All right. But I can't stay long. Buddy's out in the living room and I have a casserole in the oven."

She strolled toward his house as if she didn't have a care, pleased that at the least, she'd taken him by surprise. Underneath her calm exterior anger and hurt simmered. She didn't think all hope was lost, though. If Mark was so all-fired anxious to be rid of her, why had he cared so much whether she was hurt? And why had he kissed her as if he couldn't get enough?

MARK OPENED his kitchen door and Cat breezed past him. "What were you doing in that tree?" he asked.

"Looking for something. And I found it."

"Show me."

"It's really none of your business, but I was looking for this." She pulled something from her pocket and showed it to him. "Thank goodness Bluebell hadn't buried it under all his other treasures yet."

He stared at the object in her palm with disbelief.

"You risked your neck for a hair doodad?" He wanted to shake her for doing something so crazy.

Her hands immediately went to his scattering of mail and stacked it in a tidy pile on the countertop. "It's my niece's favorite barrette, and we agreed you overreacted." She picked up the note about the buyer he'd tossed down earlier that week and set it on top of the stack. Satisfied, she folded her arms across her chest, leaned back against the counter and smiled at him. "Okay, talk. I'm listening."

He took a turn around the room, nearly tripping on the roll of green vinyl he'd pulled up from the floor. He halted in front of her before uncharacteristically fumbling for words. "I know you're still mad at me, and I can't blame you. But I— The other day was…" *Fantastic,* he thought, though he couldn't say it. His tongue tied itself into knots. He felt stupid and clumsy, something he hadn't been with women even as a teenager.

This discussion wasn't going as planned. For one thing, she should be mad. Instead, she looked almost…bored. Her attention seemed more focused on the peeling wallpaper and bare concrete floor than on him.

She flicked him a resigned glance. "You don't have to explain, Mark. We had a…an interlude and discovered that we aren't compatible. In the bedroom, that is.'' She smiled sunnily and patted his cheek. ''Don't worry about it, I feel the same way.''

Not compatible? The hell they weren't! He started to say so, then bit back the words in frustration.

''But just because sex is out of the picture,'' she continued, ''doesn't mean we can't be friends. Right?''

Exactly what he'd wanted. Why did it make him so angry? ''You're blowing me off.''

''Technically, you already blew me off,'' she told him, taking a few steps to grab the newspaper spread over his kitchen table and tidy it. ''I'm just agreeing that we don't suit each other.'' She glanced at him over her shoulder. ''Sexually, that is.''

If she said that one more time he was going to push right up against that refrigerator and remind her exactly what— He gritted his teeth. No, he couldn't touch her. That kiss outside had been too much. If he touched her again, he wouldn't stop until he'd had his fill of her.

''You want to be friends. Just like that? Forget what happened, no recriminations, no nothing.''

''Sure, why not? After all, we're both adults. We can admit we made a mistake. It's no big deal, Mark.''

He didn't want to be friends. He wanted to drown himself in that sweet, lithe body, and make endless love to her until neither of them could move. But he couldn't. And she was offering him exactly what he'd wanted, and he hated it.

She'd been hurt the other day. He'd seen it in her eyes, heard it in her voice. Yet here she stood, acting as if what had passed between them had been nothing more than a roll in the hay. A boring one, at that.

Cat put out her hand. "So, friends?"

He took her hand and held it, keeping his gaze on hers. "Friends," he agreed. A gleam came and went in her dark brown eyes. Anger? Mischief? He wasn't sure, but he did know one thing. Cat was up to something.

And in his experience, a woman scorned was a woman bent on revenge.

CAT LEFT MARK'S HOUSE well pleased with herself. She'd retrieved her dignity and at the same time confused him. She stopped with her hand on the door, thinking. What would make a man respond the way Mark had? Fear, she decided, letting herself inside. Fear that things were getting too serious too fast. He'd said as much, after all.

Cat tried to put Mark out of her mind by working, but she met with no luck. Finally, late that afternoon she went in search of confirmation of her theory. Male confirmation. She found her brother Cameron exactly where she'd expected, behind the bar of the Scarlet Parrot, keeping one eye on the ball game and the other on a busty blonde casting him sultry glances.

Cat stopped and looked around, realizing how much she loved this place. The Scarlet Parrot looked exactly like what it was. A waterfront bar and grill with good food, loud music and a sympathetic bartender. Whose ear Cat intended to bend.

"Hey, sis, what's up?" Cam's gaze didn't leave the blonde, but he slid a coaster in front of Cat with unerring accuracy.

She climbed onto the stool and slapped her purse down on the counter. "Give me a double."

His head snapped around and he stared at her. "A double what?"

"Anything, as long as it's strong."

"What gives?" he asked. "The last time you asked for a double you and Chad the cad had just broken up." He moved away and returned with a glass of white zinfandel.

Cat frowned but grabbed it, downed a big sip and choked. Okay, maybe a double hadn't been a good idea. Trust Cam to watch out for her. "You're a bartender. You talk to people all the time. Give advice and stuff."

"Wrong. I don't give advice, I listen."

She flipped a hand. "Whatever. I have a hypothetical situation I want to talk to you about. That means no telling Gail, and especially no telling Gabe.''

He rubbed down the already gleaming bar and cast her a sharp glance. ''Does this hypothetical situation involve a guy?''

''Yes. And no fighting.''

''What happened to hypothetical?''

''Promise me no fighting or I'm out of here.''

''Hey,'' he said, spreading his hands. ''I break up fights, I don't start them.''

Sure he did. Unless he thought somebody was messing with his family. Still, she needed a male point of view and Cam was nowhere near as volatile as Gabe. She pursed her lips and tapped a finger on the bar, unsure how to begin. ''Assume you have two people who are attracted to each other. Very attracted,'' she added reflectively.

''I'm listening.'' Grabbing a clean cloth, he polished a wineglass and held it up to the light. Satisfied, he placed it in one of the overhead racks and pulled another from the sink.

''These two people, er, act on the attraction.''

He halted in midpolish and narrowed his gaze at her. ''Hit the sheets, you mean.''

She nodded, took another sip of wine, enjoying the sweet taste as it trickled down her throat. ''And say that things are really good between them.''

Cam laid his towel on the counter. "Did the earth move?"

She laughed. "Pretty much."

"So what's the problem?"

Her gaze met his and she sighed. "Dream guy dumped her the next day."

"You don't have a problem." He smacked a fist on the counter in front of her, so hard her glass jumped. "You have a dead man."

Cat curled her feet around the stool's legs and leaned forward. "Cam, you promised me no fighting."

"I'm not going to fight. I'm going to kill the son of a bitch." His eyes blazed alarmingly. "Who is it? Peters? By God, no way is he messing with my sister and getting away with it."

"Cam." She laid a hand on his arm. "It's not him. I swear it's not."

His jaw still tight with anger, he subsided. "It's that new guy, isn't it? Your neighbor. Gabe told me he walked in on something."

"Gabe has a big mouth." But she didn't deny it. She grabbed the bowl of peanuts and started tossing them down. Cat loved peanuts, but generally avoided them because of her eternal five extra pounds. Some occasions deserved an indulgence, though, and this was definitely one of them.

Cam leaned on the bar, peering at her in concern. "What exactly happened, Cat?"

"Basically what I told you. I thought we had something special." Realizing her glass was empty, she held it out, ignoring Cam's frown. He knew she rarely had more than a single glass. "Apparently he didn't." That bothered her more than she wanted to admit.

Cameron refilled her glass in silence. He considered her a moment while she sipped, then asked, "If you don't want me to kill him, or beat him up, what do you want?"

"Advice. I want to know how to get him back."

"Why?" He tossed the towel over his shoulder and his eyes flashed with anger. "The jerk dumped you after a one-night stand."

Cat circled the rim of her glass with her finger and smiled.

"Oh, I get it. Payback."

She nodded decisively. "Eventually. After I've had some fun."

Cam shook his head. "No. You're not cut out for this, Cat. Forget the guy."

"Nope, can't do it. I've already started." She gulped back more wine. Her head swam and she remembered why she didn't drink much. Two glasses made her woozy. Three knocked her out. "I told him the sex was mediocre at best, but that we could be friends.''

''Ouch. Did he buy it?''

Remembering Mark's expression, she smiled. ''I was very convincing.''

Cam glanced at the blonde, who was signaling him impatiently. ''I have to go see to a customer. Don't leave yet, and don't even think you're driving.''

When he returned, she brought up the subject that had been bothering her. ''He said he thought we should cool it. That we should back off before we became too involved. Do you think he's scared? Because we have a good thing going and he isn't ready to make a commitment? Do you think that could be it?''

Cam glanced at her, rubbed the bar with his towel, then looked at her again. ''It sounds like a line, honey,'' he said gently. ''Like I said, you're better off forgetting the bum.''

I wish I could, she thought, pressing both palms against the bar counter to steady it.

''Either way, you lose. He doesn't want to commit to anything for longer than a day. This guy isn't who you're looking for.''

Cat leaned forward, blinking to clear her vision. ''That's where you're wrong. He's exactly what I'm looking for. Do you know how tired I am of never having fun? Well, with men, anyway. What's wrong with my having a little fun? A summer fling?''

Cameron scowled. ''You're not cut out for a casual fling. You'll get hurt.''

She flipped a hand. ''Not if we state the rules going in. If we both know it's temporary, then what's the problem?''

''I'm not sure I'm following your logic.''

''That's okay.'' She drained her wine. ''I am. I just need a plan. Thanks for the wine and the advice, Cam.''

''You didn't take my advice.''

''That's okay. You never take mine either.''

''Yeah, but I'm the big brother. You're supposed to listen to me. And fork over the keys.'' He held out his hand.

''I only had two glasses,'' she protested, closing one eye to better focus.

''Forget it, Cat. You can't drive worth beans even without the wine. Hand them over. I called Gail. And since she's here now, she can take you home.''

''Oh, all right.'' She blew him a kiss as she left with her sister. A plan. Now what could she do to convince Mark that they could have a temporary, no-strings-attached relationship? One neither of them would regret.

CAT'S MOTHER CALLED the next day. Usually during work hours she let the machine take her calls, but her mother knew that. Cat sighed at the voice demanding she pick up. If she didn't, her mother would simply call back until she drove Cat crazy.

She snatched up the cordless phone and tucked it between her ear and her shoulder. "Hello, Mom. I'm right in the middle of something, can I get back to you?"

"No, you can't. You'll forget and this is important. Vitally important."

Cat groaned silently. It always was with her mother. "What do you need?"

"Darling, I'm having a party."

Obviously a matter of desperate significance. "Great, Mom," she muttered, hoping her mother wouldn't spend half an hour describing the upcoming event. She listened with half an ear while her mother chattered on.

Now where was that return she'd been looking for? Could she have misfiled it? That wasn't like her, but she'd been distracted lately.

"You must come, Cat. I've arranged a treat for you."

"A treat?" she asked cautiously. She stopped fingering the stack of papers she deemed most likely to hold the errant return. Last time her mother had arranged "a treat" it had been a date with her best friend's nephew. He'd had bad breath and octopus arms. Ick.

"Mom, I don't think I can—"

"Please don't disappoint me, darling. This Saturday. I've asked Kyle to bring you and he's simply thrilled. The Cavanaughs will be here, and the Maxwells and—"

Her words penetrated and Cat pushed herself away from the desk. *Not again.* "How many times have I told you?" she interrupted. "I'm not interested in Kyle."

"Oh, pooh. You're being so stubborn. Give the poor man another chance."

Poor man, my foot, Cat thought. "No. Call him back and tell him I can't make it."

"Cat, don't be stubborn." Her mother sounded irritated now. "I want you to come, so why shouldn't you come with an eminently eligible man?"

"Because I already have a date with another man." Or she would by Saturday. The perfect opportunity to be with Mark again.

"What man?" Her mother sounded suspicious.

Cat grinned, pleased for once with her mother's ploys. "I'll introduce him to you Saturday. Gotta go, Mom."

Cat had a plan now. Simple. Direct. And she hoped, effective.

As long as she didn't lose her nerve between now and Saturday night.

CHAPTER ELEVEN

ANOTHER MORNING SHOT, Mark thought as he climbed into his truck and cranked the engine. Big surprise, the building supplies he needed couldn't be obtained any closer than Corpus Christi. He heard a shout and saw Cat waving him down. Window rolled down, he waited, irritated that he couldn't look at her without remembering being with her...and wanting her again.

"Great, I caught you," she said as she reached him. She placed her hands on the door and leaned in, her pale green tank top gaping just enough to give him a glimpse of smooth, creamy cleavage and a white lacy bra. He groaned silently and dragged his gaze to her face.

"I need a favor. My mother's giving a party Saturday night and I've been commanded to show up. How about going with me?" Before he could speak, she rushed on. "The food will be good, I swear, and we don't have to stay long."

"I thought we decided not to date." She was up to something, he just couldn't figure out what yet.

"No, we decided not to have sex." She smiled

cheerfully. "Dating's entirely different. The thing is—" she bit her lip "—I'm in kind of a bind. I told my mother I was seeing you."

"First Peters, now your mother. Why?"

"Because she keeps trying to fix me up with Kyle, that's why. The woman lives to matchmake, and you haven't seen anything until you've seen her at the top of her form. She's very hard to withstand. So I told her I couldn't come with Kyle because I was dating you."

A plausible explanation, but he thought there was more to it. "What kind of party is it?" She leaned closer and he caught a whiff of her perfume. The same scent she'd worn the day they'd made love. Sweat popped out on his forehead. It was going to be tougher than he'd imagined not to touch her.

"Oh, it's just a bunch of the locals. The older crowd, mostly. Retired. Yachts, tennis and golf are their major interests. And they love to go to parties, which is where my mother comes in. She gives excellent parties. Since my dad died she gives them even more. That and matchmaking for her children are her favorite pastimes."

Not just older but wealthy, if they were a part of the yacht set. Collectors, possibly, the type who might be interested in rare, illegal birds. Too good of an opportunity to pass up. He'd just have to keep his hands to himself. "All right. But you're out of luck if I have to wear a suit, because I don't have one."

She laughed. "You're obviously from the city. This is the coast in the summer. Casual, don't worry. Thanks, Mark."

Taking her to a party shouldn't be a big deal. And it was the perfect chance to get a better idea of who did what in the community. So why did he feel like he'd been baited, hooked and reeled in like a speckled trout?

SATURDAY NIGHT ARRIVED, and when Mark saw Cat, he figured out her plan. To launch a full-scale war.

Alone for the moment with his chilled shrimp, he watched his date work the room. For someone who protested she didn't like social events, she handled them well. Cat's mother's place was on the waterfront, in one of the exclusive gated neighborhoods, each street separated by a water canal. Guests loitered in small groups in a huge, open room with acres of windows, expensive chandeliers, ultramodern furniture and original artwork gracing the walls. The thought of what a hurricane could do to a place like this made him green around the gills.

The doors opened out to a lighted terrace, with scatterings of tables and chairs overlooking the water. Blooming plants of all varieties were placed strategically both inside and out, including a pair of potted bougainvillea flanking the doors. A pianist played background music on a gleaming black baby grand, while waiters circulated with trays of drinks and hors d'oeuvres. Not one male guest wore a coat and tie. The women were pretty, expensive and very well maintained.

Mark had two impressions.

Cat's mother was loaded.

And this sure as hell wasn't the kind of beer-and-nachos party he was used to.

Then there was Cat. She wore a dress he itched to get her out of, and he wasn't the only one, by a long shot. Every man in the place, even the old geezers, damn near stepped on his tongue whenever she walked past, and more than one head turned to mark her progress.

The red print sundress with spaghetti straps revealed an ocean of tanned, glowing skin. Luscious, kissable skin. He wanted to start at her collarbone, head downward, and keep going until he drowned in her. His gaze dropping, he noticed she'd thrust her bare feet into sandals with skinny heels. He wondered if all she had on beneath that saucy little number was a tiny pair of panties like those she'd worn before. It was enough to make a man cry, especially when he knew all he could do was look and not touch.

Her hair was dark, shiny and smooth, and she'd done something to make her brown eyes look even more sultry than they usually did. And her mouth. Oh, man, that mouth. He groaned, watching those full red lips as she chose a strawberry from a passing waiter and playfully popped it in her mouth. All in all, a classic case of torture. He'd bet everything he owned that she knew it, too.

Business, he told himself. *You're here on business, so drag your mind and your eyes off that tidy little package and put them to work.* Peters gave him the opportunity a few moments later, when he joined him at the buffet table. Just the man Mark wanted to talk to.

Earlier that afternoon Mark's partner had called to say they'd traced the company that had put an offer on his house. The information had been buried deep, but Kyle Peters was a silent partner in that company. Coincidence? Mark didn't think so.

"You're a lucky man, Kincaid," the vet said, loading a plate with lobster rolls, shrimp étouffé, seviche, caviar and other delicacies.

"How's that?" Mark took another bite of shrimp and avoided looking at the caviar. Black, slimy fish eggs weren't anything he wanted near his mouth.

Peters used his drink to gesture at Cat, who was headed their way. "Cat. She's looking good tonight."

"Yeah, she is." If Peters didn't quit staring at her breasts like he owned them, Mark was going to drag him outside and drop him in the ocean. After he slugged him.

Cat reached Mark's side and tucked her hand in the crook of his arm before speaking to the vet. "Hi, Kyle. Nice to see you here. How are you?"

"Good. You're looking lovely tonight. I was just telling Kincaid here what a lucky man he is."

She shot Mark a wry glance. "Thank you, Kyle. What a sweet thing to say."

Sweet my ass, Mark thought.

Fortunately for Peters's face, Gabe Randolph joined the group a few moments later. They exchanged greetings, brother and sister welcoming each other with a hug.

"Are you fishing that Port Isabel tournament next weekend?" Peters asked Randolph. "It's a big one, I hear. I thought about going, but decided against it. Pregnant patient due. A very neurotic poodle." He chuckled. "Duty calls, you know."

Nice of Peters to make him a present of that information, Mark thought. Port Isabel. They'd popped someone there last summer with a trunkful of parrots.

Randolph nodded and swigged his beer. "That's the plan. I've got a client who's convinced he's going to bring in the winning blue marlin."

"Good luck," Peters said. "I hear there hasn't been a marlin sighted in two weeks, and not much else, either. Hope your fee isn't contingent on success. But then, you haven't had a lot of that lately, have you? It's a wonder you've still got clients."

Gabe's face darkened. "This guy can't be too dissatisfied, since this is the fifth tournament we've entered together."

"No offense intended, of course." Peters managed to look both superior and surprised.

Cat stepped into the breach, laying a hand on her brother's arm. "How long will you be gone, Gabe?"

"The weekend and most of the week following," he said. "I'm coming back Friday morning."

She patted his arm before turning to Peters. "Kyle, I saw my mother had you cornered earlier. I hope she wasn't bending your ear about Tizzy."

He laughed, his attention divided between Cat's face and her cleavage. "No such thing. Her champion Pekingese is doing just fine." He turned back to Gabe. "But what's this I hear about you, Gabe? Your mother was telling me about your run-in with the FWS last week. Did they really accuse you of smuggling birds?"

Gabe scowled. "They didn't accuse me, exactly. They just asked me a lot of questions. Two parrots turned up on my doorstep. I took them to Cat, but they were already dead. She reported the incident to the FWS the next morning. They've been badgering me ever since."

"I didn't realize they'd questioned you more than once," Cat said. "I'm sorry, Gabe, but I had to take the birds in." He shrugged in answer.

She turned to Mark and added, "So much for your theory that it was just routine questioning."

"Could be you have Kincaid to thank for this,

Gabe," Peters said. "After all, the story is, he's an investigator."

"You've got your facts wrong," Mark said mildly to the vet. "I'm a game warden at Grapevine Lake. We talked about it at the Scarlet Parrot, remember?"

Peters looked skeptical. "I know that's what you said. But Gilbert talked about you a lot. He always said you were some kind of investigator."

Mark forced a laugh. "Gilbert always did like to embroider his stories. Anything to make them more interesting. I'm not an investigator." Technically, his title was special agent. "As I said, I'm a game warden." Not a complete lie, since he'd been one in the past.

Peters looked unconvinced, as did Gabe. "Still," Peters continued, "it wouldn't have hurt you to stand up for your girlfriend's brother."

Nice dig, Mark thought. Before he could respond, Cat piped up.

"Gabe didn't do anything wrong, so it's a moot point. Why should Mark be involved at all? He's not even working with the FWS here. He's on a leave of absence. And why are you so interested in what happened to Gabe, Kyle? You don't even like him."

Gabe gave a bark of laughter while Peters sputtered and his face flushed. "Good point," Gabe said. "Why are my troubles of any interest to you? Or is it just ghoulish curiosity?"

Peters launched into a long explanation, the gist of

which seemed to be that he was concerned about all of Cat's family. Gabe didn't appear to be buying it.

Mark took Cat's chin in his hand and tilted that luscious red mouth up to his. "Score one for you," he said, and planted a kiss on her pretty lips.

Sexual tension leaped between them, even from such brief contact. He dropped his hand and their gazes met and held. Her eyes turned dark and heated, tempting him to lead her out of there to a more private place. Luckily for him, Peters cleared his throat and broke the spell.

"You mother's waving at you, Cat. Or maybe at Gabe." He gestured at a dark-haired woman, probably in her late fifties. "And she doesn't look happy."

"I'm out of here," Gabe said, and beat a quick retreat.

Cat glanced in her direction. "No, she doesn't." She looked at Mark. "Either she's going to lecture me about kissing men in public, or she's mad because I haven't let her talk to you since I introduced you at the door. Come on, I'd better placate her before she really throws a fit."

"See you later, Kyle." Cat took Mark's hand and led him toward her mother.

"No loss," Mark thought he heard the vet mutter as they walked away.

When they reached Meredith Randolph, Mark found himself being shrewdly assessed. "So pleased you could come, Mark. And that Cat has finally brought you over so we can get acquainted.'' She shook his hand, her grip firm. ''Cat tells me you're remodeling your uncle's place. Do you plan to be in town long?''

Amused at her direct approach, Mark smiled. ''My plans aren't firm.''

''Don't give him the third degree, Mother.''

''Darling, I asked a simple question.'' She turned back to Mark, her eyes bright. ''My daughter also tells me you're from the Dallas area. I knew a Lillian Kincaid from Dallas once. She helped plan a benefit gala I had an interest in. Any relation?''

He nodded. ''My mother.''

''Really?'' Her eyebrows raised. ''Lovely woman, as I recall. Do you share her enthusiasm for philanthropy?''

He smiled. ''Not at all.''

She seemed taken aback, then laughed. ''Well, you're honest, at least. Cat, I believe your young man needs a drink. I'll catch up with you again later. Don't leave without talking to the Cavanaughs. You know how they dote on you.''

Cat made a face. ''The most boring people in the universe,'' she muttered to Mark as they left her mother. ''And he pinches.''

''Want me to slug him?'' Mark offered.

She gave a peal of laughter. ''He pinches my cheek. And he's older than dirt, so no, I don't want you to hit him.'' After a moment she sobered. ''Did you mean what you said about philanthropy? Or were you trying to shock my mother?''

He shrugged. ''I have no reason to want to shock your mother. I meant it.''

''You don't believe in charity?''

''I didn't say that. Charity is fine, but not at the expense of your own family.''

She studied him a moment, then put her hand on his arm and squeezed. ''I think we just hit a touchy subject. Come on and let's get you that drink.''

''I could use a beer.'' He could also use some time to think about what had happened tonight. Peters had gifted him with the information about Gabe Randolph's fishing trip. That only made him more suspicious of the vet, and less of Randolph. Because if Randolph meant to make that trip a smuggling run, why would he have discussed it so freely? Mark didn't believe he would have. Even so, he couldn't afford to ignore Randolph totally. The man hadn't been cleared, even though Mark was becoming more sure by the day that he was being used. By Kyle Peters.

Tomorrow, he'd put in a call to check Randolph's boat's registration. He remembered the name from when Cat had pointed it out at the marina. *El Jugador*. The Gambler. Appropriate, he thought. Then he'd alert the Coast Guard. They'd be happy enough to help out the FWS in this case by finding an excuse to board Randolph's boat upon his return to Aransas

City. If nothing turned up, then Mark could be wrong about Peters setting up Randolph. But he'd make book that the Coast Guard would find something.

He and Cat stayed for another hour, and although Mark met a lot of people, he didn't find any more likely suspects than the two he already had. Kyle Peters and Gabe Randolph. And he sure as hell wanted it to be Peters.

Because he couldn't get Cat out of his mind. Kissing her had been a mistake. It had been hard to resist her before. That little taste of her had freshened his memories to a painful point.

And he couldn't do a thing about it.

MARK DROVE CAT HOME with the salty tang of the ocean blowing through the open windows. It didn't cool his jets one iota. In fact, the last half hour of the party had been pure torture, when all he'd wanted was to find a private place and have his way with Cat.

Instead, Cat had dragged him around by the hand and introduced him to everyone from her great-aunt Bertha on down. He seriously doubted a single one of his new acquaintances knew any more about smuggling rings than his car's engine did. The talk he'd overheard had centered on exactly what Cat had predicted—golf, tennis and yachts. With one addition. Dog shows.

Still, the scene with the vet and the information

about Randolph's trip had turned the party into a success. Professionally, that is.

Personally, he was on shaky ground.

Next thing he knew, Cat had scooted over close to him, leaned across the center console and patted his leg. His thigh muscles clenched, and he gritted his teeth, hoping she wouldn't notice what other part of his anatomy had perked up considerably.

"What's wrong, do you have a headache or something? I get them at parties sometimes, from the smoke."

"Or something," he said, biting back a groan when her hand stayed where it was.

"I could massage your temples when we get back. I've been told I'm very good at it." Her hand made circular motions on his leg, her voice sounded sultry, as if she'd just gotten out of bed.

A vision popped into his mind of Cat and him naked, giving each other a full body massage. God, she was going to kill him.

Her voice came near his ear, her breasts brushed against his bare arm. "Or I could just kiss it and make it better." Suiting action to words, her lips grazed his temple, skimmed his cheek, then halted at the corner of his mouth. "Better?" she whispered.

He was surprised sweat wasn't rolling off him. Those healing fingers of hers, not to mention her voice, took him from half-aroused to hard as a rock inside a minute. He suspected she knew it, too. They pulled into his driveway, and when he saw her sassy smile, he was sure of it.

"What are you doing, Cat?"

Her lips curved upward, a breath away from his. "Isn't it obvious?" she asked, and locked those rosy lips to his.

Just one taste, he thought. *One taste and I swear I'll let her go.* He changed the angle, thrust his tongue inside her mouth, drinking in her sweet, hot flavor. She moaned throatily and settled against him.

He wanted to loosen the tie between her breasts, fill his hands with beautiful, naked flesh. Wanted to kiss her, be inside her, sate himself with her. Instead, he broke the kiss, turned his head aside and drew in a deep, jagged breath. "You'd regret it if we made love again."

"Would I?" Her voice was soft, husky. Infinitely seductive.

He put her away from him and sucked in another breath. "Yeah, you would. It's not going to happen, Cat."

"You sound awfully sure of that—" her gaze flicked to his lap, then back to his face "—for someone who's going to spend the rest of the evening in a cold shower."

He smiled wryly. She had that right. "I don't know how long I'll be around."

"I'm aware of that. You've mentioned it before. Several times."

''I don't do long-distance relationships. Or any serious relationship.''

Cat didn't speak, she simply gazed at him a moment, then got out of the car. He closed his eyes and cursed silently, then turned when he realized she'd walked around to his window. She leaned in, close enough that her spicy scent wafted to him, close enough he could see those dark, sexy eyes and that lush, curvy mouth.

''Neither do I,'' she said, and left him.

Mark had a moment of self-revelation while watching the gentle swing of her hips as she walked away. Even if it hadn't been for the situation with her brother, he would have backed off. Cat was exactly the kind of woman he didn't want to fall for. She was too passionate, too absorbed in a career. He'd experienced that kind of obsession firsthand with his mother. He didn't intend to deal with it again.

It was too damn bad he'd already fallen for her.

CHAPTER TWELVE

CAT DIDN'T GIVE UP easily, but Mark made her want to pull out her hair. Their date the night before hadn't been a total bust, but she sure as shooting couldn't call it a success, either.

He wanted her. He'd made that obvious last night, but he'd also made it clear he didn't intend to take the relationship any further.

"What I want to know is why? Why is he so against the two of us getting together again?" she asked Buddy, who was hanging upside down from his perch and admiring his red tail feathers by fanning them.

"Kissy, kissy," Buddy responded.

She laughed. "I wish."

Buddy righted himself and flew to another stand, the one with bells and rings he loved to play with. His darting pecks at the bells played a pretty melody, if Cat had been in the mood to listen. He tired of that quickly, and spying a floppy disk on the table, swooped down to get it. Luckily, Cat reached it first.

"What's your problem, anyway?" Buddy's tone

held the perfect note of irritation and Cat had to laugh.

"Mark, that's what."

The bird's head tilted and she swore she saw a gleam of concern in his eyes. He perched on her shoulder and gave her what passed for a kiss, rubbing his beak against her cheek.

"T-t-t-trouble," he trilled.

Buddy's comments didn't always make sense, but sometimes they were eerily to the point.

She decided she wouldn't get anywhere if she didn't see Mark, so she baked a fresh batch of double-Dutch chocolate macadamia-nut cookies and took them to him late that afternoon.

He answered the door wearing a worn gray T-shirt, the color of Buddy's chest feathers, and a pair of ragged denim cutoffs. The yellow paint in his hair and splattered on his shirt gave her a good idea what he'd been doing.

"I had extra cookies and thought you might like some," she said, shoving the plastic container into his hand and walking past him before he could protest.

He scowled, looking irritated. "I'm painting."

Cat propped a hand on her hip and surveyed him. "Yes, I can see that. But the proper response is thank you, I believe."

That drew a reluctant smile. "Thank you. I'm painting."

"Want some help?" she offered brightly. "Rembrandt is my middle name."

"Rembrandt painted pictures, not walls."

Cat simply folded her arms and waited him out. He shrugged and tossed the cookies down on a coffee table that gave new meaning to the words *distressed wood*. She remembered Gilbert hadn't believed in spending money on what he called "fancy" furniture. Or fixing up the house, obviously. Mark's uncle had been a bit eccentric, to put it mildly.

Mark opened the door to the downstairs half bath and waved her in. "Right now I'm just doing woodwork. You can start on that," he said, indicating the cabinet underneath the sink. "I'll finish the door." He shut it and picked up a brush from the tray on the sink.

Cat grabbed another brush and settled cross-legged on the floor, which due to the size of the room, put her right beside Mark's legs. "So, do you hear anything from Jay? Did he get back to California?" She brushed a stroke of pale yellow on the cabinet with approval. Much better than the dingy white of the original.

"Not yet. He went to Dallas."

His voice sounded oddly troubled. She looked at him, but with his back to her, she couldn't see his face. She concentrated on the cabinet. "Is anything wrong? You sound worried or something."

His brush halted and he glanced at her over his

shoulder. "I raised him from the time he was thirteen. I'm entitled to be worried."

"What's wrong with Jay going to Dallas?"

"I think he's making a mistake. He doesn't see it that way."

"Oh, woman trouble?"

Mark laughed grimly. "You could say that. Our mother."

"You don't want him to see his mother? Why?" She'd gathered he had problems with their mother, but she hadn't realized they were quite so serious.

"More painting, less talk," he said, his back to her once again as he applied the brush to the door.

"Sometimes it helps to talk."

"Sometimes it doesn't."

She couldn't force him to open up to her, so she resumed painting, mulling over what little he'd told her about his family. He must have been awfully young when he took the boys on, she thought, since he was only in his mid-thirties now.

They were silent a moment, both painting, and then he said, "She's going to hurt him. Both him and Brian, and they're too damn naive to see it."

Cat didn't think Jay had seemed naive at all, but she let the comment pass. "What makes you think she's going to hurt them?"

He put his brush down and turned around to look at her. "Because she did it before."

"When you gained custody of your brothers?" she hazarded, getting to her feet.

He nodded. "I'd moved out several years before, as soon as I graduated high school, but I kept in touch with the boys. She wasn't—" He hesitated, as if it hurt him to remember. "She wasn't taking care of them the way she should have been. So I told her I'd sue her for custody if she didn't get her act together." He shrugged. "She didn't. Instead, she left them. She let me take my brothers, and then she walked out of our lives. She flat disappeared."

"Did she ever give you an explanation?"

He shook his head. "No. Besides, I knew. She was all wrapped up in her causes, in raising money for them. Had been since I was a teenager. When my father left, she became even worse. I figured she wanted to do her thing, and two teenage boys were too much trouble."

"That's why you said what you did about charity work. Your mother—"

"The good causes, the next donation, all those things mattered more to her than her sons did." He leaned his head back and shut his eyes. "She handed Jay and Brian over to me, without a fight."

Cat moved closer, patted his arm. "You must have been awfully young to have so much responsibility thrust on you."

"Barely legal," he agreed, opening his eyes and

leaning back against the sink. "I grew up fast." He smiled ruefully. "I was so damn scared."

"You, scared? It doesn't seem like your nature."

He laughed, not entirely happy. "Petrified, believe me. Afraid I couldn't support us, afraid I couldn't handle the boys. Afraid I'd screw them up for life. They needed a mother. What they had was me."

Her heart went out to him, imagining the struggle he'd had. "How did you do it?"

"I managed. Both boys worked part-time, after school, weekends, summers. I'd thought about working in the FWS, that had been my goal during college." He glanced at her, smiled wryly. "The jobs I qualified for didn't pay enough, so I went back to construction, which I'd been doing to put myself through school. I figured it was more of a sure thing than a new career."

"You put your career plans on hold for your brothers."

"They needed me," he said simply. "Wouldn't you have done the same thing?"

She would have, she realized. Her family meant the world to her. Yet, her mother, difficult as she could be, had never deserted them. "Your brothers are lucky to have you."

"Other way around. I'm lucky to have them." His mouth lifted at the corner. "Don't look so solemn. It's not that big a deal. I did what anyone else would have in the same situation."

She suspected it had been a very big deal to a twenty-one-year-old, barely out of college.

He ran his hands through his hair, then looked at her. "I don't know why I told you all that."

"Have you ever talked to anyone about it?"

He shook his head. "No. Never."

"You needed to talk. I'm glad you decided to talk to me."

Their gazes met and held. Her breath caught as she read the expression in his eyes. Did he want to forget... Or did he simply want her?

"It's not a good idea," he said huskily. "You and me."

"I know you keep saying that. But I think you're wrong."

"I don't want to hurt you."

"Why do you think you'll hurt me?" She knew now why she'd wanted him back so badly. Not for revenge, not to assuage her hurt pride. Because she'd fallen for him.

He reached for her, his fingers tracing her cheek. "I don't think it, I know it," he said softly.

"But that's my risk to take, isn't it?"

He didn't answer. Instead, he leaned toward her and she knew he was going to kiss her. His doorbell rang. They stared at each other, their lips inches from each other.

"Just as well," he said, dropping his hand and opening the bathroom door.

Frustrated, emotions churning, she followed him a moment later. A petite woman in her early fifties stood at his front door. Her hair was carefully frosted, her casual red skirt and white blouse, immaculate. She looked at Mark, her expression equal parts hope, longing and pure fear.

His mother had come to see him.

"Can I come in?" she asked in a soft, tight voice.

He stood aside to let her in. "What are you doing here?"

"I—I wanted to see you." Her hands twisted around the handle of her purse. "Mark, please, we need to talk."

"I don't think that's a good idea."

"There's a lot I need..." She hesitated and put out a shaky hand. "I have to talk to you."

His jaw tightened. He didn't answer, but simply stood there staring at his mother, as if he couldn't believe she was there. Perhaps he couldn't, after so long.

"You must think we're very rude," she said to Cat. "I'm Mark's mother, Lillian Monroe."

"I, uh, gathered." She didn't say it, but the set of their eyes was identical, as was the color. "Nice to meet you," Cat said, shaking the hand she held out. "I'll just be going—"

"Don't go."

"Mark, it's better if I leave you two alone."

His mother walked past him into the living room,

chose a seat on the lumpy couch, crossed her legs and waited.

"Walk me out, Mark," Cat said. She didn't intend to be a bystander in whatever was going on between them.

After a confused glance at his mother, he did as she asked. At the door, she laid her hand on his arm and squeezed. "You and your mother need to clear the air. I'll be home if you want to talk later, okay?"

The panicked look in his eyes tore at her heart. "I don't know if I can do this," he said, glancing over his shoulder, then back to Cat. "I haven't seen her since—" Breaking off, he pressed his lips together. "Since a couple of months after she left the boys with me."

"She's your mother. Talk to her."

Her heart ached at the pain in his eyes. Pressing a hand to his cheek, she said, "Remember, I'm here if you want to talk later."

MARK CLOSED THE DOOR behind Cat and waited for a moment, gathering his resolve. He'd rather face armed smugglers than the woman sitting in his living room. It was stupid, that she still had the power to affect him. After all, he hadn't seen her in twelve years.

He remembered every detail of the day she'd turned the boys over to him. Lillian hadn't even fought him. Had she felt anything—beyond relief?

He remembered his shock, too. Somehow, he'd expected her to at least pretend to care.

Mark scrubbed his hands over his face and shook off the past. The present, that's what he needed to deal with. He walked into the living room and looked at his mother, trying to reconcile this picture with his last memory of her. When she'd left, she'd been absolutely devoid of emotion. Cold, calm, her face expressionless. She'd simply handed over the boys and walked out.

By contrast, the woman seated on the couch was a bundle of nerves. Her red-rimmed eyes indicated she'd cried recently, and the hands twisting together in her lap implied uneasiness. *Uneasy, hell,* he thought. *She's scared to death.*

The thought jarred him, as did her next words.

"You look like your father."

Leaning against the doorjamb, he tucked his hands in his pockets. "Yeah, I know. Is that why you never could stand me?"

She shook her head, her expression sad. "You're so wrong. Mark. I've always loved you. And your brothers and sister, too. I just wasn't good at making you believe it."

"You weren't very good at taking responsibility, either. For your family, anyway."

She paled and sucked in a breath. "For a moment there, you sounded just like your father. Did you intend to?"

He shrugged without answering.

She asked, very quietly, "Do you hate me so much?"

He didn't know what he felt for her. Once, he'd hated her, for what she'd done to his brothers. But now, she looked small, defenseless, as if she were waiting for him to crush her. "I don't hate you. I don't...know how I feel about you."

Her eyes closed and her head bowed in defeat. He felt mean, and found he didn't care for it. "Let's just get this over with. Why did you come here?"

"Jay said—he said he didn't think you'd come to me. That if I wanted to see you, I'd have to come here. So I did." She touched a shaking hand to her face. "I came to—to make amends."

Make amends? For deserting him and his brothers? For allowing their father to drive Miranda away? "You let me take the boys like they were so much garbage. Nothing will ever change that. And what about Miranda? You never even tried to find her after she took off."

She looked startled. "Is that what you thought? I had a private investigator looking for her for months afterward. Months that turned into years."

His eyes narrowed. "First I've heard of it."

"He couldn't find a trace of her. I didn't see the point in telling you. I thought it might make it harder somehow, to hear he'd failed."

So she'd tried to find Miranda. Too little, too late. "And Jay and Brian? What about them?"

"I—" Her hands twisted together in her lap. "By the time you took custody of the boys, I was barely hanging on. I couldn't take care of myself, much less two teenage boys. Besides, I thought you'd be a better parent than I could ever be. And I was right."

He couldn't let it go, couldn't forget the anger he still held. "You let me have them because you were too caught up in your damn causes to pay any attention to them."

Her gaze fell, then lifted to his. In a low voice she said, "That isn't what happened. I let you believe it because I couldn't cope."

Why did she have to look so shaken? He didn't want to pity her, didn't want to feel anything for her. "Cope with what?" he asked.

"With my life." She gave a short, humorless laugh. "With anything." She fell silent a moment, then asked, "Will you sit down and let me tell you about it?"

He nodded, his emotions too precarious to allow him to speak. The past was over, no matter her explanation, and they could do nothing to change it. He took the only seat in the room, at the other end of the couch. "Go on."

Her gaze fell to her lap. "I'll start at the beginning. Do you know why I turned to my causes?"

He shook his head, not sure he wanted to hear her justification, not sure of anything at all.

"Your father and I—we had a difficult marriage. I don't know what you remember—"

He interrupted. "I remember the fights. About all the time you were spending away from us. How he'd get off work and blow up because you were never there."

"Do you remember him? What he was like?"

He closed his eyes and plunged into the past. Remembered the ranting, the put-downs, the digs at whatever Mark had enjoyed. "He didn't leave until I was sixteen. It's not like I can draw a blank on that part of my life." Even though sometimes he wanted to.

His mother sighed. Her hand crept up to her neck. "Sometimes I thought he lived to make me feel like nothing. He enjoyed it."

"I remember," Mark said unwillingly. "He did the same thing to me. To all of us."

"I know, and I'm sorry. I needed something, though, something that didn't make me feel small, or petty, or useless. So I turned to volunteering. That led to fund-raising, and then I became involved in different causes—too involved, I can't deny. But for the first time in years, I found something I excelled at, something he couldn't take away from me or make…insignificant."

"Meanwhile your kids were crying out for your attention."

"I lost myself, and you children paid the price."

Impatiently, he waved away that last remark. "I was grown, I handled it. But how could…how could you leave the boys? Do you know how they felt when you didn't even fight me for them?"

She lifted a hand in supplication, but he continued regardless, unable to stop the harsh words, words that had built through all the long nights of trying to be both parents to his brothers, and fearing time after time that he'd failed them. "They felt like garbage, especially when you kept letting them down. God knows how they turned out as well as they did."

"They grew into fine young men because of you."

They'd grown into fine men because he'd been lucky. "I don't understand how you could walk away from your sons."

Her head lifted, she met his gaze and said, "I spent two years in a psychiatric hospital. Being treated for depression, among other things. That's why I stopped calling."

Stunned, he stared at her. He hadn't expected her excuse to be anything like that. He didn't know what to say to her. Even if he believed her, and he did, it didn't negate everything that had happened. "Couldn't you have told me? Or have the doctors tell me? Why did you let the boys believe you didn't give a damn about them?'' *Why did you let me be-lieve it?*

She bowed her head. "At first, I was ashamed. Later, after I left the hospital, I was scared. Scared you'd reject me, scared that I deserved whatever happened to me. I believed it would be better to simply stay out of your lives."

"I'm not a monster. If you'd told me you were sick, asked me for help, I'd have given it to you. If you'd let me think for one minute you had a good reason for what you did—"

"I'm sorry. I was wrong, so wrong." She hung her head and covered her face with her hands. Her shoulders shook and he knew she was crying.

Not knowing what to say, what to do, he sat there while she cried. His emotions were roiling, his mind a jumble. Everything he'd believed for years about his mother had been wrong. Finally, he asked, "What changed your mind? Why did you decide to contact Jay and Brian?"

Her head raised. Blinking back tears, she drew in a shaky breath. "My husband. My new husband, Walt Monroe. He knew I had regrets, knew how much I hated the void in my life. He convinced me I had to at least try to make peace with my children. So I contacted Brian and Jay because I hoped they might think less harshly of me than you did."

She didn't say it, but Jay's words came back to him. "She's afraid of you, afraid you'll convince us not to see her.'' And he'd tried. But he hadn't known all the facts then. He'd only known he didn't want his brothers hurt…again.

''They've been very kind. You must be very proud of them,'' she said softly. She pulled a tissue from her purse and blotted her eyes. ''I swore to myself I wouldn't cry, but I guess I botched that, too.''

''I don't know what to say. I can't forget the past, as if it never mattered. All those years, I thought you didn't care.'' He met her gaze. ''If you'd told me the truth, I'd have understood. Or tried to.''

''I know,'' she whispered. ''I know I was wrong. I don't expect you to forget. But I hoped someday you might forgive me.''

He averted his eyes, unable to look at the anguish in hers. ''I—I don't know. I don't know what I'm supposed to feel, or think, or say.'' He'd never been more confused in his life. ''I need some time.''

''Well.'' She let out a breath. ''That's better than I expected.'' She rose, smoothed her skirt. ''Your brothers have my number if you decide…'' Her voice trailed away. ''Goodbye, Mark.''

The door closed quietly behind her. He slumped back on the couch. *What the hell am I supposed to do now?*

CHAPTER THIRTEEN

FOR THE TWELFTH TIME since she'd come home, Cat peeked out her window. Finally, she saw some activity at Mark's house. His mother walked out and got into her car. The interior light stayed on a moment, enough to illuminate complete dejection as she put her head on the steering wheel and remained motionless. Long moments later, she started the car and drove away.

The light came on in Mark's kitchen, then a few minutes later, blinked out. Cat debated whether to go see him or leave the decision to him, but when it became apparent he wasn't coming over, she said to heck with it. He needed a friend, and if he was too darned stubborn to see that, then she didn't mind making the first move.

A few minutes later, she knocked on his front door. Mark opened up just as she raised her hand to knock again. Her words of greeting died in her throat at the sight of him. A world of hurt lived in the depths of those gorgeous blue eyes. Whatever had happened with his mother must have really rocked him.

"Mark—"

"Don't say it." His eyes shifted from wounded to intense in a heartbeat. "I don't want to talk. I don't want to analyze. I don't even want to think."

"Okay." She swallowed, hard. "But...could you use a friend?"

He set the beer he was holding on the floor, took her wrist and pulled her inside. Backed her up against the front door and put his palms on either side of her face. Her heart began to thump, a slow thrill of anticipation.

"I don't want a friend." He leaned closer, his body not quite touching hers, his mouth a sigh away. "I want a lover. I want you, Cat. Right here, right now."

Her throat tightened, with desire not fear. Afraid she'd stutter, she nodded instead. His mouth came down on hers, his lips slanting over hers in a hot, hungry, demanding kiss. He drew back, cradled her face in his hands and stared at her in the shadowy silence. "You have the most incredible eyes." His thumbs caressed her jaw very gently. "Doe eyes. Big, brown. Absolutely trusting."

Her heart sprinted madly. Cat couldn't remember ever being aroused so quickly. Or ever wanting quite so desperately. Her hands crept up to latch onto his wrists and she looked into his eyes, trapped as much by the passion in their depths as by his hands, so warm against her face.

"Stay or go, Cat?" His voice emerged, husky, tempting.

"Stay," she breathed.

A devil's smile curved that beautiful mouth. "Good." His hands dropped and he began to slowly unfasten his shirt buttons.

Her hands shook, just a little, as she did the same.

He didn't speak, didn't touch her, but he watched her, his gaze unblinking as he dropped his shirt on the floor.

Cat let her blouse slide down her arms, aware her nipples had tightened and strained against her bra. She unsnapped the front clasp and peeled the cups back slowly. She felt wicked. Alluring. And more aroused than ever.

Mark knelt in front of her and his lips covered her nipple. His warm mouth tugged gently. Struggling not to whimper, Cat braced herself, one hand against the door, one tangled in the dark hair at her breast.

Teasing, tempting, he kissed and sucked her other breast, while his hands caressed her bottom and pulled her closer. "I think I should tell you," she panted, "I've never been ravaged against a door before."

He smiled against her skin. "Do you want me to stop?"

"You'd better not," she said, and he didn't.

His mouth moved down her stomach, halted while he undid her shorts and slipped them down her legs. She thought he'd rise then, but he didn't. He kissed her. Intimately. Where she ached with desire, where every nerve ending of her body had coalesced, begging for release. Kissed her again. And again. Her fingers tightening in his hair, she screamed his name.

Mark didn't give her time to do more than gasp in a breath, but swung her up in his arms and took the stairs rapidly. Midway, he stopped to kiss her mindless. "Why—where?" she managed to ask.

He smiled and kissed her again. "My bedroom. Condoms."

He kicked the door open and put her on the big bed, the sheets unmade and smelling of him. She watched him hungrily as he shucked his shorts and briefs in a rapid move. Yanking open the drawer of the bedside table, he searched it and cursed. "If Jay took them, I'm going to kill him."

"Get in line," Cat said, then laughed as he pulled a box out.

Then he was beside her, over her, inside her. Everywhere. "I want you." Another slow revolution of his hips sank him deep inside her and he looked into her eyes. "So much." Staring down at her, he pulled back, and her hips lifted in supplication.

"I want you, too." She wrapped her arms and legs tightly around him, coming apart as the tide took them both.

MARK KNEW he shouldn't have made love to Cat. But he had, and found he couldn't regret it. Of course, having a warm, naked woman snuggled up against him made it hard to regret anything.

"You're not going to dump me again in the morning, are you?" she asked sleepily.

He tugged her chin up and kissed her. "No way." This time he was keeping her. At least, until she discovered he'd lied to her about his job. And that he'd allowed her brother to be set up. Imagining Cat's reaction, he winced.

"What happened with your mother?"

The rosy glow faded still more. He'd almost managed to push that incident out of his mind.

"You don't have to tell me, and I know you're a guy and guys usually have a hard time talking about, well, talking about emotions and stuff—"

He interrupted before she became truly wound up. "I found out tonight that everything I'd believed about my mother, almost everything, was wrong."

Cat shifted, sitting up against the headboard, as he had. Her fingers fluttered gently over his face, a fairy touch of comfort. "Tell me."

Remembering, he rubbed his hand over his face and began. "I thought my mother was selfish. That she didn't love us. That she never had. Turns out she was sick. Really sick." He paused, then added, "After I took custody of the boys, she went into a psychiatric hospital for two years."

Cat put her hand over his and squeezed. "Oh, Mark. How sad. For all of you."

He looked at Cat, wanting her to believe him. Wanting to believe it himself. "If I'd known, I'd have helped her. Taken the boys to see her. But she never told us. I spent all these years resenting her for something she had no control over."

"Why didn't she tell you?"

Confession time. Mark wondered what Cat would think of him once she knew the whole story. "She said at first she was ashamed. But the main reason she stayed out of our lives for so long was me." He clenched his fist, remembering the anguish in his mother's eyes. "She was scared to death to approach us. Even now, years later, she went through Jay and Brian first, before she tried to talk to me."

Cat put her arms around him and hugged him.

He pulled out of her arms and stared at her, reading nothing but compassion in her eyes. "Didn't you hear what I said?" Why was she offering comfort when he deserved scorn?

"I heard you." Her arms closed around him again, hugging him tight. "It's not your fault, Mark. You didn't have all the facts. It was wrong of your mother to blame you for her actions."

"She didn't blame me. But I do."

"You shouldn't. It sounds to me as if you reacted the way most people would have, given the situation."

"I don't know. Maybe."

"Give yourself a break, Mark. You took care of your brothers, raised them, loved them. That's something not everyone could have, or would have, done. You should be proud of yourself."

He'd never thought about it that way. Cat snuggled up against his back, wrapped her arms around his neck. It felt good, and very comforting. "She wants me to forgive her. She has a relationship with my brothers now. She wants a relationship with me."

"What do you want?" Her warm breath feathered across his skin as she brushed a kiss on his cheek.

"I don't know. I want to forgive her, but it's not that easy. I always thought we lost my sister because of her. That she let my father force Miranda into running away. Maybe that wasn't her fault either."

"I thought your sister died?"

"For all we know, she did. None of us has seen her since she was fifteen. That was nineteen years ago. No one's been able to trace her." He laughed humorlessly. "That's another thing I didn't know, that my mother tried to find Miranda, too."

"I'm sorry. That must be so hard to live with." She kissed his cheek again, held him close. "You've been given a lot to deal with. I don't think it's wrong to take some time to figure it all out."

He loosened her arms and turned around, holding her away from him. He wanted—no needed—to see her eyes when he asked his next question. "Do you think I'm a bastard because I can't just forgive her? Because I can't tell her what she wants to hear?''

Cat smiled and shook her head. ''Not even a little bit.''

''She was sick, Cat. That wasn't her fault.''

''No, but choosing not to tell you and not contacting you for so long was her responsibility.'' She took his hand, squeezed it. ''For what it's worth, I think you will forgive her, and you will establish a relationship with her. Don't beat yourself up because you can't do it immediately. You need time, don't feel guilty about taking it.''

Mark brought her hand to his mouth, turned it over to press a kiss into her palm. ''You're really sweet, you know that?'' She laughed, then sighed as his lips moved up her arm. ''And beautiful.'' He lay down, pulling her on top of him. ''And naked. You have any ideas on what we should do about that?''

''One or two,'' she said, and proceeded to show him.

THE NEXT DAY, Mark spent all morning on the phone with the Coast Guard, double-checking the details for the sting on Randolph's boat at the end of the following week. He felt guiltier by the moment for allowing the man to be used, especially when he was all but certain that Randolph was innocent. Yet he had no choice but to follow the lead, and hope he could expose Peters as the real criminal. Shortly after he hung up, his cell phone rang again.

"Kincaid." Thinking he didn't need them, he shoved his notes in a drawer.

"Can you say *mother lode?*"

"Simpson?" Mark couldn't remember his normally laid-back partner ever sounding so wired. "What's up?"

"Okay, mother lode might be a little ambitious, but it's big. You know how sometimes the smallest lead turns into gold?"

"Yeah. But most of the time they turn into nothing."

"Too true, but this one didn't. Last night we busted a pet shop in Dallas. Small operation, we're thinking, hardly worth the time and sure as hell not worth the paperwork. Turns out this guy's a clearinghouse, involved up to his neck in the Parrot Blues case. And he's spilling his guts so fast, we're dizzy."

"That's great." He tamped down on the twinge of regret for not being in on the operation. "Did he roll over on any big kahunas?"

"Oh, yeah, and that ain't half of it. He's fingering people left and right, in places from Texas to New York to California."

"How did you guys get him?" Settling back in his chair, he propped his feet on the edge of the table and waited to hear the story.

"Dumb luck. I had some time on my hands and

followed a lead from a kid who worked for him. Something the kid saw spooked him and he came to us.''

''Not luck,'' Mark said, knowing his partner's hunches often led to good things. ''Sounds like you did a good job, there. I don't suppose he gave you a name for the man down here?''

''No, but he gave us a tip that's almost as good. There's a shipment set to come in this weekend or the first part of the following week. We don't know what, but it's a big one. Rumor is, worth several hundred thousand street prices.''

''Damn!'' His feet hit the floor and he got up to pace the kitchen. ''Here in Aransas City?'' This could be why Peters had dropped the news about Gabe Randolph's fishing trip. He wanted a decoy from the real thing.

''He didn't know the exact meeting place or the date yet. All he knows is it will be somewhere between Rockport and Corpus Christi.''

''On water or on land?''

''Unclear. His contact down there is very cagey. Our guy still doesn't know who he is, and he says the man never tells him the exact meeting place until the last minute. Guess he thinks that gives him less time to talk.''

''Can't argue with success,'' Mark said. ''Any more news on the vet?''

''None. We can't trace the money at all. Probably

has cash stashed in the islands. Nothing illegal about that.''

"Yeah, but where it came from is what I want to know,''

"How sure are you that it's the vet and not the fisherman we're looking for?''

"Ninety-five percent. You know everything I know. What do you think?

"Your reasoning about the dead birds is sound. And Peters being a silent partner in that company who wanted to buy your house is suspicious as hell, I'll admit. On top of that, the way the vet handed you the information about Randolph's fishing trip is suspect.''

"Why do I hear a but coming?'' Mark asked. "Spit it out, Simpson. What's bugging you?''

His partner was silent a moment. "I get the feeling you don't want Gabe Randolph to be guilty. Because of the sister.''

Mark frowned and glanced out the window, eyes drawn by a flash of red as Cat's pickup pulled into her driveway. "It's true I'd rather the link be Peters than Gabe Randolph. I can't deny that, but it doesn't mean I'd screw up the case.''

"I didn't think you would. But you've got this thing for the sister, it's bound to cloud your thinking. I thought you said you'd handled her.''

"I did,'' he said shortly, watching Cat take a load

of groceries into her house. He'd handled every inch of that delicious little body. And meant to do it again.

"You sound a little uptight, man. I'm thinking this chick really has you going."

Forced to agree, Mark closed his eyes. "Don't worry, I'm doing the job. The Coast Guard is set to check Randolph's boat next Friday, on his return from a fishing tournament. If they find anything, we'll go from there. Because if he has been set up, I'll prove it. And when I do, that will give us the man we're after."

They talked a bit more, going over details, comparing notes. Simpson's parting words were "Forget the chick, Mark. Once she finds out who you really are, you'll be SOL, anyway."

Forget the chick, Mark thought, hanging up. Not a chance. Rubbing his temples, he stared out the window at Cat's house. He hadn't been hit with the stupid tree, he'd been hit with the whole damn forest.

The night before, he'd suspected his feelings. Waking up this morning with Cat in his arms, he'd known for certain. He'd fallen crazy in love with her.

Assuming her brother was innocent, Cat wouldn't thank Mark for using him to further his case. Though if Peters wanted to frame Gabe Randolph, there wasn't a lot Mark could do before the fact. And he couldn't live with himself if he didn't follow through on a case that had already cost the lives of countless animals. The case he'd worked and sweated over for months.

The Parrot Blues operation was going down.

No matter what it took to do it.

CHAPTER FOURTEEN

REPLACING LIGHTBULBS was one of those household chores Cat always put off as long as possible. Consequently, by the time she replaced the dead bulbs in the kitchen fixture, she'd been sitting in near darkness. She stretched to give a final twist to the last new lightbulb, when someone knocked on her door.

"Come in."

"What is this penchant you have for unstable ladders?" Mark asked.

Cat looked at him and smiled, her heart kicking up at the sight of him. It had taken all her willpower to let him come to her, but she'd done it. She wanted to be absolutely sure he didn't have second thoughts about the night before. "This is a step stool not a ladder. And it's perfectly stable."

He pulled her into his arms and the stool fell over with a clatter. "My point," he said, and kissed her.

Mark didn't kiss her as if he intended to run anytime soon. Sighing, Cat wrapped her arms around his neck and soaked up every blood-sizzling moment.

He sat in one of the kitchen chairs with her in his

lap, nuzzled her neck and said, "How does candle-light, soft music, wine and good food sound to you?"

"Wonderful." She pulled back and gave him a saucy smile. "But I don't have any candles, or any wine."

"Not here. There's an Italian place in Corpus Christi I hear is great. Gianni's."

"It is great. Also expensive." A place Cat never went unless someone else picked up the tab. She shifted and put a hand to his cheek. "We could stay here and—" she walked her fingers down his chest "—improvise."

He caught her hand, kissed it and set her on her feet. "Nope. I want to take you out. Go get dressed. I'll pick you up in half an hour."

She decided against further argument. Half an hour didn't leave much time to find something to wear that would knock his socks off.

MARK HAD TO REMIND himself to breathe when he saw Cat that evening. She wore a little black number that clung to her curves like a lover's hand. Her scent, soft, feminine, with a hint of exotic spice thrown in, hit him with a gut-twisting punch when she kissed him hello.

Why had he been so gung ho to go out?

By the time they reached the restaurant, he'd remembered. He wanted at least one special night with her. One night where he didn't have to think about the case. One night he could romance her.

He wanted the fantasy tonight. Because in a few days the dream would almost certainly blow up in his face.

Gianni's was everything promised. Dark, intimate, romantic. Flickering candlelight, bloodred tablecloths, sumptuously upholstered chairs in shades of gold and white, fresh flowers on the tables. The black-suited waiter hovered at a discreet distance, setting dishes in front of them and whisking them away with quiet efficiency. Violin music haunted the air, at times sweet and joyous, at others dark and enchanting.

"I'm glad you brought me here," Cat said, snaring an olive from the antipasto tray and popping it into her mouth. Finished with the olive, she took a tiny sip of wine. "Are you sure you knew it was so expensive?"

He had to laugh. "Quit worrying about it," he said, carrying her hand to his mouth and dropping a kiss on her wrist. "You're worth it."

"It's perfect. And your timing was good, too. I needed cheering up after my afternoon."

He kept hold of her hand, rubbing his thumb over her knuckles. "What happened this afternoon?"

She grimaced. "I went to the FWS and asked Hargrove why they haven't sent me any birds in so long. He hemmed and hawed, and gave me a big runaound, but I think it has something to do with Gabe. Obviously, Hargrove is still suspicious of him, and that seems to have spilled over to me.''

So much for not thinking about the case. ''Do you want me to talk to him? See if I can find out what's going on?'' He had talked to Hargrove, of course, and while the FWS officer didn't believe Cat guilty of any wrongdoing, he still suspected Gabe. So he'd decided to take the cautious approach and not give Cat any more birds at present. In fact, he and Mark had argued after Mark had pointed out the other man was penalizing Cat for no good reason.

''That would be wonderful,'' she said, reaching for her water glass. ''I miss having birds around. If I didn't have Buddy, I'd go crazy.''

''I'll see what I can do,'' Mark promised. ''The FWS aren't the only people who give you birds, are they?''

''No, but it's spotty. Here and there, an occasional injured bird makes its way to me. It's a grapevine kind of thing. If I had a bigger home operation I could establish other contacts, but with my only being able to rehab part-time, I can't afford to expand.'' She glanced away and sighed. ''When I'm really dreaming, I think about a wild-bird sanctuary. Like the one for herons near Port Aransas, but smaller.''

She looked a little sad. ''Why don't you do it?''

She came out of her reverie and laughed. ''Money, primarily. I don't have any way of financing it, and with a state sanctuary already located nearby, government help isn't likely. Not that I'd know how to go about getting that.''

Mark did. He knew just the person who would. Their entrées arrived just then, and they went on to talk of other things.

''I can't eat another bite,'' Cat said a little while later, and pushed her plate away. ''As it is, I'm going to be eating salad for a week.''

''Why?'' Mark asked, and then it dawned on him. ''You're kidding, right? You don't need to lose weight.''

She laughed. ''Thanks. Golden words.''

''You're curvy. I like your curves. All of them.''

She smiled, that blinding smile that had gotten to him the first time they met. ''You just made my night.''

''Yeah? Let's see if we can make it even better. What do you want to do after dinner? Go dancing?''

Her eyes lit with mischief. She smiled and shook her head. ''I have a better idea.''

SHE TOOK HIM to a place near Aransas City, a place named Copper's Cove, far off the beaten track. Mark stopped the car and they got out, walked in silence to the water's edge. The full moon rose above the water, casting pale fingers of light across it. As always, the breeze carried the sharp tang of salt.

''What do you think?'' Cat asked Mark.

He looked at the bay, then back at her. "You're right. It would make a perfect sanctuary."

"Yes, it would," she said, unsurprised that he'd known without her telling him.

"It's beautiful." He smiled. "And deserted."

Her lips curved in response. "Not many people know it, though I'm not sure why. It's not even posted. I discovered the spot in high school."

He took her hand and began walking back to the car. "Did you bring your boyfriends here?"

"No, I didn't want to share the place."

Reaching the car, he leaned back against the hood and tugged her to stand between his legs. His hands caressed her arms, moving up and down slowly. Their gazes met. "You're sharing it with me."

"This has been such a wonderful night." She sighed dreamily. "I wanted to bring you someplace special. So I thought of this cove. I've always loved it."

He eased her closer and kissed the pulse at the base of her throat. "I can see that. It's in your voice." His lips brushed her throat again. "In your eyes." He kissed each eyelid, a feather-light touch. "In the curve of your mouth." His mouth brushed each corner of hers, then skimmed her cheek. Her heart rate picked up speed with each sensation.

She drew back in his arms, laid a hand against his cheek. "There's something else I want to share with you."

"What's that?"

"I love you, Mark."

Their gazes met and held, his dark and unreadable. He didn't speak, he simply pulled her closer, bent his head and kissed her. Slow, sweet, and tender as the dawn.

ALMOST EVERY WEEK, Cat met her sister for lunch at ChiChi's diner on Main Street in Aransas City. The broken-down sign hanging above the tiny beige brick building proclaimed it to have the "Best Burgers in Texas." As with Cam's place, the locals loved it.

Cat and Gail sat in one of the ancient booths along the wall, in front of a window looking out onto the street. Attempting, without success, to avoid a broken spring, Cat shifted on the red vinyl upholstered seat. "I don't know why I put up with this place. This seat is the pits, and forty years old if it's a day. I swear, I've complained about it the last four times running."

"We come back because the food is great and, more importantly, cheap," Gail mumbled around her hamburger.

Cat took a bite of her burger and acknowledged her sister's point. "I've done a really stupid thing," she said to Gail between bites.

Gail paused with a French fry halfway to her mouth. "How stupid? A little bit stupid, medium stupid or huge stupid?"

"Tremendously stupid." She pushed her plate

away and propped her forearms on the once-white, now-dirty beige tabletop. "You know Mark and I have grown, uh, close lately."

Gail rolled her eyes. "Close? Is that what you call it? I'd say you're having a mad, passionate affair with him. You've been gaga over him since he moved in." She paused, and added reflectively, "Not that I really blame you. He's definitely hot." She finished her French fry. "Get to the stupid part. And if you don't want your fries, I do."

Distracted, Cat glared at Gail. "If you weren't my sister, I'd hate you for eating like a lumberjack and never gaining weight. Why can't I have your metabolism? Or even an inch or two more of height?"

"Totally off the subject," Gail said. "Come on, talk."

Cat waited until the waitress had refilled their tea glasses and left. "I fell in love with Mark. Not only that, I *told* him I loved him."

Gail finished her hamburger and started in on Cat's fries. "I'll bite. Why is that so tremendously stupid?"

"Because the day after we first made love, he panicked and dumped me."

"Dumped you? As in, *Adiós, amiga,* this is way too serious for me?"

Cat nodded, pleased with her sister's quick comprehension. "Exactly. It took me forever to get him to sleep with me again."

"Obviously, you succeeded."

"I caught him at a weak moment. Night before last. He needed comfort." She closed her eyes and remembered being ravaged against his front door. She needed a fan.

"Comfort for one and all. Cat's specialty," Gail said. "And if that satisfied smile on your face is any clue, I'd say it turned out great. Is that when you told him?"

"No, I told him last night. He took me out for a romantic dinner, and then I took him to Copper's Cove."

"You never take anyone there," Gail said.

"I know. But it seemed like the perfect place to tell him."

"So, what did he say?"

"Nothing. He just kissed me, and then we got distracted."

"I bet," Gail said dryly. "And now you're afraid he's going to rabbit again."

Cat nodded. "Of course I am. He said he wouldn't, but that was before I had my attack of stupidity." Dejected, she picked up her hamburger and took a huge bite. It didn't help. "The thing is, he has very good reasons to be scared of relationships."

Gail looked skeptical, but said nothing.

Cat sighed. "I know, that sounds like a line, but Mark didn't say it, I did. He has major issues with his mother. She left her family, and he raised his younger brothers. I think he may have real difficulty trusting women. For years he believed that his mother's obsession with her work was to blame for a lot of their problems. He's come to realize that wasn't quite true, but it still affects him. It's hard to change a conviction you've had your whole life, even if you know it's wrong.''

''What, he wants a nonworking woman? That will be hard to find.''

Cat shook her head, trying to organize her thoughts. ''No, but...I think he needs the assurance that he's important to someone. That he matters to a woman.'' That someone loved him, she thought. ''He doesn't have the kind of support we have, Gail. He's always been the responsible one, and I don't think he lets his brothers help him with his problems the way you, Gabe, Cam and I do for each other.''

''Sounds like he opened up to you. You should be happy about that.''

''I am. But I don't want him to get cold feet again. What do you think I should do?''

''I don't know. Reassure him that you're not trying to pressure him.'' Gail sipped her tea, then asked another question. ''*Are* you trying to pressure him?''

''Of course not.'' Cat sighed, drumming fingers on the table. ''That would be even dumber, especially since we agreed this was just a fling.''

Gail looked confused. ''But you told him you loved him. That doesn't sound like a fling.''

"To him it is. At least, I think it is. See, I told you I screwed up."

"How serious are you about this? I know you said you loved him, but you've been in love before. Remember Chad?"

Cat held up a hand. "Please, not while I'm eating."

Gail laughed. "Exactly the way I feel about my ex-husband." She tucked a strand of hair behind her ear and tilted her head, considering. "Well? Are you serious?"

She met her sister's eyes and nodded. "I think Mark could be the one, Gail." The only problem was, he didn't know it yet. "Buddy adores him. Follows him around and wants him to play. It's the sweetest thing. Mark pretends he doesn't like him, but I've caught him sneaking him treats and rubbing his chest feathers."

"You're going to let a bird choose the man in your life? You worry me, Cat."

"No, of course not. But I do trust his judgment. If I'd paid attention to Buddy, I'd never have gone through that whole disaster with Chad." Thinking about that, she frowned. "Maybe that's why I never warmed up to Kyle. You know how Buddy hates him." Remembering Buddy's latest trick, she laughed. "He's started calling him vile Kyle now. I don't know where he heard the word *vile*."

Gail laughed, too. "Oh, that's priceless. I'd give anything to see Kyle's face when he hears that."

"I hope he doesn't. He might fire me as his bookkeeper," Cat said glumly. "I still need the money."

"You know, I always thought that was strange. I mean, Kyle's an avian vet. You'd think your parrot would like him." Gail glanced at her watch. "Oh, wow, look at the time. I have to get back to work." She dug in her purse for money to cover her part of the tab. "I'm sorry I don't have any better advice about Mark."

"That's all right. I just needed to talk."

Gail patted her hand and rose. "Do you have a plan?"

Cat nodded. "It's a simple one. I'm just going to love him, and see what happens."

CHAPTER FIFTEEN

CAT WOKE UP EARLY Friday morning in Mark's arms, just as she had every morning since the night she'd told him she loved him. Light filtered through her window and splashed over the bed. Mark's eyes were the deep blue of the ocean, and just now, crowded with shadows.

"Have you been watching me sleep?" Several times over the past few days, she'd caught him looking at her that same way. Almost…wistfully. As if he couldn't quite believe she was there.

He smiled and the shadows fled. "Yeah. I like to look at you."

"I hope I wasn't drooling or something."

"Let me check." His head lowered and he kissed her. "Nope, no drool."

She laughed, wrapped her arms around him and returned the kiss. "It's still really early. Even Buddy's not awake. We don't have to get up yet, do we?"

"No. Cat—" He stopped and looked at her, his eyes solemn. "What?"

"Nothing," he said, but he looked sad.

"I love you," she told him, and pressed her mouth to his.

Later, after they'd made love, she thought he'd never been so tender with her. She wondered what caused a niggle of worry. She was in love. Deliriously happy. Why should anything go wrong?

THAT AFTERNOON, Cat's phone rang for what must have been the hundredth time. The unfinished work before her played on her guilt. She hadn't accomplished much. Mark had left, saying he had business to take care of, so she'd really had no excuse. No excuse except being in love and unable to concentrate.

Determined to finish something at least, she let the machine take the call. Her brother's voice could be heard over the clattering background noise.

"Damn it, Cat, pick up. It's about Gabe," Cameron said, "and it's bad. Pick up, I need your help." She snatched up the receiver, fumbled and punched on the phone.

"What's wrong?"

"Good, you're there. We've got trouble, serious trouble. Meet us down at the Scarlet Parrot as soon as you can."

"Cam, what is it? Should I call Gail?"

He hesitated, then said, "Not yet. She won't be able to find a sitter and this isn't a conversation that needs to happen in front of children."

"Maybe Mom could take the girls—" she began, but Cam cut her off with a sharp expletive.

"God, no, Mom's the last person we need to involve in this. She'll freak. Just meet us at the Parrot, ASAP. We'll fill Gail in later."

He sounded worried, even a bit frantic. Not at all like the cool, composed brother she knew. "You're scaring me, Cam. Is Gabe all right? Where are you? You sound like you're at the bottom of a well."

"I'm at the jail, bailing Gabe out."

Her fingers tightened on the receiver. "Jail? Gabe's in jail? What did he do?" She heard someone speaking to Cam, but couldn't make out what they said.

"Thanks, I'll be right there," Cam said, to the other person. "I've got to go, Cat. I'll tell you when I see you."

The line went dead, leaving Cat to stare at the receiver in total confusion. Why would Gabe be in jail? He didn't drink and drive. At least, not that she knew of, and besides, she thought, glancing at her watch, it was only five o'clock. She didn't think they threw you in jail for speeding, either. What could Gabe have done?

Forty-five minutes later, Gabe and Cameron walked into the bar together. By the time they arrived, Cat had assassinated two entire dishes of peanuts, along with three Diet Cokes. She rushed over and hugged Gabe, questions bubbling from her. "Are you all right? What in the world is going on? Cam had me frantic—''

Cam interrupted sharply. "Go to my office. I'll be there in a minute. I have to check on Sally," he said, referring to the waitress he'd left in charge.

Gabe detoured by the bar, snaring a glass and a bottle of Jack Daniel's whiskey. He'd yet to say a word, but the shock and devastation in his eyes told the story. This wasn't a minor problem, but something big.

Still silent, Gabe sat in the worn office chair behind the ugly metal desk stacked high with papers. He poured a shot of whiskey, tossed it back, poured another. Head in his hands, he muttered, "God, I can't believe this is happening to me."

Desperate for something to do, Cat straightened the papers on the desktop, darting worried glances at her brother as she did so. Finished with one stack, she glanced around for more, but the two ancient file cabinets against the wall appeared to be shut tight, and she couldn't do much to the computer sitting on Cameron's desk.

Cam entered a moment later with an extra chair for Cat. "Okay, let's have the story," he said to Gabe. "I thought I'd go nuts waiting for you to finish talking to your lawyer."

"First, someone tell me what the charges are," Cat said, sinking into the seat thankfully. "It's not DUI, is it?" Surely he wouldn't be drinking if it had been.

"No." Gabe gave a humorless laugh. "It's worse." With a flick of his wrist, he tossed back more liquor, slammed the glass down and met Cat's eyes. "Smuggling. Wild-animal smuggling. I think the actual charge is conspiracy to smuggle wild birds."

Stunned, Cat sat up straight and stared at Gabe. "You were arrested for smuggling birds? But...how? I don't understand. Don't they need proof?"

"Yeah, and they have it in spades." Gabe took another drink, and his hand trembled. Cat had never seen him so unsure, not even at the height of his gambling problems.

"They struck gold. They found hundreds of yellow-naped Amazon parrots in a fake gas tank strapped into the hold of *El Jugador*."

"Oh my God." Her hand covering her mouth, Cat stared at him. Smuggled birds in Gabe's boat?

"Start at the beginning," Cam said, sitting on the edge of the desk and crossing his arms, his eyes never leaving his brother. "Everything you remember."

"Believe me, it's all crystal clear. I wish to God I could forget it." He scrubbed his hands over his face, took in a deep breath and began. "Early this morning, I came back from a fishing tournament in Port Isabel. When I pulled into Aransas Bay, the Coast Guard stopped me and boarded my boat." He waved his hand, sloshing amber liquid onto the desk. "Hell, one of the guys was Robert Wells. I've known him since high school. I figured it was a routine inspection, no big deal." He banged his fist on the desk. "Routine, my butt. They knew what they were looking for. I'm sure of that."

"Go on," Cam said grimly.

"They didn't like the looks of the gas tank in the hold. The extra one I carry on long runs. So they opened it up, and bam, there they were." Clearly still stunned, he shook his head. "I couldn't believe it. Birds, hundreds of them, in a fake tank. Jammed in there like sardines, with their beaks taped shut. Drugged, I guess, or I would have heard something." He took another drink. "I thought I was going to puke. God knows how many made it out alive, but it couldn't have been a lot."

Sickened by the image he conjured, Cat struggled to make sense of his story. "How did the birds get there?"

"I don't know! I don't have a clue. I've been racking my brain since it happened, and I'm as clueless as I was when they first opened that sucker up." Halting, he held first Cat's gaze, then his brother's. "But I can tell you this, I didn't do it. I'm not a goddamn bird smuggler."

Cameron said quietly, "Come on, Gabe. Do you really think you have to tell Cat and me that? We know you're not capable of smuggling wildlife." He grasped his brother's hand. "You've screwed up before, but you'd never do anything like this."

"Sorry," Gabe said hoarsely. "I'm a little rattled right now."

"Who wouldn't be?" Cat asked. "And of course we don't think you did it. It's just—" She pressed her fingers to her temples. "I don't understand how this could have happened. The whole thing is ridiculous."

"If they convict me," Gabe said, his voice harsh and gritty, "this *ridiculous thing* can get me jail time. My lawyer said if they believe I'm conspiring, that my involvement is more than just a onetime deal, I could get up to five years hard time and a two-hundred-fifty-thousand-dollar fine."

Cat sucked in a breath. "Five…years?" she faltered.

His skin looked ashen. He nodded. "Sixty months. In prison."

Cat knew the penalties for smuggling illegal animals were harsh, and she agreed with them. But not when her brother was being wrongly accused. "How did you get the bail money?"

"They set bail at twenty-five thousand dollars. I came up with the twenty-five hundred for the bail bondsman," Cam said, and turned to Gabe. "Why was the bail set so low, when it's obviously a serious crime?"

"Oh, that's another kick," Gabe said, and laughed harshly. "My lawyer said they must think I'm going to lead them to more smugglers. They think I'll try to get in touch with my bosses.'' He smiled cynically. ''He very tactfully told me to watch who I associate with.''

Shocked, Cat asked, ''You mean your lawyer doesn't believe you're innocent?''

''Hell, why would he? Caught red-handed with the birds, and no way of explaining them? What would you think if you didn't know me?'' He grabbed the whiskey bottle and drank from it, tilting it back and letting the liquid slide down his throat. Long moments later, he set it down with a bang and wiped his mouth with the back of his hand.

With a glance at Cat, Cam took the bottle and moved it out of his reach. Cam hadn't spoken much, instead he'd appeared to be digesting Gabe's words. He shoved away from the desk and walked around it to stand in front of his brother. ''You say the Coast Guard seemed to know what they were looking for? You're certain it wasn't a random inspection?''

''Pretty damn sure. They didn't go through the usual routine. They got right down to the search. They weren't surprised when they found those birds, either. I was shocked as hell.''

''I guess we know who we have to thank for your arrest,'' Cam said, still looking at Gabe. They were both silent, then in unison, they turned to glare at Cat. ''Don't we, little sister?'' Cam asked softly.

Until that moment, the thought hadn't even occurred to Cat, but horror struck with Cam's question.

"No," she protested automatically, gripping the sides of the chair. "No, he's a game warden, he couldn't—"

"Game warden, my butt," Cam said. "Kincaid's an investigator, and he's looking for smugglers. The whole house thing was just a cover-up. A baseball bat to the head couldn't be any more obvious."

Gabe slammed his fist on the desk, so hard the bottle jumped. "Hell, yes, of course it was him. He knew where I'd be and when I was coming back. I told him myself, the night of Mom's party."

"You two have been real tight lately, haven't you?" Cam asked Cat, his gaze turning ferocious. "Damn it, Cat! He's been using you to get to Gabe all along."

Cat shook her head, not wanting to believe, but her stomach tightened with nausea.

Cam continued hammering the suspicions into her mind. "Problem is, you boyfriend's so dumb, he's investigating the wrong man. If he had the sense God gave a goat, he'd realize Gabe is being set up."

She wanted to throw up. "I'll talk to him. I'll ask him if he's involved. There must be an explanation..." Her voice trailed away. One explanation fit the facts. And they all knew it.

"I'll go with you," Cam said.

She jumped up and put a restraining hand on his chest. "No, you won't. You'll just try to beat him into a pulp and that won't help Gabe. No, I'm going alone.''

"I'll make the son of a bitch talk," Gabe promised grimly. "He's going to tell me why he thought those birds would be on my boat."

"Gabe, he won't." She put both hands on the desk and leaned forward, speaking earnestly. "If he's the one who had your boat searched, and he thinks there are others involved, then he's not going to talk to you." Or to me, either, she thought, but she intended to force him. "It won't help your case to hurt him, especially if he really is a special agent."

She let him digest that, then confronted Cameron. "Don't let Gabe do something stupid. And don't you, either. Promise me."

Cam's eyes blazed with anger. "Damn it, Cat, you can't expect me—"

"I expect you to do what's best for your brother," Cat interrupted. "And hitting an agent isn't it. Let me handle Mark. Besides—" She broke off, drew in a deep breath. "I need to talk to him alone."

For a long moment, Cam hesitated, then shrugged. "All right, you have a point. But don't count on me keeping my hands off him forever." He lowered his voice and added, "Don't forget, I owe him for you, too."

"Give me back that bottle," Gabe said. "For some reason, I have this urge to get drunk."

"You already are," Cam said with a wry smile, but he handed him the whiskey.

"I'll call you later," Cat said, preparing to leave. "Although I don't think it will do any good to talk to you by then," she told Gabe as she hugged him. "Have faith, Gabe. You're innocent, and that has to count for something." *Please God, let it count for something.*

Cam put a hand on her arm and pitched his voice low so that only she could hear. "I'm sorry. About Kincaid, I mean. I know you're tangled up with him."

Her throat closed so tight she couldn't answer, so she simply hugged him and left. Mark had lied to her. Used her to get to her own brother.

Worse, she still loved him.

MARK DIDN'T RETURN home until late that evening. He'd spent the day in interviews with the Coast Guard, the Sheriff's Department and the local Fish and Wildlife Service officers. Everyone involved in Gabe Randolph's case.

Randolph looked as guilty as sin, he thought as he let himself in the back door. And Mark was certain now he'd been set up. One of the Coast Guard officers, a lifelong friend of Gabe's, had been extremely vocal in his defense. But several hundred birds in a fake gas tank outweighed by a factor of ten any character witness Randolph could dream up.

The worse things seemed for Randolph, the better for Mark's team. His arrest would leave the real culprit believing the FWS had taken his bait.

So all Mark had to do now was prove that someone—and he'd bet his ass it was Kyle Peters—had framed Gabe Randolph. And he needed to do it before the real deal went down.

He flipped on the light and halted at the door. Cat sat in a chair at his kitchen table, legs crossed, fingers drumming on a piece of paper. She looked beautiful. And furious.

"Busy day?" she asked, rising slowly.

He didn't answer, for the simple reason he didn't know what to say.

She stopped in front of him. "I came over here praying you'd have an explanation I could live with. Even with the facts staring me in the face, I didn't want to believe them." Her laughter rang out, harsh and hollow. "I've been so stupid, buying every line you've fed me."

"What's going on, Cat?"

"I should have let Cam come pound you into the ground. But I wanted to talk to you first because I thought you'd be able to explain. That Gabe and Cam couldn't be right about you." She waved the paper in his face. "Then I found this. Gabe's boat's registration number. It was lying on that stack of papers," she said, indicating a pile she'd obviously tidied. "In plain sight, so don't think I went through

your drawers. That would be dishonest, wouldn't it?''
Her gaze heaped scorn on him. ''But you know all
about deceit, don't you, Mark? You're a regular master of it.''

''Why don't you tell me what you're talking
about?''

''I'm talking about you having my brother's boat
boarded today. I'm talking about Gabe being arrested
for smuggling birds, *Mr. Secret Agent*.'' She said the
last three words with a heavy bite of sarcasm.

He kept his expression stony. He couldn't confirm
or deny a thing. Not when pursuing an active investigation, and especially not to the suspect's infuriated
sister.

Angrily, she turned away, pacing the room before
coming back to him. ''Do you deny it? Are you denying that you had Gabe's boat boarded? That you're
in town to investigate smugglers?''

Leaning back against the counter, he crossed his
arms. ''I'm not denying anything. Or confirming anything.''

''I'm so dense, I never even connected you until
my brothers did.'' She crumpled up the note and
threw it at him. ''I guess this means you're not going
to tell me why you suspected Gabe. Why you had
the Coast Guard search his boat.''

Again, Mark said nothing. If Peters thought the
FWS and Coast Guard didn't believe Gabe guilty,

then he'd kill the real deal and they'd never have a chance to break the smuggling ring.

Cat whacked his chest with her fist. "I've got news for you, *Mr. Secret Agent.* Gabe is innocent. He's been set up. Why aren't you out there doing your job? Looking for the real culprit?"

"You're his sister. You're not exactly an objective witness. If your brother was arrested for smuggling, then the authorities must have had good reason."

"Someone framed him," she repeated. "They put those birds on his boat without his knowledge. I know him. Gabe would no more smuggle birds than I would."

"It's a moot point, Cat. I'm not involved in this investigation." There, now he'd added out-and-out lying to skirting the truth.

"I don't believe you."

"Your choice."

She fisted her hands on her hips. "You used me to get to my brother. You used me to get information." Tears glistened in her eyes but she didn't let them fall. "Wasn't it convenient of me to fall for you like a ton of bricks? Sleeping with me just made it that much easier for you to spy on my brother, didn't it?"

"That's not why—"

She interrupted swiftly. "That's not why you had an affair with me? Don't make me laugh, Mark. It's exactly why."

His heart twisted. He'd known almost from the beginning that she would believe he'd used her. Hearing her put it into words, hearing the pain in her voice, made the reality much, much worse.

"If you believe nothing else, believe that I didn't have an affair with you to get to your brother. I wanted you. I still do."

"Wasn't the sex enough? Damn you! Why did you have to make me fall in love with you?"

Tears rolled down her cheeks, each one a knife in his heart. He'd hurt her, lied to her, made her cry. And he could do nothing to change it. He took hold of her arms, wanting to pull her closer, knowing he didn't dare. "You're not the only one who fell. I'm in love with you, Cat."

She twisted away from him, staring at him with total disbelief. "Do you honestly expect me to believe you love me? After this?"

"I'm crazy in love with you."

She dashed away tears and looked him dead in the eye. "Then that's too damn bad, because I've just fallen *out* of love with you."

She slammed the door behind her.

Bright, really bright, Kincaid. Wait until she's furious and then tell her you love her. Like she's going to believe it?

CHAPTER SIXTEEN

MARK DIDN'T NEED ESP to know who pounded on his door at 8:00 a.m. the next morning. The only thing that surprised him was that Cameron Randolph had waited until morning to confront him.

He opened the door and the man stalked through. In silence, they measured each other for a long, intense moment. "The only reason you're not on the ground," Randolph said finally, his gaze as harsh as black ice, "is that I promised Cat I wouldn't hurt you. She thinks if I beat the hell out of a FWS special agent it wouldn't be good for our brother's case."

"It won't go any further than right here. Take your best shot," Mark offered, glad for the distraction.

Randolph's fists clenched, but he shook his head. "No, I'm not going to do it, not this time. I'll make this short, Kincaid. Are you too goddamn stupid to figure out a setup when you see one?"

"I told Cat and I'll tell you, I'm not involved in your brother's case." A big fat lie, but necessary. Even though none of the Randolphs would believe him. "If you think he's been framed, take it up with the Coast Guard."

"Say whatever you want, I know you're on Gabe's case. I know you're an investigator with the FWS, even if you won't admit it. What I don't know is why you're letting Gabe take the heat for this. The real smuggler's going free, while you're jacking around my brother."

"If Gabe is innocent, then it will come out," was all Mark said.

"You're damn right it will, and then you'll be exposed for the incompetent bastard you are. But while I'm here, there's something else I want to talk to you about. I can't force you to do the right thing for Gabe." He jammed his forefinger into Mark's chest and faced him squarely. "But Cat's a whole other story. If you *ever* touch my sister again, you're dead meat. Come within five hundred feet of her and you're mine."

"Don't you think that's her choice?" Not that he held any hope of her forgiving him. Not anytime, say, this century.

"That *is* her choice, bucko, and you're hearing it from me. You've had your fun, you've gotten what you wanted from her. So now I'm telling you, leave Cat the hell alone or I'll make damn sure your Romeo days are over. Permanently."

Great way to start the day, Mark thought. Nothing like having the brother of the woman you loved threaten to castrate you if you ever saw her again.

LATER THAT MORNING, Mark sat in a cramped office at the back of the Coast Guard facility in Corpus Christi. A beefy, sandy-haired man with a permanent tan sat across from him. Robert Wells, one of Gabe Randolph's arresting officers as well as his old friend, gave a snort of disgust and glared at Mark.

"I'm glad you called," Mark said, "because I needed to see you, as well. I wanted to yesterday, but you weren't here when I interviewed the other arresting officers. I need to know where Randolph might have picked up that load." The man's mutinous expression didn't bode well for cooperation. "In order to verify that he received the birds himself."

"Good luck, because you're not going to be able to verify anything. I'm telling you," Wells said, "I know Gabe Randolph, and he wouldn't smuggle birds. He doesn't have it in him. Somebody set him up to take a fall, plain and simple."

"I agree."

Wells started to continue, halted abruptly and stared at Mark. "You do?"

Mark nodded. "Yes, but I can't let Randolph know that's what I—or the FWS—believe. As far as the general public is concerned, we think he's guilty as hell."

"Why the charade?" Wells asked. "He's bound to be going crazy—"

"We're still trying to break the smuggling ring. That's our primary objective." Mark rubbed the back of his neck to get the kinks out. "It's necessary to my operation that the smuggler in Aransas City thinks he's safe now. Randolph's arrest will do that, we believe."

Wells frowned heavily. "So you're using Gabe to further your case. I don't like it. I don't like putting Gabe and his family through this crap. Do you know how I felt, having to arrest him?" He shook his head, looking upset. "I've known him since high school, for God's sake."

"We're using Randolph's arrest," Mark corrected, "not the man himself. Besides, what else would you have us do? At this time we don't have any proof that Randolph is innocent. He was caught red-handed with those birds in his boat."

"I already gave a statement about that. I saw Gabe's face when we found those birds. He's not that good an actor. He didn't have a clue they were there."

"Yeah, but the point is, we can't prove his innocence. Not yet." Wells started to say something, but Mark held up a hand. "For what it's worth, I don't like it, either," Mark said, thinking of Cat. "I don't like anything about it. But if Randolph's arrest will help us take down this ring, then he's just going to have to deal with it." He leaned forward, planting his hands on the desk in front of him. "Now, do you have anything concrete to justify your statement that

Randolph's being framed? I don't need a character witness, I need facts.''

"As a matter of fact, I do." Wells steepled his fingers and flashed Mark a wintry smile. "You put the Coast Guard onto him, but did you know the FWS also got a call? An anonymous tip about Randolph's boat bringing in an illegal load.''

Eyes narrowed, Mark sat up straighter. "No. I never heard a word. Why the hell didn't they tell me when I talked to them yesterday?''

Wells laughed. "Typical screwup. A new clerk took the call and she went home sick without telling anyone. We only found out this morning. That's why I called you in. A little too coincidental, wouldn't you say? Seems you weren't the only one interested in the contents of that boat.''

"Our man wanted to make sure somebody boarded Randolph's boat.''

"Seems like," Wells agreed. "You think you know who it is?''

"I've got a good guess going. But I need proof.''

"Why would anybody frame Gabe?''

"Diversion is my guess." Thinking, Mark stood and paced a few steps. "My team has information that points to an operation going down here either this weekend or the first part of next week. Randolph's arrest was likely intended to make us think that his load was the cargo we heard about. That way we won't be looking for anything else.''

"Makes sense. Another thing," Wells said, leaning back in his chair. "Ninety-five percent of the birds we found on Gabe's boat were dead. Not much money in that."

Mark nodded. "Happens all the time. It's one of the really lousy parts of my job. Seeing the waste." He rubbed the bridge of his nose and swore softly. "One thing that bothers me, though. It's an expensive frame job." Frowning, he looked at Wells. "Those Amazons wouldn't bring as much as some other species, but it's still not pocket change. These guys are greedy, I can't see them wasting a load of valuable birds, even to implicate someone else."

"Maybe when they first dreamed up their scheme they didn't plan to use as many. Just enough to get him busted. Then this bunch turns up mostly dead, so they figured why not, and used them instead."

"Good point. It could have happened that way. But we're still speculating. I need to know where Randolph picked up that fake gas tank. And since I'm still theoretically undercover, I can't ask him where he gassed up." Not that he'd be likely to talk to Mark, anyway. "The last place is the most logical, so he'd have less time to discover the switch. Can you find out?"

"Hell, I don't have to ask him. Not if you're looking for the closest stop. Red Covey's place here in Corpus. Can't miss it, it's under the causeway bridge.

Cheap diesel. Red's been around forever. Gabe goes there all the time.''

RED COVEY was a huge hulk of a man in his late sixties, with grizzled dark hair, leathery skin and green eyes permanently bloodshot from squinting across the ocean into the harsh coastal sun. He punctuated his Texas drawl by shooting an occasional stream of tobacco juice in the general direction of a coffee can. It didn't appear to faze him when Mark introduced himself as an officer with the FWS.

Mark had debated the wisdom of interviewing the man himself, but decided the risk of discovery was low, especially if he gave a false name. For all the owner knew, Mark was simply an FWS flunky.

Thanks to the grapevine, Red had already heard the news about Gabe Randolph being arrested and carted off to jail. ''Musta been a mistake,'' Red told Mark, leading him inside a murky room filled with marine supplies, foodstuffs and what had to be the grimiest sailfish Mark had ever seen, hanging on the wall with an old fishing cap perched on its head.

The old man gestured at a decrepit chair, and took his own seat in an equally battered rocker. ''I sold that boy his first fishin' pole. He used to work here summers when he was growin' up. The boy's no smuggler. Drugs, wasn't it?'' He spat explosively. ''Nope, I don't believe a word of it.'' After setting his can down, he wove his fingers together over his stomach.

The grapevine had it wrong. Or else Red was playing dumb. If the switch had taken place here, Mark thought, then he could be involved in the scheme. "Not drugs. Birds."

Red shrugged. "Birds, drugs, whatever. Boy's no smuggler, I tell ya."

Randolph was around Mark's age, hardly a boy. But he supposed to someone who had dandled you on his knee, you remained young for a long time. "I'd like to ask you some questions about yesterday. Did you wait on Gabe Randolph yourself?"

"Well…" Red scratched his nose and thought about that. "Can't say as I did. He came in and jawed with me, like he always does, but I didn't gas up *El Jugador*. That woulda been George."

"Is George available for me to talk to?"

"Will be when he gets back from his break. Might not do you much good, though." He winked. "George ain't the brightest kid I ever had work for me, but he tries."

"How long would it take to gas a boat the size of Randolph's?"

"Depends." He scratched again, spit again. "Maybe twenty minutes, maybe more. Gabe didn't seem to be in any hurry," he offered.

"Where did you talk? In here?"

"Yup. Always do."

His glance around the dark interior of the store held pride of ownership. Given the shape it was in, Mark couldn't imagine why.

"Randolph stayed with you the entire time the boat was being serviced?" Red nodded and Mark asked another question. "Does he usually keep an eye on the boat while it's fueling?"

Red picked his teeth and considered that a moment. "Nah, why would he? Even George can fill up gas tanks."

"How did Randolph seem to you? Nervous? Distracted?"

"Nope. Fact is, he came in full of tournament talk. Seems his client caught the winning marlin." He slapped his leg and laughed. "Got hisself a bonus, he said, and offered to buy me a brew if I'd come to his brother's bar."

"Did you have other customers at the same time as Randolph?"

The old man sat up straighter and pinned him with a glare. "Not as I can recall. And so what if I did?"

"Just trying to establish the sequence of events, Mr. Covey."

"Now, listen here, sonny, you're beginnin' to get on my nerves. Sounds to me like you're fishin' and I don't much like what you're trollin' for. What are you tryin' to say, that you think Gabe took on that load of whatever the hell it was at my place of business?"

"It's a possibility," Mark said. "That's one of the things I'm investigating."

"You're sayin' *I* had something to do with it?" he demanded incredulously.

"I'm not accusing you of anything, Mr. Covey." Having talked to the old man now, Mark's gut instinct told him Red had nothing to do with framing Gabe Randolph. "But I do have to check out all the possibilities."

"Possibilities?" His voice rose in wrath. "I'll give you possibilities, you son of a bitch!" He bounded to his feet with fists clenched. "Put 'em up, sonny. I may be old, but I can wipe the floor with you with one hand tied behind my back."

Mark didn't laugh. The old man was big as a tree and no doubt tough as an old bootstrap. He suspected if Red landed one of those punches, it would hurt like hell. "There's no need for that, Mr. Covey. As I said, I'm not accusing you, I'm simply looking into the matter." He waited a beat to let his words sink in. Red subsided, apparently somewhat mollified.

After a moment, Mark continued, "There's another scenario, one I believe is more likely. Your place could have been used for the transfer without your knowledge. Without Randolph's knowledge, for that matter."

Covey's eyes widened with realization. "Somebody used my station to— And used Gabe's boat to— Used my place of business to—" His complexion ruddier by the moment, he broke off, too furious to continue.

Taking hold of himself, he said, "By God, they better not have or I'll know the reason why." He stood for the moment, mental wheels turning, then spun and strode out the screen door, slamming it behind him with a bang.

"George! Where the hell are you? Get your scrawny butt in here right now!"

He reentered and gave a decisive nod in Mark's direction. "We'll get to the bottom of this. George ain't smart enough to think this up on his own, you know. But he'd be an easy man to use." His head shook regretfully. "Too dumb to live, that boy is."

A gangly teenager with bad skin and a vacuous expression entered the room. "Did you want me, Red? I still have five minutes to go on my break. And I didn't smoke near them gas tanks, neither," he added virtuously.

"Thank God for small favors," Red muttered. "George, I'm gonna ask you a question, and I want the truth when you answer. Did you put anything on Mr. Randolph's boat yesterday when he was fueling up?"

If anything, the kid's expression grew blanker. "Yes, sir. I put the fuel in, like he asked me."

"Did you do anything else?" Mark asked.

"Well, just switched out the empty extra tank, like the man told me." He scratched his head. "I said I could've filled it in the hold, but he didn't want me to. Said it had to be replaced with the one he gave me.''

''What man?'' Mark asked sharply.

Adam's apple bobbing, George said, ''It was Dr. Peters. The vet from over there at Aransas Pass.'' A chagrined expression crossed his face. ''Dang it, I forgot! He told me not to tell no one, and for sure not tell Mr. Randolph. Dr. Peters didn't want him to know nothing about it.'' He slapped his forehead in dismay. ''Dad blame it, I forgot I wasn't supposed to tell no one. He even gave me fifty bucks so I wouldn't. I wonder if I have to give it back now?''

He looked from his employer, staring at him with openmouthed shock, to Mark's expressionless face. ''Did I do something wrong?''

As bad as it was, Mark had a hard time not laughing. The poor kid didn't have a clue what he'd done. ''Didn't you find it odd that Dr. Peters would ask you to do something to another man's boat? Without his knowledge? And then pay you to keep quiet?''

George looked increasingly befuddled. ''Heck, mister, it was fifty bucks. I didn't think about nothing but spending it.''

Red put his hand on the boy's shoulder. ''Son, I'm afraid you're in a boatload of trouble.''

''Unfortunately, that's true. I'm going to have to take you in for questioning, George.'' To the old man Mark added, ''The fact that he came forward willingly will work in his favor. And I'll put in a good word for him.''

"I'd better go with him," Red said. "Just let me close up shop and I'll be right along.'' In an aside to Mark he added, "His parents ain't none too smart, neither. Be better if I'm there.''

Mark knew where to place the majority of the blame. On Kyle Peters's soon-to-be-arrested head.

Before he took George in, he made a call to the FWS. "Put a tail on Peters. He's the one.''

CHAPTER SEVENTEEN

So MUCH FOR that vow, Cat thought that evening, tossing a tissue into the trash can by her desk. She'd sworn she wouldn't cry over Mark. Told herself she'd only been infatuated and would get over him in no time.

It wasn't true, though, and she knew it. She would never get over him.

But she couldn't hate him. Not totally. Because even if she didn't like Mark's methods, she believed in his job. Through her work with the FWS, she knew that the illegal exotic-animal trade was a huge industry worldwide. Wild animal populations, particularly birds, were being decimated at a tremendous rate, many of them pushed to the brink of extinction. She wanted Mark, and other professionals like him, to stop the people responsible for the devastation.

But she didn't intend to watch her innocent brother go to jail for a crime he didn't commit. And she didn't enjoy being used and betrayed by the man she loved, either.

Her doorbell rang and Buddy trilled in imitation.

Grasping at anything to distract her from her misery, even a 9:30 p.m. business call, she answered it.

"Is this a bad time?" Kyle asked when she opened the door. "I know it's after work hours, but I brought some receipts for you." He paused, and added, "If you'd rather I come back tomorrow, I will."

"No, that's all right." She let him inside. "Buddy's out in the living room, though, and I don't feel like chasing him down. We'd better go to the office."

Upon spying the vet, Buddy began hurling curses from his perch. "Kyle is vile," he shrieked at the top of his lungs. "Vile Kyle, vile Kyle."

Cat cringed with embarrassment at the parrot's latest invective, feeling especially guilty because she'd laughed the first time he'd said it, undoubtedly encouraging him. "Don't pay any attention to Buddy. I don't know what's gotten into him lately," she said uneasily.

Kyle followed her into the office and closed the door, muffling Buddy's taunts. "He seems to like me less each time I see him. I wish I knew what I'd done to make him dislike me so much." He set a large manila envelope down on her desk, then turned to look at her closely.

"Cat, what's wrong?"

She hunched a shoulder, then finally said, "It shows, huh?"

"That you've been crying? Yes." He put his hands

on her shoulders and gazed at her in concern. "Tell me what's wrong. You look like you could use a friend."

Reminded of what she'd said to Mark not long ago, she began tearing up. Not trusting her voice, she shook her head.

"Sometimes it helps to talk."

Cat burst into tears. Kyle put his arms around her and let her cry on his chest, making comforting noises and patting her back. Eventually she pushed herself away from him, too drained to be embarrassed any longer. Picking up a box of tissues, he handed them to her, saying nothing while she mopped her eyes and blew her nose.

"Thanks." She blew her nose again and attempted a smile. "I thought I was through, but apparently not."

"It's Kincaid, isn't it?" His mouth turned grim when she didn't deny it. "What did he do to you?"

"Had my brother arrested, for starters." At Kyle's exclamation of surprise, she nodded and continued, "I'm surprised you haven't heard. Gabe was arrested yesterday for smuggling birds."

"I hadn't heard a thing. Good God. That sounds serious. You say Kincaid's responsible?"

"Yes. It's bad, Kyle." She added sharply, "I don't have to tell you Gabe didn't do it."

"Of course not."

Eyes narrowed, she crossed her arms over her

chest. "Mark thinks he did. That's why he cozied up to me. He wanted to get to my brother."

"Good Lord, Cat, I can hardly believe—"

"It's true," she cut in. "Humiliating but true." She sank into her chair, spent of emotion for the moment. "Not that he'll admit he's involved or that he had anything to do with Gabe's arrest."

"I always thought Kincaid was up to something. A little too shady for my liking. Sorry you had to find out in such a painful way."

She pressed her fingers to her eyes. "It gets worse. Mark doesn't believe Gabe was framed. Won't even look for anyone else."

Kyle made a sympathetic noise. "Is the evidence against your brother so clear-cut?"

"Yes." She laughed humorlessly. "They caught him red-handed with a load of birds in his boat." As she said the last words, she glanced up at Kyle. She could swear she saw a gleam of satisfaction in his eyes, but it faded so quickly she decided she must have imagined it. "And whether he admits it or not, I know we can thank Mark for that arrest."

"Kincaid's not worth your tears." Kyle cupped his fingers around her chin, then trailed them over her cheek. "Maybe you'll give me another chance now," he murmured. "What do you say, Cat?" Before she realized his intent, he bent his head and gave her a lingering kiss that did nothing but inspire mild distaste. "I can make you forget Mark Kincaid ever existed."

Not in a million years, she thought. She smiled wanly, not quite meeting his eyes. "Thanks, Kyle, but I don't think so. At the moment, I'm sort of sour on men."

"If you change your mind, you've got my number." His fingers stroked her cheek one last time before his hand dropped.

Reminding herself how nice he'd been, she tried not to be irritated, but it was no use. The last thing she needed right now was to fend off a pass.

"Well, I'd better be going. How about walking me out? Protect me from your bird," he added with a laugh.

After a few choice words from Cat, Buddy subsided into a mostly silent sulk. Cat knew she'd pay for it by having to endure his pouting, but her head pounded and she just couldn't deal with the noise. As they reached the door, she smiled at Kyle. "The shoulder helped. Sorry I cried all over you."

"I consider it an honor. Tell Gabe good luck. There can't be anything much worse than being caught by the FWS with a load of yellow-naped Amazons."

Confused, Cat gazed at him a moment. "I thought you said you hadn't heard the news?"

"I hadn't. Not until you told me."

"Then how did you know what kind of—" As

comprehension dawned, she dropped her gaze swiftly
and reached for the door, turning her back on Kyle.
"Thanks again. You were sweet to let me cry all over
you," she babbled.

Cat hadn't mentioned which species of bird Gabe
had supposedly been smuggling. So how had Kyle
known? Unless he was the one who'd put them there.
Which must mean...Kyle Peters had framed her
brother?

"Don't open the door yet, Cat," he said, his voice
pleasant and deep.

Cat turned around slowly. Kyle held a gun, the
barrel pointing directly at her chest. "What gave me
away?"

She stared at him and the gun in shock. "I never
said what kind of birds they were."

"That wasn't very bright of me, was it?" he asked,
his tone conversational. Just a shade regretful. "I
can't afford to have you running to your erstwhile
lover with the news that I'm responsible for Gabe's
difficulties with the law."

"I don't— I wouldn't— Don't point that thing at
me." *My God,* was all she could think. *Kyle Peters
is holding me at gunpoint.*

"Yes, you would. That's the first thing you'd do."
Still smiling pleasantly, he stepped forward and
touched the gun barrel to the center of her chest, nest-
ling it between her breasts.

Her mind raced, searching for a way out, but she

was so scared, so astonished at the rapid turn of events, she could hardly think.

"Too bad I'm going to have to do more than point this thing at you." Stroking the barrel lovingly across her breast, he added, "You're a beautiful woman, Cat. I really did want a taste of you."

She couldn't prevent a shudder of revulsion.

He laughed. "Oh, get over yourself, Cat. I'm a smuggler not a rapist."

"And a murderer." She stared at him in disbelief, at the burnished blond hair, the handsome face, the charming manner, even when threatening to kill her.

The gun bobbed, conceding her point. "A reluctant one, but yes."

"Why?"

"Why do I do it?" He smiled, enjoying himself. "Why do you think? I'd say the answer's obvious."

"How can you be a party to bird smuggling? You know smugglers' methods, you know what harm you're doing. You know how many of those birds die in the process. You're a vet, for God's sake. You're supposed to be saving animals, not causing their deaths."

"Come on, Cat, you're a smart woman. Figure it out."

Wondering how she'd ever thought she knew him, she shook her head.

"Money. One hell of a lot of money. I have a shipment coming in tonight at eleven-thirty. A ship-

ment of one hundred palm cockatoos that, once dis-
tributed, will be worth around seven hundred thousand dollars." The gun touched her chest again, and
Kyle's eyes hardened. "Think about it. Seven hundred thousand dollars," he repeated slowly, dis-
tinctly. "No one is going to screw that up for me.
Not even if it means I have to kill you."

WHY COULDN'T PETERS be easy to find? Mark wondered on his way home. It had taken several hours to
process George and fill in both the sheriff and the
local FWS about the latest developments on the case.
The tail they'd put on Peters—a part-time cop named
Winslow—had yet to locate him. Mark wanted the
vet found, and found fast, before the deal went down.
For all they knew, it could be taking place right now.

He punched in Winslow's cell phone number.
"Any luck?" he asked when the man answered.

"I was about to call. Found him just a minute ago.
His car, at any rate. Parked outside his accountant's
house. Pure luck I saw it, I'd checked maybe fifteen
minutes before and it wasn't there."

Cat's house. Damn, why did he have to be there?
Peters could have a hundred reasons to see Cat, half
of them perfectly legitimate, but Mark didn't like it.
He didn't want the man anywhere near her. "Any
signs of activity?"

"No."

"All right, I'm headed that way, about ten minutes

out. Keep me apprised of any further developments. Anything at all, got it?''

"Will do."

Three minutes later, when his phone rang, Mark had thought of enough scenarios, from bad to truly horrendous, to scare the hell out of him.

"Peters and the girl are leaving the house," Winslow said.

Mark's stomach tightened. He had a bad feeling, a very bad feeling about this. "What do they look like? What's their manner? Is she under duress?"

"Hard to say. He's got her snugged up against him, I'll say that. Good thing the moon's full, or I couldn't see a thing. No sign of a weapon, as yet."

But that didn't mean the vet didn't have one. Though Cat didn't know of Mark's suspicions, she did keep Peters's books. What if she'd found something suspicious and asked him about it? Cat tended to blurt things out first and think about them later... Swearing silently, he sped up.

"Bad news," Winslow's disembodied voice said a moment later. "They're getting into his Jag, from the passenger side. She's crawling through to the driver's side."

"Goddamnit!" Mark slammed his fist down on the steering wheel. "The son of a bitch is abducting her!" And Mark couldn't do a thing to stop him.

"Odds are," the cop agreed. "Not the usual way

to get into a car, is it? I can try to approach the vehicle—"

"Negative. Too risky. At this time, we have to assume he's got a gun. I'm calling for backup." Tucking the phone between his ear and shoulder, he reached into his shirt pocket for the two-way radio, talking rapidly to Winslow as he did. "Keep them in view, and for God's sake, don't let him spot you. Peters knows my car. You'll have to give me directions so I can stay out of his sight. Let me know as soon as they're on the road."

He broke off to speak into the radio. "Requesting assistance. Take it to private." Switching over to the private channel, he continued, and with each word his fear for Cat increased.

"Abduction in progress. Repeat, abduction in progress. Officer Winslow and Agent Kincaid in pursuit and requesting backup. Do you copy?"

They copied, all right. But as short-staffed as the sheriff's department and the local FWS office were, and with any other police assistance half an hour away, minimum, Mark pegged the chances of getting the help he needed at about ten percent. If that.

Cat's life was in danger. Her best hope, possibly her only hope, lay in the hands of a part-time cop and him. Mark Kincaid, an FWS special agent with a lot of experience busting smugglers, and none at all in halting an abduction. A man who was very much in love with the kidnapper's victim.

WHY THE HELL did I get in the car with him? Cat asked herself. She should have made a scene, screamed at the top of her lungs, thrown a convulsive fit outside her front door, anything except get into a car with the man holding a gun on her. She was an idiot.

"Shit, Cat, can't you do better than that?" Kyle snarled at her as the Jaguar shuddered and lurched forward. "If a cop stops us because of your driving, I promise you'll be sorry."

Tightening her sweaty hands on the wheel, she threw him a look of disgust. "Oh, excuse me. I hadn't realized driving well was a requirement for being abducted. I'm nervous. Sue me." The car surged forward, halted, shuddered and moved forward again, rubber squealing as it did so.

"Damn it, nobody drives this badly. You're doing it on purpose. Stop it." He pressed the gun against her side and dug it into her ribs. "I mean it."

"I can't help it! You know I don't drive very well at the best of times." Her fingers clenched into a white-knuckled grip on the steering wheel. "How do you expect me to function now, when I'm scared to death?"

He cursed, but backed off.

They continued, with an occasional order from Kyle, punctuated by more curses about her driving. Cat frantically tried to think of a way out of the mess she still couldn't believe she'd stepped into.

Her gaze darting away from the street for a moment, she shot him a sideways glance. "You said you didn't want to kill me. You don't have to, you know."

"How do you figure that? Turn left at the next corner."

Where were they going? she wondered. The industrial waterfront, consisting of abandoned warehouses, dilapidated docks, and for all she knew, drug deals galore, wasn't an area of Aransas City she frequented.

"You're not planning to stay in town longer, are you?" she asked him. "Aren't you leaving after tonight?"

"I hadn't decided. Possibly. But Aransas City has been good to me. I've made a lot of money in the past two years."

Stifling nausea, she tried not to think about how many birds had passed through his destructive hands. "Mark's going to realize that Gabe was framed. Then things could become dangerous for you. I think you should leave town. Tonight, after your deal, if not before."

"You're giving Kincaid more credit than he deserves," Kyle scoffed, his tone superior. "You said yourself he's convinced your brother did it."

"He might change his mind. Investigate further. Can you take that chance?"

"Say that I do get out of town, so what? I can't leave you here to spill everything you know."

"Why not? I don't know where you're going. All you have to do is make certain I can't talk until after you're long gone."

He hesitated, then shrugged. "By then you'll know too much. You'll have seen my contacts, seen the deal going down. Sorry, Cat, you're too much of a liability alive."

From his tone, she'd have thought he was discussing the weather. Could he really be that callous? How could she get through to him? Make him see reason? The longer she kept him talking, kept him thinking about ways not to kill her, the better.

"You could take me with you."

"Stop here," he said, ignoring her last words. "Right here, behind this building."

She parked the car where he indicated, in the deep shadows of an abandoned warehouse. He forced her out of the car, taking her arm in a painful grip.

"Kyle, did you—did you hear me?"

"I heard you. What's in it for me? Give me a reason to take you with me." He walked rapidly toward the building, dragging her along with him. She realized with a sick start that he was a lot bigger and stronger than she'd ever given him credit for.

"I'm an accountant, I can tell you all sorts of ways to hide money."

"More likely you'd get me caught on purpose. Try again."

"The birds. I could—" Choking, she made herself finish, "I could help you with them."

"Not good enough. Try again."

An undercurrent of enjoyment rang in his voice. *He's getting a rush from having me at his mercy,* she realized. She forced herself to say it, a last, desperate attempt to delay the inevitable. Out of ideas, she whispered, "You said you wanted me."

Kyle stopped walking and pocketed the gun. In the moonlight she saw the feral grin that slashed his face. He grabbed her, pulled her tightly against him, his arms hurtful bands around her. One hand raised to bracket her throat, as if to throttle her. His voice emerged, husky and evil on a whisper of wind. "That sounded like an offer to share your body with me, Cat. Was it?"

Afraid she'd throw up, she nodded. Out of self-defense, her thoughts veered away. She closed her eyes, willing herself not to shudder. *Be strong,* she told herself. *Convince him not to kill you.*

He kissed her brutally, grinding his mouth over hers, thrusting his tongue inside. She told herself not to fight him, told herself to respond to him, but when he didn't stop, she began to struggle against him, desperate to get away. Finally, years later, he released her.

They stared at each other in the shifting moonlight, his eyes glittering wildly, his breathing labored. He was, unmistakably, turned on.

"You can't even kiss me like you want me," he said savagely. "Do you think I'm so stupid I'll believe you want to have sex with me?" He pulled the gun out of his pocket, jamming it into her side as he grasped her arm and jerked her along with him. "You'd run at the first chance, and lead the cops straight to me."

Flinging open the door, he gestured with the gun. "Get in the damn warehouse. Now, before I decide to take you up on your tempting offer." He smiled, an evil, twisted smile. "One last fling before you die."

He means it, Cat thought, truly believing for the first time that unless a miracle occurred, Kyle Peters would kill her.

CHAPTER EIGHTEEN

FROM THE MURKY shadows of an abandoned building several yards away, Mark and Winslow saw Peters haul Cat up against him and kiss her. Enraged, Mark sprang forward, but he halted even as he felt the other man's hand on his arm, restraining him.

His fists clenched and his blood heated to a rapid boil as he watched the vet manhandle her, yet he knew he could do nothing to stop Peters. *You're going to pay, Peters,* he swore silently, *for everything you've done.*

But saving Cat came first. Because if he couldn't save Cat, then nothing else mattered.

"Guess we know what his plans are for after the deal goes down. Must not have had time before they left," Winslow said, shaking his head as they watched them enter the building. "At least that means he isn't likely to kill her right away. Not until he's had his fun."

"Plans can change," Mark said grimly, "and I intend to change his. He's going to pay for ever laying a finger on her." For abducting her, scaring her, hurting her. For framing her brother. Peters would pay, for all that and more.

"That threat sounds personal."

"It is. Believe me, it is."

"He's definitely got a gun," Winslow said. "I saw him pocket it before he grabbed her. That's why I stopped you from going after them."

"I know." He'd known it from the first, with a sick feeling in his gut.

Both men studied the warehouse where Cat and Peters had disappeared a few moments before. Tempted to rush in, Mark forced himself not to, but instead analyzed the situation as quickly as he could. He made a mental note of at least two entrances, and a couple of broken windows. Breaking in shouldn't present a problem. Once inside was a different matter.

"Do you have experience in hostage situations?" Mark asked Winslow, afraid he knew the answer.

The cop shook his head. Middle-aged, brown-haired, with a doughnut belly, Winslow seemed like an average small-town cop. Not stupid by any means, he appeared solid and unpretentious, but not necessarily capable of handling a major crime.

As if to confirm Mark's thoughts, he said, "Aransas City doesn't run to much serious crime, not like Corpus and the bigger cities. Mostly I deal with drunks and domestic disturbances. Occasionally some petty theft." After another glance at the warehouse, he turned to Mark, brightening. "But I learned about hostage situations at the academy."

Cop school. Fifteen or twenty years ago, Mark thought. No way was he letting this man take charge. "This isn't a classroom. And that woman in there—" the woman he loved "—is in danger of losing her life if we screw this up."

"I realize that, Kincaid." Winslow cast another worried glance at the building. "Maybe we should wait for backup. He's armed and dangerous, with a hostage. I think we need a SWAT team."

In Aransas City? Mark thought. Fat chance. "The closest SWAT team is thirty or forty miles away. Without a miracle, we won't have backup at all, much less a SWAT team. Not in time. It's up to you and me. We have to get the hostage to safety as soon as possible. The longer we wait, the greater her danger."

"But we can't just bust in there—"

"Damn it, Winslow! Her chances of dying increase with every minute we stand here talking! Peters is about to take on a cargo of smuggled birds, and we're not talking spare change. Once his associates show up, anything can happen. Anything, including a gunfight, with her in the middle of it."

"Still, we need backup," the cop insisted.

Mark realized he'd made his decision long before. "I'm through arguing." He pulled his weapon, a Glock 29 10mm auto, from the holster in the small of his back and checked it. "I radioed our location when we arrived. They'll be here when they get here. I want you to call in again and reiterate the need for a silent run. I don't want to spook Peters. He's bound to be jumpy, waiting for this bundle."

Winslow shook his head dubiously, but didn't interrupt when Mark continued. "Then I want you to keep an eye out for the people Peters is meeting. Most likely they'll bring the cargo in by water. I don't know why he'd be here, otherwise."

The cop looked up from checking his own weapon. "What are you going to do? Do you have a plan?"

"Yeah. It's simple." He looked at the building, his gaze hardening with resolve. "My plan is to go in that warehouse and get the woman I love the hell out of there."

MARK GAINED ENTRY with no problem, and located Cat and Peters just as easily by following the sound of their voices. Then his luck wavered. Instead of tying up Cat and leaving her alone, in preparation for his meeting, Peters dragged her around by the arm, proudly showing off his facility.

From his hiding place, behind a partially closed door in one of two adjoining rooms, Mark could see both of them. Cat looked shaken, but thank God, she was alive and as far as he could tell, unhurt. And growing angrier by the minute, which Mark thought was a good thing.

Most of the warehouse was in keeping with the exterior, broken glass and trash everywhere, pieces of pipe lying around, dirt and disorder the norm. But the room he found Cat and Peters in was a whole different story.

Brightly lit and sparkling clean, on first glance it looked more like a zoo's aviary than a smugglers' operation. Rows of cages filled with perches, clean straw shavings, water bottles and food trays stood against one long wall, plainly awaiting the next cargo of birds.

Veterinary supplies were stacked high on a shelf, a stainless-steel exam table stood in one corner of the room. No backstreet, small-time operation this, but a place through which the man could run thousands of illegal birds.

"What is this?" Cat asked, looking around, her eyes shocked and haunted. "I've never seen anything like it."

"It is impressive, I think," Peters said smugly. "And I did it all myself, for obvious reasons. I suppose you'd call it a halfway house. The birds make their way here, I work my magic on them and—"

Cat's sickened exclamation had him smiling. "The birds are no use to me dead, Cat, after all. I make sure they're healthy and then send them on their way to hundreds of bird lovers."

Cat said something Mark couldn't hear. Peters's eyes narrowed, and he took hold of her chin with his free hand, pinching her cheek. "Watch that smart mouth, honey. Your death doesn't have to be easy or clean. My associates wouldn't think twice about sampling a tasty pigeon like you, willing or not." She paled and a sadistic smile widened his mouth. "Three of them," he added. "Think about that, Cat, and then I'd say you owe me an apology."

Mark blocked his anger, concentrating instead on how to move Cat out of harm's way. All he needed was one clear shot, to take Peters out.

"I'm...sorry," she finally whispered.

"Not very gracious, but I suppose that will do. Now, where was I?" the vet asked, and dragged her away to admire more of his toys.

Cat didn't remain silent for long, interrupting his self-satisfied monologue. "They're going to know you killed me. You'll be a fugitive the rest of your life. Is that what you want? To be on the run forever?"

Good girl, Mark thought. Keep talking logic.

"No one will know. Really, Cat, you'd say anything at this point." He sounded slightly put out.

She continued to bang away. "I left my house with you. In your car. Someone will have seen. And I didn't put Buddy back in his cage. Once Mark knows that, he'll know something's wrong. Then it will be just a matter of time before everyone figures out you're the one who killed me."

"You're forgetting there's trouble in paradise."

Peters wagged a finger in her face. "Kincaid isn't likely to bother with you, not when he has your brother. Gabe's the one he wanted, after all."

She shrugged, not responding to the dig. "The police then. Because if you think my family won't realize something funny's going on and drag the police into it, you're crazy."

"It won't matter if they do," Peters said. "Not once it's obvious that your brother isn't the only one involved in bird trafficking."

Peters turned his back to Mark, leaving Cat directly facing him. He'd never have a better chance, he thought, and pushed the door open just far enough to show himself to her. Just quickly enough to signal her to get out of the way the minute she could.

Her eyes widened, and she looked stunned, but Mark hoped Peters would attribute that to what he'd just said.

"Wh—what are you talking about?" she asked a little breathlessly.

"Didn't I tell you?" Toying with her now and obviously enjoying it, he grew more careless with his gun, letting it dangle from his hand rather than point directly at her. "You're involved up to your neck in a smuggling ring. You must have gotten greedy and tried to rip someone off. That's why you buy it during the exchange."

Cat stared at him a moment, then burst out laughing. Peters didn't seem to notice her edging closer to the door behind her, but Mark did, and silently cheered her on.

"No one will believe I'm smuggling birds. No one who knows me."

"No? Then ask the FWS why they haven't given you any birds since your brother found those Amazons on his doorstep."

Her eyes widened. "You're the one who put them there, aren't you? I should have realized. You've been framing Gabe all along, haven't you?"

The vet smiled, nodded. "He seemed the most logical choice. And you *are* his sister. So don't be too sure no one will think you're guilty."

"Mark won't," she said, and dived out of the way.

Peters squeezed off a shot the instant before Mark's bullet caught him in the right arm, spinning him around. The vet's mouth fell open. In total shock, he stared at Mark as blood began to pour down his arm and his pistol hand sagged.

Mark trained his gun on the center of the man's chest. "Drop your weapon! Slowly. Do it! Before my finger slips on this trigger."

Still openmouthed, Peters released the gun and it fell to the floor with a clatter.

"Kick it over here, easy," Mark commanded.

A cunning expression replaced the surprise as the vet started to obey.

"Try something," Mark invited him, both hands wrapped around the gun, arms held straight in front of him. "Give me half a reason to kill you. And if you hit Cat with that round you got off, praying's not going to help you."

Apparently, Peters believed him, because he did as Mark told him. Keeping him under cover, Mark picked up the vet's weapon and stuffed it into his holster. "Cat? Answer me, Cat, are you all right?" The longest moments of his life passed before he heard her shaky reply.

"I'm okay. Can I come out now?"

Relief swept through him like a riptide. "Let me cuff Peters first."

"I'm bleeding," the man protested as Mark forced him to the floor and cuffed his hands behind his back. "I'm in pain, I could be dying."

"Yeah, too bad I'm fresh out of sympathy. You'll live, it's just a flesh wound." Mark leaned close and spoke very softly in his ear. "You're one lucky bastard to be going to prison, Peters. You'd better hope you stay there for a long, long time. Because what I want to do to you makes prison look like paradise."

"You're threatening me! That's illegal!"

"Tell it to a lawyer," Mark advised. "And don't move. Not one inch, you got it?" The vet nodded, and babbling agreement, subsided into a moaning mess.

"Cat, it's safe. You can come out now."

She peeked around the door, and the next thing he knew she'd launched herself at him, her arms clamping around his neck in a convulsive grip. He clasped her against him with one arm, the other still holding the gun on Peters. He wanted to kiss her desperately, but he couldn't take the chance that Peters would bolt.

"How did you know?" she asked in a choked whisper, her cheeks wet against his neck. "I didn't think anyone would know he'd—he'd abducted me."

"We had a tail on him and saw him take you. I'll tell you all about it later. I promise, you'll hear everything. Cat—" He stopped, knowing he couldn't afford to let his emotions take over.

He gazed into her eyes, dark as midnight, with deep smudges of exhaustion beneath them. "Did Peters hurt you? At your house, did he—" Mark broke off, not wanting to put his fear into words.

"No. He, uh—" Her gaze skittered away. "I'm okay. He didn't...do anything like that."

"He should be damn glad he didn't," Mark said, glancing at the vet, who was still writhing on the floor. He put her away from him and looked at her, checking to see if she was all right, and then he realized blood dripped down her arm. "You're hit! God, why didn't you tell me you were hit?" With a quick jerk, he pulled his radio from his pocket and barked into it. "Winslow, get in here now. We may need an ambulance."

Cursing Peters with every breath, Mark examined her. She simply stood there, looking dazed. "Why didn't you say something?'' he demanded again, his hands shaking as he patted her down.

''I didn't realize it. I— Is it bad? It doesn't hurt…much.''

The only injury he found was on her arm, a small tear of flesh. ''No, thank God, it's just a scratch.'' His heart still beat uncomfortably fast, the adrenaline surge inspired by fear for her fading slowly. ''His bullet must have hit that door. I think a wood splinter caught you.''

''What about me? I'm bleeding to death, and you're worrying about a scratch,'' Peters said, groaning. ''You shot me, you bastard. I could die.''

''Don't tempt me,'' Mark said as Winslow appeared.

The cop took in the scene quickly. ''Good job,'' he told Mark briefly. ''ETA for back up is four minutes.''

''Good. We can use the help when Peters's friends show up. It should be a hell of a bust.'' He glanced at Peters, then motioned to the supply shelf. ''Better pack that wound. We want him nice and healthy for the trial.''

''You didn't read me my rights, Kincaid! This is an illegal arrest! My lawyer will get me off!''

Winslow tended to the vet's wound quickly, then pulled Peters to his feet, none too gently, waiting for Mark's response with lips twitching.

''Sorry to disappoint you, but you're not my collar.

Officer Winslow has that pleasure, and I'm sure he'll do everything right. Aggravated kidnapping with intent to commit murder takes precedence over illegal bird trafficking.''

Mark smiled as the blood drained from the vet's face. "But don't worry, Peters. We'll add smuggling charges, too. You won't be sprung from prison before you're ninety-five.''

"You have the right to remain silent..." Winslow said as he led him away.

Mark watched him go, trying to channel his blood-thirsty thoughts into more productive channels. It wasn't easy. He wanted to beat the hell out of the bastard for what he'd done to Cat.

His arm around Cat, Mark realized she'd sagged against him. "We need to get you out of here before those other smugglers show. I don't want you near this place when the bust goes down.''

"Mark?" Her voice sounded weak and shaky. "I think I'm going to be sick.''

CHAPTER NINETEEN

CAT CLOSED HER EYES and fought back another wave of nausea. Why was she sick now, when it was all over?

Mark made her sit down and put her head between her legs. His strong arm wrapped around her, soothing, comforting, supporting. "It's all right, baby," he murmured huskily. "You're safe now. Deep breaths."

He continued to hold her, talking to her quietly until the nausea gradually receded and she was able to raise her head. "I'm okay now. Sorry, I don't know why that happened. I mean, it's over."

The smile that curved his mouth was as tender as she'd ever seen. "Delayed reaction. You kept the fear at bay until you could afford to deal with it. You did great, Cat. Most people would have fallen apart long before this."

He got to his feet, then swung her up in his arms. "And now you're getting out of here. The place will be crawling with cops and agents any minute. We'll find someone to take your statement and then take you home."

Her head nestled against his shoulder. Her hand clutched his shirt as he carried her out of the warehouse. "Wait. I want to see it through. I want to know those people are going to get what they deserve."

He looked down at her and his gaze turned grim. "Trust me on that one. I've been working on this case for two years. I'll make sure everyone involved is punished to the full extent of the law. Peters's arrest is going to blow this ring wide open. They'll never recover from the blow."

"What about Gabe? He's innocent, Mark. I don't have proof, but Kyle admitted it. That's why he was going to kill me, because I knew he'd framed Gabe."

"So that's why he took you. I thought you might have found something fishy in his books." He shifted her in his arms as he walked out of the warehouse. "Don't worry about your brother. I have proof Peters framed him. That's why we put a tail on him and were able to find you. By tomorrow all the charges against Gabe will be dropped and he'll be completely exonerated."

She turned her face into his shoulder and drew a deep breath. "Thank God."

He didn't say anything else, just continued walking with her in his arms.

"What about the birds?" she ventured after a moment. "I can help them."

"We have FWS agents in place, or will any minute. They'll take care of the birds. Besides, you need someone to take care of you, not the other way around.''

''Mark, please. Let me stay. And you can put me down now. I'm perfectly capable of walking.''

He ignored that and continued striding relentlessly across the shadowed gravel driveway. ''You've been kidnapped, threatened, shot at and scared to death. Don't you think you've had enough excitement for one night?''

A man, the one Mark had said was a policeman and who'd led Kyle away earlier, reached their side. He nodded at her and said, ''Glad to see you're all right, ma'am. Your fiancé here was tearing his hair out, trying to get to you. Peters is lucky Mark didn't rip him apart.''

Her fiancé? Before she could request enlightenment, the man continued, telling Mark how many men had arrived, and asking for instructions on how to place them.

''Tell them to secure the perimeter of the warehouse. I want men placed in strategic positions inside. Watch the water. Like I said, I don't think they'd come by land if this is the meeting place. Three men, possibly more, and we have no idea of the timing. Also, I don't know how large the cargo they're bringing—''

Cat touched his face, causing him to break off and look at her. ''He told me.'' Remembering the conversation, she shuddered. Surely with time it would fade from her memory, but right now she recalled every chilling word. "He said they were meeting him at eleven-thirty. And they're bringing in a hundred palm cockatoos."

"A hundred palm cockatoos?" Mark repeated. "Good God, we thought it was big, but we had no idea how big." To the policeman he said, "Okay, Winslow, you heard the lady. Eleven-thirty." He shifted her in his arms to glance at his watch. "That's in about fifteen minutes. I'll be there as soon as I take care of Miss Randolph."

Cat sighed. She hadn't really thought he'd let her stay. Those poor birds… *Birds.* "Oh my God, I can't believe I forgot about Buddy. He must be frantic by now."

"He was," Mark said. "We had the cops check your house after you left, for clues to where Peters might be taking you, or what exactly had happened. One of them is a bird lover and he took care of your parrot." One side of his mouth lifted. "Seems Buddy doesn't much care for Peters, either. Kept screaming Kyle is vile and vile Kyle at the top of his lungs."

"Buddy hates him. He always has. I guess he sensed something about him, something twisted. I should have listened to him," she said soberly.

Mark carried her to his truck, opened the passenger door and placed her on the seat. "Stay here and lock the doors. If I see one hair on your head, or the tip of that pretty nose, anywhere outside this truck before I give you the all clear, I'm grabbing the first available man to take you home. Understand?''

''You're letting me stay?'' she asked him, astonished.

''Under those conditions. Well, is it a deal?''

She nodded. ''I won't leave the truck,'' she promised. ''What changed your mind?''

His jaw tightened. ''You deserve to be in on the bust. You've been through hell, and the rest of your family, too. If watching these guys go down helps you, then I'm all for it. I just don't want you in any more danger. My heart can't take it.''

''Thank you,'' she said softly. ''Mark?''

Clearly impatient to go and do his job, he glanced at the men silently surrounding the warehouse before turning his attention back to her. ''What?''

''Why did that man call you my fiancé?''

He paused a moment. ''Something I said must have confused him.''

''Oh.'' She wouldn't ask for more, though she was dying to.

He smiled, cupped his hands around her face and tilted her head back. His lips covered hers in a slow, thorough, spine-tingling kiss.

''Probably when I told him I was going to get the woman I loved the hell out of that warehouse,'' Mark said, and left her.

TALK ABOUT ANTICLIMATIC, Mark thought as he walked to his truck. The bust had gone down with two shots fired, and those into the air. Not that Mark minded, but these guys hadn't been nearly as tough as Peters had indicated. All three men were in police custody, where they'd cool their heels until tomorrow, when Mark questioned them. Not that he expected to gain much useful information. Flunkies, every one of them.

But that didn't matter so much now that they had Peters. The vet would sell out his grandmother if he thought it would reduce his sentence. Mark predicted Peters would spill everything he knew, finger everyone even remotely involved in the ring on the chance it would work in his favor. Fortunately, the even more serious charges against him made it reasonable to hope he wouldn't see daylight for a long, long time.

The birds were under FWS care. Probably because of their value—Mark pegged it at seven or eight hundred thousand—they'd been handled more carefully than a lot of smuggled cargo. The majority of them had made it alive. Whether they'd ever be returned to the wild was doubtful, though not impossible. The FWS would return them to their native country, and the authorities would take it from there.

Winslow and Mark had given their statements to the police, who had agreed that Cat could give hers the following day.

When Mark reached his Blazer, he found Cat curled up in the seat, asleep with one cheek pillowed on her hand. Her bare arm already showed bruises—finger marks the bastard had left on her. She looked young, completely exhausted, and so vulnerable it broke his heart.

He cursed Peters for what he'd done, then cursed himself for allowing it to happen. It didn't matter that Mark had put a tail on the man the instant he'd had reason to, didn't matter that smugglers tend to be greedy more often than violent. Didn't matter that no one, least of all him, had expected the vet to take a hostage.

What mattered was that Cat had been in danger and very nearly lost her life. And Mark had been damn lucky to get to her in time.

She didn't wake as he drove home, but slept restlessly, her head turning back and forth on the seat, whimpering, muttering unintelligibly, then subsiding. He thought the dream had passed and then she said, "No! No, don't touch me, don't! I don't want to—"

Then she screamed and his blood chilled.

Mark pulled off the road and jammed the car into park. Taking hold of her arms, he tried to speak firmly and soothingly at the same time. "Cat, wake up. You're dreaming. Wake up, baby."

She whimpered some more, choked, then her eyes blinked open and she stared at him. "Mark?"

"Yes, it's me. You're okay, it was just a dream."

She drew in a shuddering breath and shook her head. "No, it was real. Kyle—"

"He's in custody," Mark cut in, wanting to spare her. "You're safe from him. I swear it."

Cat closed her eyes and slumped back, leaning her head against the seat. "I can't get it out of my mind."

"Cat—" Unsure how to proceed, Mark hesitated. "I saw you outside the warehouse. Saw Peters grab you. If there's more, if he did something else—"

"He didn't rape me."

At this point, Mark was no longer certain of that. Deeply troubled, he rubbed his hands gently up and down her arms. "If he did, we need to get you to a hospital." He stroked the soft skin of her jaw. "Tell me the truth, baby. Let me help you."

"He didn't. Nothing happened, not really. But he, um, he wanted me." Her eyes squeezed shut, tears trickled from the corners. "And I knew it. So I...offered to...go away with him...to...be with him. If he wouldn't kill me." Her eyes opened, anguish leaping in their depths. "I didn't mean it. I only told him because I thought...I thought it might buy me some time. I didn't want him to—to kill me right then and there."

"And now what? You're feeling guilty because you told the bastard whatever you had to in order to survive?"

She shook her head and said so quietly he almost

didn't catch it, "Not guilty. Ashamed." A shudder swept through her. "How could I have told him I'd—do that? What kind of person does that make me?"

Mark couldn't believe she was blaming herself. "Listen to me, Cat. You have nothing, nothing at all to be ashamed of. You were in a desperate situation. You knew Peters had the hots for you and you used the knowledge to try to save yourself. There's nothing wrong with that."

"I offered...myself. What if I'd done it?" she whispered.

"Then it would still have been rape." Their gazes locked. "You're the victim in this situation, Cat. None of this is your fault. None of it."

Her breath drew in with a catch. "I know that. In my mind."

He was an idiot. Why hadn't he realized she'd need help? Why hadn't he gotten her help at the scene? He'd been so damn grateful she was alive and unhurt, he hadn't thought about the psychological consequences of what she'd been through.

He forced himself to speak calmly, gently. "It's just going to take a while for your heart to know it, too. You need counseling, Cat. A professional who can help you. Let me take you home and call the police. They have people who help victims of violent crimes."

She shook her head. "Not tonight. I'll talk to someone tomorrow, I promise."

''Tonight would be better.''

She smiled, not the beautiful, beaming smile he'd grown to love so much, but a different one. Tender, loving…wistful. Heartbreaking. ''Tonight, I don't want to talk, or analyze, or even think.'' She touched his face, her fingers warm against his cheek. ''I want you, Mark. Make love with me. Tonight.''

HE DIDN'T ARGUE with her. He pulled back onto the highway, took her hand and held it as he drove. Cat didn't know what he intended until he spoke.

''My house or yours?''

She blessed him for understanding and allowing her to have control. A control she desperately needed right now. She took a deep breath and answered, ''Mine. I want to replace those bad memories with good ones.''

A short while later they pulled into her driveway. ''It looks so normal,'' she murmured. ''I wasn't sure…''

Her hand tightened on his as they walked to the door. She gave a shaky laugh. ''I hope it's not locked. I don't have my keys.''

''I do. You gave me one, remember?''

''I remember. Good thing I didn't demand it back when I was so mad at you.'' She stopped under the porch light and looked at him. ''It seems like that happened so long ago, and it was only yesterday.''

''A lot has happened since then.'' He turned her

face to his. "I told you before and you didn't believe me. Will you believe me now?"

"I want to," she whispered. "Tell me again."

He gazed into her eyes, his expression more solemn than she could ever remember seeing it. "What happened between us had nothing to do with your brother. Not now, not then, not ever. I made love to you because I wanted you. And then I fell in love with you."

Cat fell into the endless blue sea of his eyes, and she believed. "I love you."

He smiled then, and kissed her.

"It doesn't look any different," she said when they walked inside. "I don't know why I thought it would."

Buddy was quiet, his cage covered with a cloth. She peeked beneath it to reassure herself, and had to laugh to find him snoozing away.

"That cut on your arm needs to be cleaned," Mark said. "Where's your disinfectant and bandages?"

"It's only a scratch," she protested. "You said so yourself."

He didn't answer, just gave her the look she knew meant she might as well give in. Rather than waste time in argument, she led him to the bathroom, washed her face and hands, brushed her hair, and let him tend to her cut.

"Feel better?" she asked when he smoothed the bandage into place.

His mouth lifted at the corner. "Yeah. How about you?"

"Much better," she said, and walked into the bedroom. She stood at the dresser, staring into the mirror. She didn't look any different, not really, but inside...she'd changed.

Mark took off his shoes and socks, then came up behind her, his arms sliding around her waist, pulling her gently back against him. He held her carefully, as if afraid she'd break. "I'm kind of fumbling, here," he said, and kissed the side of her neck. "I'm not sure exactly what you want from me."

She couldn't help smiling. "Oh, I think you have a pretty good idea." Her arm raised to curve back around his neck. "We've done this before, you know."

"It's different this time. You've been through hell tonight. I don't want to make it worse. I don't want to hurt you, Cat."

"You won't." He still looked concerned. Doubtful. "Trust me, Mark. You won't hurt me."

He said nothing, but kissed her neck again. "Your shirt," she said. "Take it off."

His head raised. Their eyes met in the mirror. His smile was slow, and wonderfully wicked. Letting go of her, his hands went to his buttons, and he began to unfasten them. He undid each button slowly, very slowly, then shrugged, and the shirt slid down his arms to drop to the floor.

"Your jeans," she demanded, and noticed how husky her voice had grown. "Lose them."

Her heart, already thudding, picked up speed as she watched him. The button first, then the slow glide of the zipper, and then he pushed his jeans down his long legs and stepped out of them. Unable to speak, in fact, having a hard time breathing, she gestured at his briefs.

He slipped them off and stood before her, saying nothing, waiting. His eyes blazed deep blue and hot as fire. Now she had a naked, beautiful and very aroused man standing in her bedroom, apparently willing to do anything she wanted. And oh, she wanted.

She reached out and wrapped her hand around him. Stroked him, smiling at his response.

His voice emerged, husky and strained. "I'm not going to last thirty seconds if you keep doing that."

She didn't think she'd last long, either. So she shed her clothes and wrapped herself around him. He walked backward to the bed, landing on it with her on top of him. She kissed his mouth, deeply, drinking in his flavor, loving it, loving him.

His hands were everywhere, touching, teasing, tempting. Hers were everywhere, touching, feeling, wanting. They kissed, and kissed, and kissed, each one deeper, longer, more intense than the one before. Finally, she rose above him, took him inside her. She threw back her head and gave herself to the rushing

river of desire, and exploded with a scream of pleasure. He shuddered, groaned her name, and with a
last desperate thrust, followed her.

When she could think, when she could breathe, she
kissed his neck. "I...needed to be in charge. Thank
you."

"Cat?" He tugged her hair so she raised her head
to look at him. He flashed her a grin and said, "Not
a problem. You can be in charge anytime you want."

CHAPTER TWENTY

MARK CAUGHT Cat's hand as she walked by him to fill her coffee cup. It was eight in the morning and neither had slept much the night before. At least the haunted look had left her eyes, he thought, but he didn't think she was nearly as solid as she acted. She wore a pale blue terry-cloth robe, which shouldn't have looked sexy but somehow did.

"We can't avoid talking about it any longer, Cat. You need to call your family so they can be there with you when you give the police your statement. So someone can drive you home." And especially so they could take care of her while Mark interviewed the smugglers and made sure that no judge was crazy enough to let Kyle Peters out on bail.

"I can drive myself, Mark. I'm not made of glass. I'm fine."

He simply raised an eyebrow and waited.

She pursed her lips, then puffed out a sigh. "Okay, I'm still shaky. But I'm a lot better." She set her cup on the table and laid a hand on his bare chest, over his heart. "Thanks to you."

He tugged her into his lap and kissed her mouth, those sweet lips that had teased every inch of his body the night before. "You promised you'd see a counselor today."

"I know, and I will. But I don't need baby-sitting. If I call my family and tell them the story, they'll go ballistic. I'd rather wait until after I talk to the police. Maybe when you tell Gabe the good news."

He wrapped his arms around her and leaned his forehead against hers. "I can't be with you all day. There are too many things I have to take care of. I don't want to worry about you being alone."

"You're very sweet," she said.

Gazing into her eyes, he took her face in his hands and kissed her mouth slowly. "I'm very in love. So humor me and let your family take care of you today."

"Say that again."

He smiled. "What, that I love you? The five hundred times I told you last night weren't enough?"

She shook her head, an impish smile curving her lips.

"I love you, Cat," he said, suddenly serious.

Her arms twined around his neck and she kissed him.

A few moments later, the back door crashed into the cabinets and a male voice roared, "What in the hell is going on here?"

Another male voice said, "Get out of the way, Cam. He's mine first. You can have what's left of him."

Mark and Cat both turned their heads. *Oh, man, both her brothers.*

"Move," a feminine voice said. "I can't see a thing from behind you."

And her sister. The Randolphs were out in force. And though he'd wanted her to call them, he hadn't intended to be caught with Cat when they showed up.

"You must have a death wish, Kincaid," Cameron said. "Or are you just terminally stupid?"

"Move, Cat," Gabe said, "so we can deal with this bastard the way he deserves."

"Cat, get up," Mark said, trying to shift her without hurting her. "I can handle this."

Her arm tightened around his neck and she hung on determinedly. "Not if you're lying out cold on the floor. And it's two against one, so no matter how tough you are, I don't think you can take them." To her brothers, she said, "I'm not going anywhere until I have your promise you won't fight. No hitting. There are a lot of things you don't understand."

"Quit hiding behind my sister, you miserable coward," Gabe said, ignoring her.

"Gail," Cat appealed to her sister, "tell them to listen to me."

Gail checked her nails, then flashed Mark a look of pure disgust. "Why? I want to watch them take him apart."

Cat sighed. "Mark, tell them about Gabe. I'm not moving until you do."

He couldn't help smiling. "I don't think Gabe's the only reason they want my blood, honey."

Cam stared at them a moment. "Wait a minute, Gabe, there's something weird going on here." He shot a dark glance at Mark. "Let's hear it."

Might as well get their attention, Mark thought. "The charges against Gabe have been dropped. He should be completely exonerated by this afternoon."

There was a stunned silence, then everyone began talking at once. Finally, Gabe made his voice heard above the rest. "Why? What kind of game are you playing?"

"No game. I have proof that Kyle Peters framed you for smuggling illegal birds."

Once again, the Randolphs were silent.

Cameron pulled a chair out and sat in it. "I need a cup of coffee." He propped his elbows on the table and scrubbed his hands over his face. "Start at the beginning, Kincaid."

"I'll get coffee," Cat said. "And I have some questions, too, Mark. I haven't heard the whole story, either."

"Okay, but this has to be the short version. We

can go into more detail later." He looked at the others. "Cat and I have to be down at the police station this morning. She needs one of you, maybe all of you, to be with her."

"That's not a problem," Gabe said, "but why? Don't be so damn cryptic. I can't figure out what's going on."

"Me neither," Gail said. "Cat, why do you have to go to the police station?"

Cat handed out mugs of steaming coffee, then sat on Mark's leg. He wondered if she wanted to show him support, or draw support for what would come later. Probably a little of both. He put his arm around her hips to steady her. She took his other hand and held it tightly, drew in a deep breath and said, "Kyle Peters kidnapped me yesterday."

"The hell you say!" Cameron shot to his feet, while Gabe and Gail stared at their sister in shock. "I never liked him...but kidnapping?"

"And attempted murder," Mark added.

When the tumult that statement caused finally died down, Cat and Mark told them the story. An expurgated version, but essentially the full story.

"So Kyle's arrest will bring down the ring?" Cat asked as Mark finished up.

"Yes. We won't get everyone involved, of course, but Peters will be fingering people so fast it will make you dizzy. He won't go down alone, and he had connections nationwide, though most are in Texas.''

''I'm glad,'' Cat said fiercely. ''It makes me feel as if I had a part in breaking up that ring.''

''You did. A crucial part,'' Mark told her. ''But I'd a hell of a lot rather you'd been on the sidelines.''

She didn't say anything, but laid her palm against his cheek and smiled.

''What I don't understand,'' Gail said to Cat, ''is how Kyle could threaten to kill you. I always thought he liked you.''

''He did,'' Mark said grimly, his eyes meeting Cat's. Her hand dropped to his shoulder, and squeezed. He read the message in her eyes as easily as if she'd spoken aloud. *Don't tell them. Please don't tell them.*

''Apparently, he liked money more,'' Mark said.

Cat nearly sagged in relief. Mark frowned, but held his tongue. She would talk when she was ready. He hoped.

''Is there a possibility Peters will get off?'' Cameron asked Mark.

''I don't see how. With two eyewitnesses, me and Winslow, the cop we had tailing him, not to mention Cat's testimony, he doesn't have a prayer in hell. On top of aggravated kidnapping and attempted murder, we'll load him down with smuggling charges, conspiracy charges and whatever the legal charge is for framing someone for a crime they didn't commit. So no, I don't think he'll see daylight as a free man for fifty years, if ever.''

''What made you suspect me?'' Gabe asked. ''I want to know why I was on your shortlist. Was it my boat?''

''Partly, but it was really a combination of factors. After you found those birds on your doorstep, I had my team run a background check on you.''

Gabe stared at him a minute, then frowned. ''You turned up the gambling, right?''

Mark nodded.

Gabe's eyes flashed bright with anger. ''I guess your check didn't show that I haven't so much as bought a lousy lottery ticket in two years.''

''Actually, it did. There was no evidence of further gambling, which was a point in your favor. But I suspected almost from the first that you were being framed. Your behavior, bringing the birds to Cat, didn't make sense if you were really guilty. It would have been much smarter simply to get rid of them.''

''If you thought I was being framed then why the hell did you have the Coast Guard board my boat and arrest me?''

''Because I couldn't prove it. I had to act on the information, on the facts. Regardless of whether I believed you were the link or not, the facts pointed to you. And the local FWS suspected you, no matter what I told them." Gabe didn't look happy, but then, Mark couldn't blame him. "You would have been boarded even if I hadn't talked to the Coast Guard. Somebody called and left an anonymous tip with the FWS. You were screwed no matter what I did."

"But Gabe's out a lot of money, from hiring the lawyer and court costs," Cat said. "They also impounded his boat. And all for a crime he didn't commit."

"I know. I can't change anything that's happened, but I can petition the court to order Peters to pay for your court costs, lawyer's fees and whatever other money you expended resulting from your arrest."

"You think that will fly?"

It cheered Mark to see a gleam of hope in the other man's eyes. "I think so. We can sure as hell ask." He turned to Cat. "I've got to go. I'm going to my place to catch a quick shower, then I'll see you at the station later."

She kissed him, and he tried not to think of her brothers, and their probable plans to draw and quarter him.

After putting on his shirt and shoes, he went back to the kitchen, managing to catch Gail's eye while Cat talked to her brothers. Gail looked puzzled, but slipped out a moment later.

He took her to the living room and asked, "Can you stay with Cat today? She needs to talk to a woman, one she loves and trusts. Looks to me like she's a lot closer to you than her mother. Will you be there?''

The blue of her eyes deepened in concern. ''What happened to her, Mark? I saw that look that passed between you when we were talking about Kyle. Did Kyle—did he assault her? Is that what you're trying to say?''

Mark shook his head. ''No. I was afraid he had, but no. But it's kind of related.'' He paced away a step and glanced back at her. ''Hell, what am I saying? Of course it's related. She feels violated. She's been the victim of a violent crime and she's not dealing with it as well as she wants all of us to believe.'' How to explain it, quickly, without saying too much?

''It's complicated. Cat has…issues to work through. I think she'll tell you. I hope she will. She said she'd see a counselor today, but she needs you, too.''

Gail stared at him. ''You really do love her, don't you?'' she asked in amazement. ''You weren't using her at all, you're in love with her.''

''Yeah, I am.'' He smiled ruefully. ''Not that it's going to matter to your brothers, though. They still want to rip me apart. Hell, I can't blame them.''

Gail flicked her wrist. ''They'll get over it, once they figure out you really care about her. Don't worry, Mark. I'll be here for Cat.''

"Good. I'm counting on you."

"Telling secrets?" Cat asked from the doorway.

He smiled at her and held out his hand. "I was just telling Gail to be sure and let me know when you arrive at the station. I want to be with you when you give your statement."

She didn't look as if she believed him, but she didn't call him on it. "We will, don't worry. Don't you need to get going?"

"Half an hour ago," he said. He kissed her, said, "Remember what you promised," and forced himself to leave her.

As soon as Mark left, Cat pounced on Gail. "Mark told you, didn't he?

"Told me what?" she asked, a shade too innocently.

"About—about Kyle."

"No." She shook her head. "Mark told me you needed to talk to a woman you loved and trusted, and he hoped you'd talk to me." She paused and added, "By the way, he's madly in love with you. Did you know?"

"I'm beginning to believe it." Cat smiled. "He's very convincing when he wants to be."

Gail squeezed her hand. "I'm happy for you. He's not the bum I thought he was."

"No, he's not. He was...wonderful to me. Last

night especially.'' She dropped Gail's hand and turned toward her bedroom. ''I guess I'd better get ready so we can go to the station.''

''Cat?''

Cat waited, not looking at her.

''Tell me what happened.''

''You know the story. Mark and I just told you.''

Gail came up behind her and put her hand on Cat's shoulder. ''Tell me the parts you left out. Please, Cat. Talk to me.''

Her eyes filled with tears. She turned around, let Gail enfold her in her arms. ''Oh, Gail. It's going to take a while,'' she said, and the tears began to fall.

''That's all right,'' her sister said, patting her back. ''Take as long as you want.'' She let go and gave Cat a gentle push toward her bedroom. ''Go on. I'll be there in a minute.'' She flashed Cat a mischievous grin. ''I'm going to tell Gabe and Cam they can clean the kitchen while they wait for us.''

MARK MOVED IN with Cat that evening and they spent a great deal of the next three weeks together. During the day, he worked on his uncle's house, but the nights belonged to her. They made love everywhere, slow, fast and everything in between. They talked about everything, from books, to music, to childhood fears and ridiculous dreams.

Everything, that is, except marriage.

Cat tried to tell herself she didn't mind. She knew Mark loved her. He told her often, and showed her. No, love wasn't the problem.

The problem was his mother. Or more accurately, Mark's feelings about his mother. The more Mark told her about his childhood, the more obvious it became that he had issues with his mother, issues that extended to Cat, as well. He saw his mother in Cat, in Cat's love for her birds. To put it simply, Mark was afraid the birds were more important to her than he was. She didn't know how to convince him she could love them both.

So she loved him, and gave him space. And hoped someday he'd trust her enough to want to make their relationship more permanent.

Mark picked up her hand and nibbled on her knuckles. "What are you thinking about? You're a million miles away."

She smiled at him. "Just in the kitchen. I need to ice that cake for Roxy's birthday tomorrow."

"Icing, huh? Need some help?" He raised his eyebrows in a suggestive leer.

She laughed and got up. "Don't you ever think about anything but sex?"

"No." He grinned. "Am I supposed to?"

"I have to go out of town for a few days," he told Cat after she began icing the cake. "My boss wants to see me."

"Your FWS boss? You're going to Dallas?"

He nodded. "Yeah, I've got to clear up the details of the Parrot Blues case."

She knew she shouldn't say it, but she did anyway. "But you're...you're coming back?"

He pulled her in between his legs and kissed her. "Yes, I'm coming back. Technically, I'm still on a leave of absence."

His hands started doing interesting things to her bottom. "Mark, I have to ice this... Maybe I can do it later."

CHAPTER TWENTY-ONE

"I'M TELLING YOU," Cameron said, sliding a coaster in front of Cat and placing a glass of white zinfandel on it, "the son of a bitch has split. Wake up and smell the coffee, honey."

"I don't think he has," Gail said, and tossed a few peanuts back. "You're still mad at him, so naturally you think everything he does is suspect."

"He's been gone a week," Gabe said. "Cam's right. Sounds like *adiós* to me."

"Tell you what, Cam," Gail said, "if you're right and he's split for good, I'll wait tables for free for a week. But if I'm right—" her eyes glinted with mischief "—then you have to tell Mark you're sorry you've been a suspicious jerk and to make up for it you'll give him free beer for life."

"Don't take it, Cam," Gabe warned. "If I were still a gambling man, I wouldn't do it."

"You were a notoriously bad gambler," Cam reminded him. "You're on, little sister," he told Gail.

Cat didn't argue with her brothers. What was the point, when she couldn't prove they were wrong? She sipped her wine and tried to ignore the continuing discussion. Mark had called her every night, told her he missed her. Told her he loved her. Why would he do that if he didn't mean to come back?

And if he did intend to return, then why was she so uneasy?

"We were wrong, Gabe," Cam said, looking toward the door. "Look who's back. And he's brought a woman with him this time."

Cat swiveled on her stool, and she stared at the two people entering the bar. Definitely Mark. She drank in the sight of him thirstily. What had Gail called him all those weeks ago? Tall, dark and gorgeous. And hers. Her pulse scrambled and joy blossomed in her heart.

"We have to take this outside, Gabe," Cameron warned. "I'm not busting up my bar over him."

"Oh, lighten up," Gail said. "She's nice-looking, but she's old enough to be his—" she hesitated, gazing at them "—older sister, at least."

"That's his mother," Cat said, stunned. "His estranged mother."

Cameron snorted.

Cat couldn't say a thing. She stared, mesmerized, as he walked toward her, his gaze locked on hers. He didn't speak, but walked right up to her, put his arms around her and kissed her. Long, slow, thorough. She wrapped her arms around him and kissed him back the same way.

"Bad news, Cam," Gabe said glumly. "I don't think he's leaving her."

"Told you so," Gail put in.

Eventually, Mark drew back and smiled at her. "Sorry it took me so long. I had to see a woman about a bird sanctuary."

Confused, she blinked at him. "What?"

With his other hand, he reached for his mother, bringing her up beside him. "Cat, this is my mother, Lillian Monroe. You didn't exactly meet under the best circumstances before, so why don't we pretend this is the first time?"

"Pleased to meet you," Cat said dazedly, offering a hand. "Won't you sit down?"

"Thank you. And I'd love a glass of white wine, if you don't mind," she told a bemused Cameron as she perched on the proffered stool. She smiled at each of the Randolphs in turn, before her gaze returned to Cat. "So tell me, how much funding do you think you'll need for this sanctuary of yours? Have you worked up any kind of prospectus?"

"Pro-prospectus?" Cat looked at Mark. He didn't say a word, only smiled at her.

"No? A ballpark figure, then?"

"I don't understand."

"Didn't Mark tell you? No, I can see he must not have. I'm here to help you obtain funding for your bird sanctuary." She took a sip of wine and nodded her approval to Cameron. "Very nice."

"My…bird sanctuary?" Cat whispered. She looked at Mark. "You—you brought your mother to help me…?"

"I thought you might want a little help with that dream we talked about. So I went to the person who knew how to make that happen."

Lillian laughed. "Thanks for the vote of confidence. But seriously, Cat, I don't think we'll have too much trouble finding funding for such a worthy project. Why, I know four people in Corpus Christi alone who might be just the ticket."

It finally began to sink in. Mark had gone to his mother for her. So she could have her dream. "But what about land? We have to have someplace to put it, assuming we do get the money."

"The land's not a problem," Mark said. "I'm closing on Copper's Cove next week."

"You bought Copper's Cove?" Her special place. The place where she had told Mark she loved him for the first time. "How? How did you know who owned it, or if they wanted to sell?"

"I had help," he said, and smiled at her sister.

"That would be me." Gail looked smug. "And I've never had as hard a time keeping my mouth shut in my life." She smirked at Cameron and said, "Pay up, big brother."

"Insider knowledge," he muttered, but he turned to Mark. "I'm a suspicious jerk, and to make up for it you can have free beer for life,'' he recited. ''Damn it.''

Everyone laughed. As the others started talking, Cat said, ''Mark, you can't buy that land. It's so sweet of you, and I love you for it, but I can't accept such a big gift. No telling what that land costs.''

''There is a way around that, you know. I'm thinking we can call it something else.'' He pulled a small jewelry box out of his pocket and opened it. A simple gold band with a single diamond sparkled on the black velvet.

A hush fell. Cat covered her mouth with her hand, tears springing to her eyes. She looked at Mark, the ring, then back to Mark again. A smile curved his mouth, but she thought he seemed anxious.

''We could call it a wedding present,'' he said. ''Will you marry me, Cat?''

''Yes!'' She threw her arms around his neck and kissed him. Between kisses she said yes, breathlessly, over and over. They both laughed and then she held out her hand for him to slide the ring onto her finger.

''I've never done this before,'' Mark said, his hand shaking. ''I didn't know I could be so nervous.'' Finally he managed to get the ring on her finger. ''I love you, Cat.''

''I love you, too.'' She turned to his mother, whose eyes were suspiciously bright, to Cameron and Gabe, who had the biggest, sappiest grins she'd ever seen on their faces, and finally to Gail, who was unabashedly wiping her eyes with a tissue. Cat waved her left hand and said, "Look, I'm engaged."

"You certainly are," Gail said. She blew her nose. "This time to the right man. I love a happy ending." Her eyes widened. "Oh, no, this means Mom will be on my case again!"

"Brace up," Cat told her, laughing. "You're up to it."

"Beer, hell, we need champagne," Cameron said. "And I've got just the bottle in the back. Let me ice it down."

"I hope you two were taking notes," Gail said to her brothers. "This guy knows how to do it right."

"Dance with me?" Cat asked Mark after everyone had toasted them. He led her out to the tiny floor and held her in his arms. The band was on break, and the jukebox grated out a nasally country tune. Cat didn't care. To her it sounded like the most beautiful music she'd ever heard.

They danced in silence for some time, simply enjoying each other. A question occurred to her after a while.

"What about your job? What are you going to do?"

"I'm transferring to the FWS office here. I tried to convince my partner to come, too, but he says he likes the city too much."

"What about you? Are you going to miss the city?"

Holding her right hand pressed against his heart, he smiled at her. "Nope. I have everything I want right here. You, me." Eyes gleaming, he added, "Your parrot. Maybe even someday, kids."

"Definitely kids someday," she said. "And birds."

"And birds," he agreed, and kissed her. "But not at 6:00 a.m."

"I'll train them to wait until seven," she promised. "I've discovered there are better things to do at 6:00 a.m."

"Absolutely," he said, smiling wickedly. "Let's go do them."

HARLEQUIN *Super*ROMANCE®

Old friends, best friends...
Girlfriends
Your friends are an important part
of your life. You confide in them,
laugh with them, cry with them....

Girlfriends

Three new novels by Judith Bowen

Zoey Phillips. Charlotte Moore. Lydia Lane.
They've been best friends for ten years, ever
since the summer they all worked together at a
lodge. At their last reunion, they all accepted a
challenge: *look up your first love.* Find out what
happened to him, how he turned out....

Join Zoey, Charlotte and Lydia as they
rediscover old loves and find new ones.

Read all the *Girlfriends* books! Watch for
Zoey Phillips in November, *Charlotte Moore* in
December and *Lydia Lane* in January.

HARLEQUIN®
Makes any time special ®

Visit us at www.eHarlequin.com

HSRG

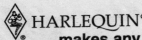

CALL THE ONES YOU LOVE OVER THE HOLIDAYS!

Save $25 off future book purchases when you buy any four Harlequin® or Silhouette® books in October, November and December 2001,

PLUS

receive a phone card good for 15 minutes of long-distance calls to anyone you want in North America!

WHAT AN INCREDIBLE DEAL!

Just fill out this form and attach 4 proofs of purchase (cash register receipts) from October, November and December 2001 books, and Harlequin Books will send you a coupon booklet worth a total savings of $25 off future purchases of Harlequin® and Silhouette® books, AND a 15-minute phone card to call the ones you love, anywhere in North America.

Please send this form, along with your cash register receipts as proofs of purchase, to:
In the USA: Harlequin Books, P.O. Box 9057, Buffalo, NY 14269-9057
In Canada: Harlequin Books, P.O. Box 622, Fort Erie, Ontario L2A 5X3
Cash register receipts must be dated no later than December 31, 2001.
Limit of 1 coupon booklet and phone card per household.
Please allow 4-6 weeks for delivery.

**I accept your offer! Enclosed are 4 proofs of purchase.
Please send me my coupon booklet
and a 15-minute phone card:**

Name: _____

Address: _____ City: _____

State/Prov.: _____ Zip/Postal Code: _____

Account Number (if available): _____

---

097 KJB DAGL
PHQ4013